The Mystery of the Weeping Friar

by

DJ Park

DORRANCE
PUBLISHING CO
EST. 1920
PITTSBURGH, PENNSYLVANIA 15238

Dorrance Publishing Co
585 Alpha Drive
Pittsburgh, PA 15238
Visit our website at www.dorrancebookstore.com

ISBN: 978-1-4809-4767-2
eISBN: 978-1-4809-4744-3

To Keith and Suzanne with love

Prologue

New Mexico is a layered mixture of peoples, legends, myths, and stories descending from the past as the summer rain falls from the clouds, sometimes wispy and lacelike, sometimes dark and ominous, delighting and surprising. From even the tiniest hamlet emerge histories of ghosts, hidden treasure, heroes, and scoundrels. One of these is the legend of the Weeping Friar of Chimayo.

In August 1680, the peaceful natives of the northern pueblos revolted against the terrible oppression of Spanish colonial rule. Hundreds of colonists were massacred; the revolt was so widespread that the Spanish actually abandoned all of New Mexico and fled south. It was the only successful native revolt in the history of the Americas.

In the aftermath, a story made the rounds amongst the survivors. It was the story of a simple friar, the only survivor from the Pecos River mission. His name is lost but not his vocation: He was a *carpentero*. When he wasn't engaged in repairing carts and wagons or making furniture, he whiled away his time carving figures of the saints, called *santos*. His carvings were of exceptional beauty and craftsmanship and became much sought-after among the colonists of the Pecos Valley.

When the revolt erupted, the friar escaped to Santa Fe, carrying for protection one of his carvings, a figure of St. Francis he'd rescued from the flaming ruin of the Pecos mission. It was said he survived only by the intercession of

St. Francis. Arriving at the governor's residence after his perilous journey, he presented the statue to the governor. When the governor unwrapped the santo, he discovered that the placid face of the saint was now stained with tears from weeping in sorrow at the deaths of so many. The friar carried the santo with him on the long retreat to Mexico.

During the journey, the friar died. However, his St. Francis survived and was returned to New Mexico ten years later when the Spanish reoccupied the territory. There it stood in a place of honor on the altar in the personal chapel of the governor. Then, as happens in these tales, the santo disappeared — lost or stolen, no one knew.

It reappeared in the Santuario de Chimayo in the 1860s, displayed on a side altar, acquiring the name Weeping Friar of Chimayo. During one of the many remodels of the Santuario, the santo disappeared again — lost or stolen, no one knew.

As legends always do, over the years the tale of the Weeping Friar took on many odd twists. There were stories of secret societies who kept the Weeping Friar hidden in a crypt far back in the sand hills east of the village of Chimayo, where they conducted strange rituals and mysterious rites. Old believers told tales of ghostly friars who walked the hills searching in vain for their compadre and his cherished santo. It was said the Weeping Friar possessed inexplicable powers and to touch it with an unclean heart meant death.

In the nineteenth and twentieth centuries, santos began to be recognized as a legitimate art form in themselves; santeros and santeras, the creators of these wonderful figures, were sought out by collectors who cared little for the religious significance of the figures but appreciated their creative genius. At the same time, the legend of the Weeping Friar took on new relevance. For Latinos it came to represent a tie with their Spanish heritage. For Native Americans it symbolized pride in throwing off the yoke of Spanish enslavement (the young) or a reminder of past humiliations (the old). To collectors the Weeping Friar was of immense historical value and, therefore, a prize to be sought at any price. And to one man, the legendary santo became a crucial pawn in the labyrinthine milieu of international politics.

What if the legend was true?

One

August, this year
Near the Okayh Owinge Pueblo, northern New Mexico
The evening air was cool and thick with the sweet bouquet of parched earth drinking in the life-giving rain that had just fallen. Crickets creaked faintly in the rabbitbrush along the dusty road; thunder roiled the darkness, and lightning flickered across the skyline. It was a delicious night.

Tires crunched on gravel as a midsized SUV approached. Blacked-out, it stopped in the deepest of the shadows. The engine purred; there was a soft snick as a door was opened, but no blaze of light pierced the blackness. A figure quietly emerged and opened the rear hatch; plastic rustled as a sheet was spread on the blacktop. There were a series of breathless grunts as a heavy burden was dragged from the interior and dropped onto the sheet with a thump. Quickly the driver slid behind the wheel and put the car in gear; one, two, three times the car jolted back and forth, each time with a ghastly thud. Returning to the road, the driver dragged the sheet into the weeds adjoining the pavement. A moment later, plastic scraped against plastic as the sheet was stuffed into a bag brought for the purpose; no traces of blood would be left as a signpost to murder. The bag was dropped neatly into the car, and now all was finished. The door closed, and the SUV moved slowly away into the darkness — less than three minutes had elapsed. The night was left to the crickets, their song muted by the horror they'd witnessed.

· · · · ·

Carrer Bisbe Silva 17, Girona, Spain
Señor Estefan Portilla de la Vaca enjoyed these early evening moments. The lively sounds of Girona wafted through the open windows of his fourth-floor apartment, fading along with the sun. Often he would stand in this place and drink in the twilight, casually studying the expansive Parc Central below, allowing his thoughts to settle from the hectic pace of the day. A smile spread across his face. In a few months, God willing, he would stand here as the prime minister of Spain.

He was a handsome man — short, well-built, black hair tinged with gray, swept back and revealing a high forehead. At the corners of his brown eyes, one thin line turned slightly upwards — giving the impression of perpetual mirth — while his delicate nose was an exclamation point above his rounded mouth. His face radiated self-assurance and small tolerance for foolishness; beneath this was a dark pool of impulsive energy.

A door opened behind him. Luis Jose Mirada, his confidant and aide, approached and stopped at a respectful distance.

"Your car is waiting, sir," Mirada said dutifully.

"In a few moments; we have plenty of time." De la Vaca turned back to the window. "Have you received confirmation of the meeting with the archbishop?"

"Yes. He's asked you to meet him at his private residence. He is very pleased with your engagement and sends his blessings for a joyous union."

"Excellent." La Vaca turned and peered at Mirada. "You still have reservations about my relationship with Mrs. Patrick, Luis?"

"I do, sir," Mirada said evenly, careful to mask any sharpness in his tone. "I am always concerned because you can be too trusting of people, particularly women."

"And you are very suspicious of people, particularly women…and perhaps a little jealous too? That is why we work well together, eh?" La Vaca said without rancor.

After five years with La Vaca, Mirada was no longer surprised that the man tried to judge his thoughts. He was taller and younger with a thin face, fawn-colored hair, and lips that, on the rare occasions he smiled, curled slightly upward. He saw the world as a hostile place where people were tools to be used and discarded; to him La Vaca was a pawn. Mirada was La Vaca's intellectual equal; for all of La Vaca's intelligence, he lacked Mirada's facility of insight. Mirada could accurately judge La Vaca's mood at any moment; he had mastered the ability to tailor thoughts and ideas in such fashion that La Vaca embraced them as his own. The subterfuge kept their relationship balanced and, for Mirada, profitable.

"You agree that we must enlist the aid of the Church in our project?" La Vaca asked.

"Yes, once our project has succeeded. When we present the evidence of our success, the endorsement of Mother Church will follow. Be cautious: I fear Archbishop Pena is too liberal in his views and ought not to be trusted completely."

A streak of light from the fading sun slashed across La Vaca's face as he turned.

"You forget his heritage, Luis. He traces his family back to Francisco Silva, loyal lieutenant of Cortez and a great conqueror in his own right. Pena's loyalty to his lineage runs deeper than his ties to Rome. Blood never lies." It was one of La Vaca's favorite axioms.

"The archbishop's loyalty carries a stiff price," Mirada responded.

"He earned my trust in the lean years. You allow personal dislike to influence your opinion. I have been blessed with great good fortune; I share with those who are worthy. Pena knows what is expected of him; when the time comes, he will stand with us. I intend to receive his endorsement while we are in America." There was resolve as well as anger in his voice, the anger cool and measured.

"You are right. I'm sorry." Mirada lowered his head, annoyed at his own carelessness. La Vaca took this as humble deference. He waved a hand, indicating that the matter was closed.

"The arrangements for the reception are moving forward?"

"Yes. You may look over the guest list on the plane."

"It goes well then. Come." La Vaca smiled and strode from the room; Mirada dutifully followed.

·　·　·　·　·

Highway 582 snaked through the heat and haze like so much black ribbon carelessly dropped across the landscape. New Mexico State Police Sergeant Mike Charles squinted against the glare. Just around a bend he saw a black-and-white state police Explorer flanked by a white tribal police Tahoe.

Trooper Alan Gomez ignored the buzzing flies and the heat rising through the soles of his boots and looked up as the car stopped. Charles squeezed his thick body from the seat of the Chevy Impala. Disordered brown hair fell across his wide forehead. His eyes were ringed with dark circles.

"Hi, Sarge. Good to see you. How's Daddy today?" Gomez said.

Charles glared at him. "Sergeant Daddy is grumpy; why are you so damned cheerful?" Waking up every three hours to feed seven-week-old Mike Jr. had made the usually even-tempered sergeant scratchy and cross. Gomez smirked and looked away.

Charles was rightly considered one of the best investigators with the state police, always driven to his best efforts to solve a case. His parents, Olan and Alice, had instilled in their only son a strong sense of duty, and it showed in his unceasing hard work. Mike didn't care about clearance rates; his focus was to wring out every case until the perp was caught or all leads had dried up and been blown away by the winds of fortune.

Investigator Phil Ortega, Charles's partner, got out of the passenger seat and walked over, grinning broadly. He was relishing Charles's discomfort at losing sleep feeding his firstborn. Ortega had five kids and knew the drill all too well. He was slightly taller than Charles, on the wiry side, with stark black hair, sunken cheeks, and light brown, kindly eyes.

Phil grew up in the rough neighborhoods of south central Albuquerque, the middle son of five boys. His parents, Guillermo and Agueda, worked long hours at multiple jobs. To them family were far more important than money. Each of their sons learned to appreciate the essences of family life: empathy, honor, and togetherness. In an environment where the police were deeply mistrusted, the Ortega boys stood out. Four became officers. The fifth and youngest son, Jose, was a respected and successful soccer coach. More affable than Charles, Phil had an infectious grin and a wry sense of humor that masked a direct way of thinking that kept him and his partner "on track" when things got tough.

"Okay, you called me out here in this heat. What's up? Dispatch said it was a hit-and-run," Charles grumped.

"That's how it was first reported, but I'm not sure. Come over here, some things I want you to look at."

Charles followed the shorter Gomez into the ditch that ran along the edge of the road; dry weeds crackled against their legs. A few feet off the blacktop, a thin, well-muscled tribal police officer was squatting next to what appeared to be a dark bundle of old clothes.

"Hi, Corporal," Charles greeted Corporal Rick Hayes of the San Juan Tribal Police, who looked up, frowning.

"Hi, Sarge. How's little Mike?" Hayes asked.

"Hungry."

"Good for him."

"Mmph," Charles grunted. With some difficulty, he squatted his 225-pound frame next to the slightly built Hayes. "Okay, what do we have?"

"Maintenance crew found her. They thought she might be a hit-and-run victim, but things don't add up. Look," he said, pointing down. There were superficial scuffs on the asphalt; something had scraped across the surface.

"See these marks? She was dragged here, not thrown by an impact. Those aren't consistent with an impact — and the way she's laid out, not like she would be if she landed after being hit." Hayes pointed at some faint scratches in the soil. "I'm not convinced it *is* a hit-and-run. There's no blood on the road. You ever see a hit-and-run driver who stops and moves the victim off the road?"

"Nope."

Gomez chimed in. "There's no purse, no ID, no keys, nothing personal. And look at her shoes. Those aren't walking shoes. What was she doin' out here? Nights out here, it's really, really dark. There's no bars or clubs close by. Where was she walking from? Where was she going?"

Charles bent over for a closer look; the shoes were thin flats, comfortable for lounging — hardly the kind of thing someone would wear for a walk on a country road. A single-strand, silver bracelet dangled from one delicate wrist, obscene in its contrast with the death scene; long, gray hair, blood-soaked, was draped across her face, which appeared to have been crushed by something heavy. The clothes were nice, if not fashionable, and seemed well-kept.

"You call the coroner?" he asked Gomez.

"On his way."

Charles stood and stretched. "Ouch!" he swatted a horsefly that had bitten a chunk from his nose. "You two are full of questions today, so here's one for you: Whadda you think?"

"She was riding with someone." Gomez said. "They were coming from somewhere, had a fight, she gets mad at him and gets out of the car, starts walking down the road. He follows her and runs her down. Then he stops, drags her off the road, takes her purse to delay identifying her, and drives away."

Ortega nodded. "Could be the way it went down. *If* it's a him. Could be a her, you know. Let's figure for now it's a him. Pretty calm behavior for someone who just killed his wife or girlfriend. And you're right, why here? Like you said, there's nothin' around. This scene was staged."

He turned to the tribal officer. "Corporal, you take any missing person reports today?"

"Nope," Hayes answered.

"You check with the county?" Ortega asked Gomez, who nodded.

"And SFPD. And Espanola PD. No missing females for the last two weeks."

"Of course not. Damn."

"Who is she?" Charles muttered to himself, exhaling in disgust; he hated these kinds of whodunit cases. Sweat trickled across the flat expanse of his nose, but he ignored it. "Whose jurisdiction is this?" he asked the two officers.

Hayes stood, plucking rice-grass heads from the legs of his cargo pants. "That's a problem. There's no way to tell what jurisdiction this is. The pueblo boundary runs along that fence; then it wanders back and forth across the road. The GPS in my car says it's county, and his says it's tribal," he said, motioning to Gomez. "Her body is on a state-highway easement, but this road follows an old pueblo footpath from a few centuries back. Technically the easement could be considered tribal land."

"Messy," Ortega interrupted.

Hayes nodded. "I talked with Santa Fe County, and there's no way they want this. They're so shorthanded with their budget problems, they can barely staff the road. Then I called a guy I know at Santa Fe FBI. Thought we could hand it over to them."

"And?" Charles asked. He removed a notebook from one pocket and began scribbling.

"He begged me not to ask them for help. Our tribal treaty says we're supposed to request the feds to take over an investigation even though they can step in if they want to. You know how it is since 9-11 — most of their guys are on the East Coast or overseas."

"How'd you leave it?"

"I told him not to worry about it after Alan suggested we call you out."

Charles glared at Gomez. "Thanks, buddy. Okay, Phil, get on the horn to the lab. Tell them what we've got and see how long it'll take for 'em to get here. I'll call the captain." He pulled a cell phone from his belt and hit the autodial.

"Think Captain Villalva will squawk?" Gomez asked.

"If he does, I'll remind him this was your idea. Maybe he'll transfer you to Clovis." Charles was unsympathetic. Gomez winced at the thought. At best Clovis was considered a rustic back of beyond; troopers who had been stationed there described it using more evocative adjectives.

"Captain? I've got a situation to run by you..." Charles began.

• • • • •

Near the Plaza, Santa Fe
"About another mile, then we turn on Paseo de Peralta." David Harrowsen squinted at the note in his hand. "At least I think so. Your sister's handwriting is worse than mine!" He shifted his six-foot frame uncomfortably in the seat.

David spoke with the muddled accent born of his Colorado upbringing. His staunchly Catholic parents, Sue and John, believed he was marked for the priesthood. But his Scottish roots gave him a strong sense of self-direction. After graduating from the University of Colorado, he announced his intention to become a police officer, following a boyhood friend who'd joined the Denver PD. Initially his parents were taken off-guard and not at all happy with his career choice; once he was successful, their viewpoints evolved into an abiding pride that they harbored until they passed away. It was inbred in him to resist the cynicism typical of veteran cops; like his folks, he nurtured an unequivocal approach to life. Come what may, his attitude was, deal with it and move on.

"Her writing used to be so good too. I was so jealous!" Althia "Tee" Harrowsen said from behind the wheel. She rolled her head from side to side, stretching her neck. "Glad we're almost there. I'm getting stiff." Nine hours in the confines of her Subaru Legacy were torture enough for the long and lanky Tee. Her tone recalled her Midwestern childhood in Wisconsin with sister Anne and their parents, Bert and Mary, which was moderated by years of professional voice training in her previous life as an actress. Bright and attractive, Tee painted life from a sensitive palette; for her, emotions provided color and light to the world.

David moaned his agreement, reached across the back of the seat, and scratched the ears of Anastasia, their bichon, who stirred, shook herself, and began to squeak in anticipation of arriving. "How about you, Taz? You've been such a good girl today!"

"Here's the turn," Tee said.

Ignoring Anastasia's rising chorus of squeaks, they rode quietly for a few moments. The streets surrounding Santa Fe's central Plaza squeezed traffic like water through a funnel, and Tee slowed as she concentrated to make out the street signs.

"Okay, there. Right onto Alameda." David pointed. "East on Alameda to Delgado. Right over the Santa Fe River, then the first left — it's a dirt street. The address is 526."

"'Kay." Tee wormed the car through the press of late-day traffic.

"I see it. There's the sign." Up ahead a carved, wooden sign swayed gently. "One Horse Dorp" it announced in elegant, flowing script painted deep ochre against a sky blue background. "Studio and Gallery" was added in smaller letters across the lower half.

Tee swung into a large parking area, stopping in front of a sand-colored adobe wall. A heavy, wooden gate was swung wide, through which a stone walkway wound between yucca, claret cup cactus, and blue flax. At the far end perched a stone porch shaded by a simple pergola that backed onto a single-story Spanish colonial house. The porch railings were lined with a parade of wonderful clay pots, some plain orange, some dun-colored and adorned with delicate, hand-painted, yellow daisies. A thick stand of white tidy tips filled a rusty, iron bucket, smiling up at arriving guests.

"I never understood that name. What's a dorp?" David said.

"Ask and you shall receive," Tee said. As she stepped from the car and stretched, her sister, Anne Patrick, appeared on the porch. Tall and slender, although shorter than Tee, with light brown hair worn long, her intense, brown-black eyes sparkled, producing an air of joie de vivre on her thin, companionable face. With quick, graceful steps, she swept off the porch and across the patio.

"Oh it's so good to see you!" she cried, embracing Tee in a tight hug.

"Anne!" Tee gasped, tearing up. Watching the two of them together, David was always surprised how much they sounded alike.

Releasing her younger sister, Anne turned. "David! You look great!" She disappeared in David's arms, stretched, and gave him a sloppy kiss.

"I like receptions like this," David said and grinned.

Anastasia's frantic yelps had reached a crescendo of anger and excitement.

"Taz!" Anne cried; she grabbed hold of Tee's hand, and they hurried to the Subaru. Anastasia fairly leapt into Anne's arms when released, smothering her with kisses amidst high-pitched squeaks. "I'm happy to see you too," Anne cooed at the bichon, laughing. "She looks good, Tee. So do you both. Too bad I can't say the same for myself."

"Sis, you look marvelous," Tee shot back. "Why do you get lovelier with age?"

"Your eyes must be going." Anne laughed a deep, throaty laugh of pure happiness that echoed around the courtyard. "Come inside. There's sun tea waiting." Cradling Taz in one arm, she kept Tee's hand and led them into the delicious cool.

· · · · ·

The three of them sat in sturdy, driftwood chairs on the rear porch; Anastasia sprawled full-length on the cool, stone floor, dozing. David sank back in the chair and stretched his legs out front; Tee sat erect and demure with feet together, belying her years of discipline as a dancer. Anne was more casual and sank back in her chair, cradling a glass and savoring the company. Her back garden was a delight of slender, orange blanketflower, lavender Bigelow's aster, cheatgrass, and green ephedra "Pueblo Tea." Just beyond at the rear of the lot, a low adobe bungalow nestled beneath a towering ponderosa.

"David has a question," Tee said.

"Oh yes?"

"What's a 'One Horse Dorp'?" David asked.

Anne laughed; when she did, a half-dozen squiggles of joy spread across her face.

"That was my cousin's idea, something her husband picked up when he was in South Africa years ago. It means a one-horse town, small and unpretentious. Too many galleries in Santa Fe have such grandiose names. I wanted something earthy, simple. I started this place with a hundred dollars and hope. It just fit."

Seven years prior, the death of Anne's husband from pancreatic cancer had left her physically drained and emotionally bankrupt. She'd recovered herself through photography, a casual hobby she'd indulged over the years. A new world emerged through the eyepiece of the camera. She learned to control and balance life through the frame, refining the environment around her by blending light and shadow with her natural affinity for people. She was skeptical when an acquaintance encouraged her to take up photography full time, but her confidence blossomed when she sold several prints at local art fairs. Moving to Santa Fe to open a gallery, she'd reached for a new life and discovered one. Then had come the Osgood Prize, a national award recognizing new talent in the photography world. Winning had validated her decision.

"Great name," David said. "Okay, tell us all about your fiancé. What's his name? What's he do?" David asked as he sat forward. Anne's announcement of her engagement after years of widowhood had taken David and Tee completely by surprise. They'd been convinced she'd never marry again.

"Just like a cop. No casual conversation, bull right ahead!" Tee said and smirked.

"Some problem?" David frowned with mock anger. "I want to know about my future brother-in-law, that's all."

Anne's expression changed from the smile of a happy sister to the delighted joy of a fiancée.

"His name is Estefan Portilla de la Vaca. He's Spanish and lives in the city of Girona. He comes from a family of leather traders, but he made his money selling olive oil."

"What a name! Does he have a nickname?" David exclaimed.

"No. I call him *mi cariño*. It means sweetheart."

"Nice. Your letter said you met him through the Museum of the Southwest."

"Yes, about a year ago. He's a great patron of the arts here in New Mexico. His support for the museum has been very generous. He is passionate about the history of the arts in the Southwest. I met him at an executive board meeting when he outlined his plan for creating a sustaining fund for the museum."

"What's he like?" Tee asked.

"He's fifty-six, a little shorter than me, very fit, *very* handsome. Estefan is a gracious, intelligent man. I was charmed from the beginning."

"I'm sure. But what's he *like*?" David said. "You know, is he serious, is he giddy, shy, what?"

"No one with a name like that would be giddy, you goof," Tee snapped. Her eyes narrowed as she studied Anne's response closely, trying to read Anne's feelings.

"Maybe his friends call him Steve," David said. Anne ignored him.

"He's very educated and well-spoken. He reads a lot, all sorts of topics. We've had some amazing conversations about art, culture, history. He even likes police officers," Anne teased. "Best of all, he worships the ground I stand on!"

"Bah!" David exclaimed, but he smiled.

"So he has some faults." Tee laughed. "When can we meet him?"

"I've invited him for tea tomorrow afternoon, if that's all right. I know you want to go to the Market while you're here."

"Anne, we came down here to celebrate your engagement. The Market is for later. When did he propose?"

Anne blushed. "This spring was the fourth time. I finally gave in. He flew in from Girona yesterday. I wouldn't be surprised if he gave me the ring while he's here."

"Finally getting down to the loot." David smirked. Tee pinched his arm. "Ow!"

"Behave yourself."

"Yes ma'am," David said with mock deference.

"That's wonderful. I'm glad we're here to share this with you." Tee reached and took one of Anne's hands in hers.

David stood. "Seriously, we're so happy for you." He stooped and gave Anne a hug. "You know we wish you great joy."

Tee's eyes teared up; she wanted to speak, but her emotions interfered.

At that moment, a young woman appeared in the doorway from the studio. She was of medium height, fair skin with brown, flowing hair and bangs draped across her forehead that nearly concealed her eyes. She wore a loose, tan blouse and paint-stained jeans; her clothes were as commonplace as she.

"Excuse me. Anne. I've finished putting together the display stand. I'd like to start setting things out if that's okay with you."

"Sure. Phyllis, this is my sister, Tee, and her husband, David Harrowsen. They just got in from Denver. This is Phyllis Van Houten, my assistant."

"Very nice to meet you," Phyllis replied warmly; her smile was fetching and bright, quite out of character with her appearance.

"Phyllis is a treasure," Anne added. Phyllis sheepishly lowered her head. "You know you are."

"Thank you." Her reply was soft. "I'll start on the display. Nice to meet you both." She left in an embarrassed rush.

"Shy, isn't she?" David said.

"Very. But she has a great eye for organizing things in the gallery. And she's a hard worker."

"Where'd you find her?" Tee asked.

"About two years ago, she came into the gallery browsing. I'd been thinking about hiring someone to help out. Ever since the Osgood Prize, I've had so many interruptions and was neglecting things around here. We started talking, and it turned into sort of a job interview. She wants to paint but needed a paycheck. Her references are really good. One was from a friend of mine at the diocese, Father Bob. He's a great judge of character; he knows that's important to me. Phyllis did some volunteer work with a youth group he organized. He told me he was okay with me stealing her from him." She laughed.

"What a bit of luck to find her," Tee said. "Is her art any good?"

"She's funny about it, really self-conscious. But I've seen a couple of small watercolors she's done, and I think they're excellent. I offered to display them here, but she doesn't want to. As you saw, she's very shy."

"Moving ahead, ladies, what are we doing for dinner?" David announced.

· · · · ·

Antonio Patricio, governor of the Taos Pueblo, was working over a stack of kindling at the rear of his "apartment" when there was a knock at the door. He walked through to the entryway and pulled back the thin curtains that covered the front window. It was Leo Sanchez, the pueblo's commercial enterprise director as well as Antonio's half-brother, so he opened the door immediately. Tourists were always wandering around, and into, the dwellings that composed the extensive pueblo. They were a necessary annoyance, for the money they brought was welcome, but one had to be careful.

"Come in. Will you eat?" Antonio said and extended a bowl filled with sweet fry bread. The tradition of offering food to a visitor was older than the pueblo and of great significance. They both knew that Leo's visit was not social, but Antonio made the offering all the same, and Leo gratefully accepted a morsel. To not make the offer, or decline to eat, would be an insult. Leo nibbled as Antonio guided him into the kitchen.

"Good to see you. Any news?"

Leo sank onto a chair and swallowed the last of his fry bread. "Word from the Market is that a few customers have been asking questions about the Weeping Friar. They tell the old stories we have heard before. There is rumor of lots of money."

"Are they collectors?"

"Of course. One is Oriental — very polite, very clever. The other is a fat white man who is rude and persistent. He's the one hinting at big money for anyone who can find the Friar for him — or at least provide him information about how he can acquire it. There might be others; those are the only two I know of."

"And what have our people told them?"

"Very little, as far as I know. But I'm worried someone may tell them a tale, string them along. If it comes out that they were being lied to, these men might be the type to make trouble. It would look bad for us."

Antonio shrugged in the dismissive manner so common among Native Americans.

"The Market is open to everyone. If someone buys, they take the risk on themselves. If someone cheats one of these men, we would simply make it clear that the pueblo does not condone cheating. If a wise man relieves a rich fool of some of his cash, is that our problem? It has nothing to do with us. But I'm concerned that people are asking about this relic again. The revolt was a long time ago. We should leave the memories there and look to the future."

"I agree. I'll talk to our vendors, the trusted ones. I'll tell them that they are not to get involved and that they are to let me know if anyone approaches them asking about the Friar."

"Good."

"I have to go." Leo stood.

"We should have a cookout and roast a goat. I look forward to visiting your house soon."

"Good. Peace to you and your family," Leo said and left.

Antonio returned to his kindling; however, his mind wasn't on the work. In spite of what he had said to Sanchez, Antonio held a long-harbored, secret hope. The leaders of the northern pueblos did not encourage talk about the revolt — the years of degradation that had followed were a shameful distraction for a people determined to move forward. Younger tribal members were more open-minded; many felt the revolt should be celebrated rather than forgotten. Despite his public pronouncements, Antonio believed that ignoring the revolt stood in opposition to his people's pride in their past. As an elder, he believed it his duty to nurture pride in the pueblo way of life, and important to this idea was an appreciation for the path they had followed to the present day. The legend of the Weeping Friar was inseparable from the story of the revolt, even if there was no evidence the relic actually existed. But what if this santo did exist? It would be terrible if it ended up in the hands of a collector, someone with no appreciation for its significance to the people who had staged the only successful native revolt against Spain. On the other hand, what if *his* people could lay their hands on the Friar?

An idea began to take shape in Antonio's mind. He needed information, the kind of information that required subtlety and intimate knowledge of the undercurrents of the trade in artworks. That meant certain risks, but the reward could be worth it. Obviously he couldn't do anything officially; this had to be a closely held secret. He knew someone who had the knowledge and the skill to make this work. Pulling his phone from a pocket, he scrolled through the numbers until he found the one he wanted.

"Good morning, nephew. How are you? Good. I need a favor from you."

· · · · ·

Two

NMSP Zone 1 Investigations office, Cerrillos Road, Santa Fe

Mike Charles slumped in his chair, chin on chest, staring at the litter of photos scattered across his desk. Bright morning sunlight filtered through the windows of the Investigations Office, softening the pasty, fluorescent light with tints of lemon and orange. Offhand a passerby would say Charles was asleep. Phil Ortega knew better; he'd seen this before.

"Coffee, Sarge." He set a cup on the desk.

"Umm, thanks." Without looking Charles picked up the cup, sipped, and continued staring at the photos.

Ortega sat and draped one long leg over the edge of his desk. He was one of those folks whose easygoing manner masked a directness of thinking and focused intensity that admirably suited him as an investigator, traits Charles treasured in a partner.

Charles took another sip. "Thought I'd go over the photos before we head to the autopsy."

"And?"

"Nothing here, or I'm not seeing anything. Until we ID the victim, we're stuck."

"Too soon to put out a bulletin?"

Charles shook his head. "Nope, you're right. You handle that. Make some notes."

Ortega picked up a legal pad.

"Victim in her forties or fifties, Caucasian, shoulder-length, gray hair. Wearing a blue embroidered blouse, plain blue jeans, and brown flat shoes. Two pieces of jewelry: wearing a silver, single-strand bracelet with no markings and a plain, gold wedding band. May be the victim of a hit-and-run that occurred last night. Send it statewide."

"Right. Should we mention it may have resulted from a domestic gone bad?"

"Mmmm. No, let's not speculate right now. Just say it could have been a hit-and-run."

"Got it." Ortega got on the phone to dispatch while Charles resumed his study of the photos. These moments of tedium were maddening for all but the most jaded of detectives. Every scene would speak if you listened closely enough; every photo would tell all if you looked closely enough. But the images before him weren't talking. He sighed and kept at it.

Ortega hung up. "Bulletin's sent."

Charles gave one last glance at the photos and stood.

"Off to Albuquerque."

· · · · ·

Office of the Medical Examiner, 1105 Camino Del Salud, Albuquerque
Charles and Ortega walked into the too-familiar starkness of the coroner's facility: harsh lighting, glistening tables arrayed with the unmistakable shrouded forms of corpses, and the envelopment of a cloyingly fetid cocktail of chemicals and body fluids — the odors of death. Attending autopsies was a critical but always nauseating task. They donned masks and gloves and entered what they referred to as the "dead room." Dr. Evan Ten Daam looked up from one of the tables. He was one of those rare folks who looked neat no matter what he wore, even if it was a blood-stained smock, like now.

"Good morning, guys. Just finished my walkaround. Third case this morning," he said cheerfully.

"Busy, huh? Anything for us?" Ortega asked.

"Oh I've fleshed out a few thoughts," he said firmly. Ten Daam's buoyant mannerisms compensated for the genuine sadness murder and mayhem evoked in him. Death in all its ugliness was his daily companion. He understood the necessity of his work and the role he played in bringing to light the unexplainable mysteries of death. Even so, were it not for his really bad jokes, he knew he'd probably crack up.

Charles stood next to the coroner while Ortega took the opposite side of the table, notebook poised.

"Cause of death: severe head trauma. Her skull was crushed by a wheel, maybe a fifteen-inch tire. Could be a car or a light truck; if it'd been heavier, the skull would have been ground to powder. I found faint black marks across the blouse that *might* be tread marks." He pointed to an adjoining table where clothing, shoes, and jewelry were arrayed. "Hard to see without magnification. It's all been photographed. You were correct that the body was placed on something and moved. There are several fibers stuck to the blood on the skull. The strands are blue, like from a plastic sheet or drop cloth you'd find at any home store. I've already collected them."

"The lab might be able to trace the manufacturer," Ortega said as he scribbled nonstop.

"Maybe. I can't say for certain, but the tires seem to be pretty worn with a medium tread, not something aggressive."

"Time of death?" Charles asked.

"Sometime after midnight and before 5 A.M. This time of year, the soil never really cools down at night, so rigor is accelerated. The low temperature last night was 65."

"Umm." Charles sighed.

"When we get into the body of the case, it gets more interesting," Ten Daam said, his eyes twinkling, waiting for a response. Nothing. "There are some bizarre aspects."

"Terrific! Just what we wanted to hear," Ortega chirped.

Ten Daam picked up a probe and used it as a pointer. "Look at her hands. See the burns? Between the second and third finger on the right hand, three on the left palm. Through the epidermis into the papillary region of the dermis. *Extremely* painful."

"Could they come from a cigarette?" Charles muttered.

"Likely. The ones on the palms are particularly deep. I've seen burn marks a few times before on chronic alcoholics or drug users. They get drunk and accidentally burn themselves when they're smoking. Typically those types of burns are superficial. But I've never seen anything like these. I'll go out on a limb and speculate she was tortured before she was killed."

Ortega's pen stopped above the page. "Jesus!"

"When I examine the lungs, we'll know if she smoked. But these burns appear to have been inflicted at the same time, not at random intervals like I'd expect from a careless smoker. If they'd happened at various times, some would have begun to heal."

"Tortured? So much for my theory." Charles shook his head. "I thought it was a domestic that went bad, and the partner ran her down. Torture takes this to a whole new level."

Ten Daam nodded. "There's a large abrasion on the back of her neck that also occurred before death. There was bleeding beneath the skin. Something struck her: a blunt object or a fist."

"Strong enough to knock her out?"

"Yes, but not strong enough to kill. It'll be difficult to tell because there's so much trauma to the head. She was a small woman. It wouldn't take a lot of force to knock her out."

Ortega was shaking his head. Charles stared down at the cadaver.

"I'll be able to tell you more once I've finished my rituals. Care to stick around?" Ten Daam grinned beneath his mask. Most detectives refused the invitation. The teeth-rattling noise of saws, the crackle of breaking bones, and seeing organs lifted and turned over like meat in a market were generally too much for any but the most hardened. Charles and Ortega would stay only if compelled.

"Thanks anyway, doc," Ortega mumbled, disgusted at the thought. Every police cadet had to attend an autopsy during training and generally agreed it was their most disagreeable experience.

"Talk about the clothes and jewelry," Charles said.

"Nice clothes but not expensive. Well-worn. The shoes are size five and show a lot of wear. The labels are standard, things you'd find at any Walmart or secondhand store. Two pieces of jewelry. The bracelet is a single strand, looks like silver, nothing unusual there. However, the ring is interesting."

"Why?"

"Solid-gold wedding band, nicely made, fairly valuable. There's an inscription inside. 'Filia de Deus.' It's Latin. And a date: 9-24-79."

"Can you say what that means?" Ortega asked.

Ten Daam smirked. "My Latin is confined to medical terms, I'm afraid."

"Any maker's mark?" Charles asked.

Ten Daam shook his head.

"Okay, we'll wait for your report."

"We'll get everything to the lab by close of business today. Sure you won't stay? I'll be done before lunchtime. I'll even buy. The enchiladas at Mario's are to die for. It's just across the street. Convenient, you know, just in case…" Ten Daam chuckled.

Charles blanched white beneath his mask. "Nice of you to offer," he said through clenched teeth. Breakfast had parked itself at the top of his windpipe.

"Take a rain check," Ortega grunted. "We've got a lot to do."

"Well like I always say, we'll be seeing you." Ten Daam laughed as they walked out.

"Guy's a real comic, isn't he?" Charles said after several deep gulps of the hot, outside air had revived him. The pale greenish tint of his lips began to disappear. "Bah!" he shook his head violently and spat. "I HATE those things!"

"Ten Daam just loves his work, that's all." Ortega was amused at his partner's discomfort. These events were distasteful for him, but his partner? It was incongruous for a homicide detective to have a flighty stomach. "I like someone who's enthusiastic about their job."

"Great, empathy from a partner. How special!" Charles snapped.

In the car, Ortega drove while Charles reviewed his notes. After a time, he spoke.

"We should set up a roadblock on 582 starting tonight. Between 2300 and 0500. I'll call Captain Michaels and get it approved. We're looking for anyone who drives that road frequently. Maybe they saw something. Looking for a small car or light truck with worn tires."

"Kind of a long shot."

"Yeah it is, but sometimes long shots pay off. Killers return to the scene. It happens."

Ortega shook his head. "Not this one. Someone who tortures a victim and crushes the head to make it difficult for identification is too smart to come back."

"They might be curious to know what the cops are up to."

Ortega shrugged. A grin slowly spread across his face.

"I was thinking, it must be lonesome work being a coroner. I mean, what do you talk about at supper? Honey, I saw the most amazing thing today. This body was so decomposed it..." he began. The frosty glance from Charles was enough. Ortega returned his focus to the crowded traffic ahead.

Three

One Horse Dorp Gallery, 526 Delgado Street

Estefan Portilla de la Vaca smiled. "It is a joy to meet you at last." He bowed and kissed Tee's hand. "I had the pleasure of seeing you dance at the Albert Hall some years ago. Your performance was captivating."

Tee blushed. "Thank you. That was a long time ago." She turned to David, who extended a hand. "This is my husband, David Harrowsen."

"Señor." David smiled.

"You are a police officer. It is an honorable profession and so important in today's world," La Vaca said, returning the handshake with a firm grip.

"Thanks."

"I'm so glad you all can meet at last." Anne said, happy in the moment.

"So am I! I'm also looking forward to meeting Sara and Elizabeth," La Vaca replied. Anne's grown daughters lived in New York and Iowa, respectively. She'd hoped they could be there when Tee and David visited.

"They're both very busy people. Sara's so busy now rehearsing her new role, it's difficult to say when that will happen. She wanted to be here this week but couldn't get away. She said to tell you how sorry she was."

"And Elizabeth?" La Vaca asked.

"Finishing her master's degree and working at the Humane Society. It wasn't practical for her to come."

"That's all right. Another time," La Vaca said.

"We have tea and treats on the patio." Anne led the way.

When they were settled, Tee opened the conversation. "How long will you be in Santa Fe, señor?"

"I must return to Girona next week. Business matters. I had hoped to stay longer, but..."

"We were thrilled when Anne told us of the engagement. Have you set a date?"

"Next spring," Anne interjected. La Vaca smiled.

"Yes, I think that will be perfect. I have a small villa in the Pyrenees, the ideal place for the wedding. You will be attending of course?" His smile was winning and amiable.

Tee nodded. "We wouldn't miss it for anything!"

"Very good. Anne has told me about your family. She says you are devoted to her happiness."

"We've always depended on each other, looked out for each other. It's just our way.

"I intend to make Anne very happy."

"Speaking of family, is yours a family business?" David asked. He had been studying La Vaca, watching the interplay, the gestures. While they went with the tailored magenta shirt, the fawn-colored slacks, and the handmade Italian shoes, the thought occurred to him that this could all be a put-on. He shoved the notion aside as a typical cop's reaction.

"No." La Vaca's cell phone jingled. He examined it and said, "I must answer this. Please excuse me." He rose and walked outside to the garden.

Tee nudged David. "Stop sizing him up!" she whispered.

"Hazards of the profession. Sorry."

Anne laughed. "Go ahead. I want to know what you think of him."

"See? Your sister understands."

Tee sipped her tea and sat back frowning. She was about to comment when La Vaca returned.

"I must apologize. My business often intrudes."

"I know the feeling," David answered. "We were talking about your profession."

"I own a small firm that trades in olive oil. I have many clients, and they require attention, sometimes at inconvenient moments. However, it has its rewards, and I enjoy it."

"It's important to enjoy your work," Tee said.

Anne patted La Vaca's arm. "You're being too modest."

Clearly the remark embarrassed La Vaca; he cast his eyes downward. "Am I?"

"Yes." She turned to Tee and David. "Estefan is not only very successful but very generous, far beyond his support for the arts here in New Mexico. He does marvelous work with an orphanage in his hometown. He's enlisted the diocese to cosponsor several fund-raising events here in support of the orphanage school."

"That's wonderful!" Tee exclaimed.

"I have been much blessed in my life. There are so many children who have so little. I feel compelled to give back and help them." It was easy to see that in spite of his embarrassment, Anne's praise touched La Vaca; his eyes glinted. "It's true I have a successful business and wish to share my good fortune."

David was determined to keep the conversation focused. "You trade in olive oil? Is that lucrative?"

La Vaca took a sip. "It is. I also dabble in wine."

"You have your own label?" Tee asked. She had cultivated a growing enthusiasm for wines, which David was just beginning to share.

"Wine is more of a pastime than a business. Have you lived in Colorado long?" he asked David.

"Most of my life. How is…" he began. La Vaca interrupted.

"You're a senior investigator with the Colorado Bureau of Investigation who has worked many cases, some of them very controversial. You have put yourself at risk because you are a man who believes in the rightness of what you do. I admire such character," he said. "I know this because there have been times when you've nearly lost your job."

David felt a twinge of anxiety; La Vaca had done a little sleuthing of his own. *This guy's been checking me out!* he thought. He began to feel uncomfortable, the way a foot starts to ache from a too-tight shoe. La Vaca's comments made him edgy, and in spite of himself, he squirmed in his chair. Reacting like a suspect being interrogated annoyed him; he forced himself to hide it. "I've been with the bureau twenty years now. I suppose I'm as committed as any other agent."

"You investigate many types of crimes," La Vaca said.

"All sorts. Whatever they assign to me," David answered.

"You must enjoy the work to do it for so many years."

"I do. Like your work, it has its rewards."

"The people of Colorado are fortunate to have such a dedicated guardian." La Vaca made his point graciously, adding to David's anxiety.

"I try to do the best I can."

Tee had observed David's discomfiture and changed the subject.

"Anne says you've been particularly generous to the Museum of the Southwest. What stirred your interest in this part of the world?"

La Vaca beamed. "I have twin passions: the arts and my dear Anne." He smiled across the table at her.

"That was how we met," she interjected. "Estefan was sponsoring a reception to raise funds for the orphanage while visiting the archbishop here. I attended the reception afterwards." La Vaca's face showed his delight at the memory.

"Althia, you no longer perform?" he asked.

"No. Please, call me Tee. I gave up performing when David and I married. I do some teaching, and I serve with a couple of volunteer organizations supporting dance and theater."

"I am sorry you are no longer performing. It is the world's loss."

Now Tee felt self-conscious. "That's very kind."

La Vaca continued. "You also have a passion for the arts. It is in your blood, as well as your family's. Here is Anne with her success in photography. And Sara doing so well in the New York theater."

"Yes. The role she's rehearsing is for an off-Broadway play. It opens late this fall." Anne smiled proudly. "She's so excited."

La Vaca turned to David. "You are a most handsome couple, David. And an unusual one: a policeman and an actress. I am marrying into an intriguing family!" He smiled and sat back.

He's an absolute charmer, no doubt about it, Tee thought. She returned the smile, but uneasiness crept into her mind, though she couldn't say why.

"Do all of your family live in Spain?" David asked, determined to know more about the man.

"Yes." La Vaca's phone jingled again. The cane seat of his chair crackled as he sat forward, examining it. Then he stood.

"He has a sister who…" Anne began.

"Pardon me, Anne. I am sorry, but I must go." La Vaca interrupted. "My phone has a function that reminds me of my schedule. I have a pressing appointment. I am pleased to finally meet my future in-laws." He bowed slightly at David and Tee. Anne took his arm, and together they walked to the porch. She kissed him on the cheek.

"Mi cariño," she breathed. "I'm so sorry you can't stay."

La Vaca squeezed her hand. "So am I. David and Althia are wonderful people. I hope we can be together again before I leave."

"Me too," Anne answered, kissing him. La Vaca smiled and walked to the waiting car. Luis Mirada ushered him in, and they drove off.

Back inside Anne carefully sat down. Worry lines creased her cheeks.

"I'm sorry he couldn't stay longer. He's so busy. So what do you think of him?"

Tee thought for a moment.

"Charming, intelligent, handsome, obviously crazy about you and you about him. That counts the most."

"David?"

"Oh I agree. Seems like a nice guy. Wealthy too. Quite a catch." He smiled even though his comments were anemic, and he knew it. But he couldn't say more without revealing his apprehension.

"That's all?" Anne sounded disappointed.

David leaned forward, took her hands, and looked directly into Anne's eyes.

"If you're happy, we're happy. And I can see you're *very* happy." He smiled.

Tee watched him closely. She sensed there was more to come but not now. Best leave it for later. She drained her cup and reached for a scone.

"These scones are wonderful. Don't let me leave without the recipe," she announced.

· · · · ·

Ellis Rubaldo, a.k.a. Monje, slumped around the sidewalks of the Santa Fe Plaza, eating a peach and watching the crowds carefully. He was medium height, nicely but not flashily dressed, with an angular face, pale gray eyes, and drab brown hair, and he made a practice to never stand out. With his sloping shoulders, shuffling gait, and downcast eyes, he resembled a simple monk, hence the moniker. Uninterested in the displays themselves, he took notice of conversations. He was adept at sidling up to people unseen and listening in. It was a talent that served him well.

Always on the alert for the undercurrents, today he paid particular attention to anyone selling santos. What he'd heard and read convinced him now was the time to make money in this segment of the market. At the moment, he focused on a man and woman who had stopped to examine several of these exhibited on a table. The vendor was a tiny Navajo woman wearing a striking, red blouse embroidered with sunflowers and a stunning, turquoise necklace (iliigo naalyehe in literal Navajo — jewelry). The couple sported well-cut designer jeans and matching pairs of alligator-skin, handmade Western boots. The woman's wrists were encased in broad, silver wristbands embedded with dime-sized rubies while the man flashed a platinum Movado Parlee wristwatch. Such people would be indifferent to money but extremely interested in commodities; their conversation could be valuable. Ellis slid up behind them.

"These are nice," the woman said in a soft voice tinged with an East Coast accent.

"Umm. I didn't think religious stuff interested you," the man replied, his tone short and snippy.

"No, but they're very well done. You agree?"

"I suppose so."

"How much is this one, honey?" the woman asked, pointing. The vendor's face belied nothing at the woman's casual rudeness — such things were expected from such people.

"This is a carving of San Miguel. The artist is well-known: Juan Demontes. He took a year to make this."

"That's nice. How much?"

"Four thousand."

"Ah too much!" the man snapped.

"Earl, that's not bad. It's really nice."

"No way, Alice! I can't tell one of them from the other. Four thousand? How do we know it's genuine? You ever hear of this Juan whatshisname?"

"Earl, my Aunt Nancy used to have a table full of these. It was like an altar: saints, candles, everything. She prayed every day. I'd like to do the same thing in the Catskill house. In her memory, you know."

"Sounds very Catholic," the man blustered. "It's hot; let's get a drink some-wheres."

"Hang on, I want..."

Ellis grinned, enjoying the argument.

"Monje?" There was a tap on his shoulder; he whirled around to see Luis Mirada standing there.

"Luis?" His surprise was obvious. "How'd you find me? Oh I know. Portava."

"There are ways. Yes, I spoke to Portava. He told me you came home to Santa Fe."

"Yeah. My mom and dad lived near here before they died. I haven't seen Portava in a long time. How is he?"

Mirada shook his head. "Cancer. He won't last the year."

"Too bad," Monje said and dismissed the thought. Neither of them really gave a damn about Portava. "What do you want?"

"Let's go somewhere and talk." Mirada's hand tightened on Ellis's shoul-der, guiding him around a corner and down the street, stopping at a green GMC Acadia.

"Get in."

Monje slid into the passenger seat, admiring the upscale, tan, leather seats and lavish sound system with its blue-white digital display. "Some ride."

"One of the benefits of my job."

Driving away from the environs of the Plaza, Mirada began to talk. "What are you up to these days?"

"A little of this and that," Monje hedged.

"Still at it, eh? How's the game here?"

"Depends. The cartels have most of the drug trade. I stay away from that; they're real badasses! The dope cops are always around. There's money to be made in other ways."

"Such as?"

"Like I said, this and that. What about you?"

"I have several interests at the moment." Mirada wheeled into a dirt park-ing area off Bishops' Lodge Road. The lot was deserted; signs announced, "Protect your valuables and lock your car. Thieves are everywhere."

"Appropriate, don't you think?" Mirada said and chuckled with a nod at the signs. He stepped out and motioned Monje do the same. "It's a nice afternoon for a walk." Monje knew Mirada's mercurial personality too well to refuse. Side-by-side they strolled along a path lined with ponderosas; flies buzzed in the scrub, and the stifling heat wrapped around them like a blanket.

"What're you interested in? What're you looking for?" Monje perked up. "Tell me what you want, Monk will get it."

Mirada stopped and faced Monje. "First let's talk about the Saud."

Monje blanched.

"What….what do you want to know?"

"You betrayed me and my brother," Mirada growled nastily.

"I didn't. I DIDN'T!"

Mirada's hand was a blur as he jabbed a thumb to the side of Monje's neck just below the jawbone, forcing his head back and upwards. "With you it's hard to tell where the truth ends and the lies begin. Let's find out," he said in a low, menacing voice.

"ARRGH!" Monje squirmed as he tried to resist.

"When they brought Elias's body home, I saw what they did to him. Hijo de puta (son of a bitch)! You're responsible."

"NO! It wasn't like that."

The veins in Mirada's neck protruded.

"Veryle…Veryle was the one," Monje bawled.

"Convince me I should believe you," Mirada snapped.

"Before I got arrested, she told me Elias talked to the Saudi police. I don't know how she knew that. Elias and I were friends, remember? We'd never snitch on each other."

"Maybe you're the one who talked," Mirada snarled. "You never could stand pain. Like now." His thumb dug deeper into Monje's neck.

"Ah! Agghhh…." Monje began to choke.

Mirada chuckled, a snapping, angry sound that trailed away into sinister nothingness. Monje's face was turning purple; his eyes began to roll back. Mirada relaxed the pressure slightly.

"Can't breathe," Monje gasped.

"Of course you can. You're speaking. Talk." Mirada said quietly.

"I didn't tell them anything. It was Veryle."

Mirada mulled this over. Perhaps Monje was telling the truth.

"Pezado de merda (piece of shit)! I should kill you right now."

"NO! Let me go. Please."

"Talk," Mirada ordered with a shove. Monje slumped nearly to the ground, rubbing his neck while glaring at Mirada through watery eyes. Mirada chuckled again, enjoying the damage he'd inflicted. "Well?"

"Ugh…ugh," Monje coughed. Forcing himself upright, he faced Mirada like a scolded child, trying to appear defiant but actually looking sheepish and afraid.

"After the Saudi cops arrested me, they took me to this shit hole of a jail. They beat the hell out of me. One time after they'd worked me over, I heard two of the officers talking. I guess they thought I'd passed out. One of them was talking about me and Elias. I knew 'cause he said our names. I couldn't make out most of their gibberish, but I heard them mention 'shitan zu el oudon.' It means 'devil with the green eyes.' I'd heard that before; a guy I knew in the Army said the Iraqi POWs called Veryle that 'cause she was so brutal with them."

Mirada nodded. "Okay. *Maybe* they were going to arrest her next. Or *maybe* you gave her up to get yourself out. Which was it?"

"No. They threw me in this nasty cell while they decided what to do with me, kept me there for a couple of weeks. I kinda got to know one of the guards and offered him a bribe. I told him I'd take him to my stash, and he could have anything he wanted if he got me out. It worked."

Mirada stared at Monje. The man seemed credulous enough.

"It's the truth!" Monje said. "He got me out and took all my shit."

"You say. Still, if you gave up Veryle in exchange for your own freedom, I approve. Miserable bitch! Ever hear what happened to her?"

"No. I split when I got out. Later Portava told me he heard she got out through Lebanon but never could confirm it. She just disappeared."

"All right," Mirada said. He wasn't completely convinced by Monje's escape story although Portava had told him the same thing about Veryle. He set this aside for later.

Monje saw the hesitation in Mirada and moved in. "How'd you get out?" he asked.

"I heard you'd been arrested. I snuck onto a boat with a bunch of pilgrims going to Iran. I lost everything though."

"You with a bunch of pilgrims? Whew!" Monje laughed.

Mirada cupped Monje's chin and examined the side of Monje's neck. "You can tell your friends it's a hickey," he said and sniggered. "I had to make sure I could trust you."

"Do you?"

At this Mirada threw back his head and laughed. "No." It was time to move ahead.

Monje laughed too. "Me neither. So what are you doing here?"

"I said I have several interests, but they don't concern you right now. I'm here with my boss. He wants a particular santo. It's supposed to be a relic from the colonial period. It's even got a name: the Weeping Friar of Chimayo. He wants to be the prime minister of Spain, and he has this stupid idea finding this thing will help him somehow. I told him I'd find it."

"Really. Weird. This guy must be loaded for you to hook up with him. Rich guys have such stupid ideas. 'Course that's profitable for us, right? So who is he?"

"None of your business."

Monje shrugged this off. "If I get this santo for you, what's the money?"

Mirada grinned. "First you get it for me *somehow*." He stared at Monje. "Understand?"

Recognition spread across Monje's thin face. "Yeah. I can arrange it."

"We'll talk money later."

Monje shook his head. "I don't work for credit."

Mirada flexed his thumb. At this Monje winced. Mirada was right — he couldn't take pain and knew he was a coward at heart.

"Okay, okay. I know people who can help us."

"How do you know them?"

"I have this arrangement. I do private auctions for collectors who have certain needs and don't ask questions. I take care of them. There's a guy that brings santos to the auctions sometimes. They're pretty good. Some are even genuine," he chirped. "I don't know where he gets them, but they're very good. He's working with somebody else but won't say who. And there's a woman who acts as an agent for people who don't want to get their hands dirty dealing with someone like me. She hasn't been around Santa Fe long but seems to know her stuff. She's sold a couple of nice pieces. Bought some stuff too."

"Names?"

Monje shook his head. "No. If I say, you might cut me out. Nice try."

Mirada chuckled. "All right. I'll meet you at the Market tomorrow at three. Have something for me by then."

"How can I get ahold of you?"

"I'll find *you*. This way neither of us knows too much." Mirada turned and walked toward the car. Monje stared at his back, thinking hard. There was no reason to tell him anything else....this could be profitable in more than one way. He followed Mirada back to the car.

Four

New Mexico State Highway 582 near Okay Owinge

Officer Brian Inez checked his watch. One-seventeen. He sighed.

"Long time to go," Officer Rick Hayes mumbled, rubbing his eyes. Overtime was always welcome, but working a double was brutal. He'd already worked the afternoon shift and was tired beyond imagining. He squinted into the night, shifting uncomfortably in the seat against the hard vinyl. They were parked at the side of Highway 582 near where the woman's body had been found the day before. It was hot and quiet.

Trooper Melanie Smith walked slowly along the pavement, heel-to-toe, killing time and fighting fatigue like the others. She was the state police contribution to the roadblock.

"How long since the last car?" she called.

"Half an hour."

Smith continued walking. Then headlights appeared just beyond the skyline.

"You got this one?" Hayes called.

"Yeah." Smith stepped to the center of the road. A light-colored sedan rounded the curve and slowed. Smith waved her flashlight, motioning the driver into the lane of cones set up just for this purpose. The sedan moved into the lane and stopped. The driver was a woman. Smith approached and spoke to her.

Another set of lights flickered against the darkness.

"Okay, Brian. We're up." They stepped out of their Tahoe, and Hayes walked to the center of the road. A small SUV emerged from the dark, slowed, and stopped. Inez flashed his light at the driver. The car didn't move.

"Come on. What, we got a drunk here?" Hayes said in disgust. Just what they needed! He flashed his light and gestured for the driver to pull over. "Come on!"

A head appeared through the driver's window. In a millisecond, the world exploded with light and sound. Hayes saw two flashes and dropped, rolling left while drawing his Beretta 9-mm pistol.

CRACK! CRACK!

His most-enduring recollection was the heat of rounds whizzing above his head and the slap of concussion against his face. He rolled off the pavement. Inez dived behind their unit.

"SHOTS FIRED! SHOTS FIRED!" Inez shouted into his radio. "HIGHWAY 582! SHOTS FIRED!"

Smith ducked, screaming, "STAY DOWN!" at the woman. She dropped behind the sedan, drew her Glock, and worked her way to the rear of the car. A quick peek — the SUV was sitting in the road, driver's door open.

"Rick, you okay?"

"Yeah! Brian?"

"Yeah!"

"Get your rifle!" Smith shouted. Inez worked his way to the driver's door of the Tahoe and quickly unracked the AR-15 mounted behind the driver's seat.

Hayes crawled crablike along the hard sand to Smith. Staying low, together they moved along the ditch paralleling the road until they were even with the SUV. The engine was running. There was no movement inside.

Hayes pointed two fingers at his eyes, then to the rear of the car. Smith nodded.

"Cover!" she called.

"Cover!" Inez answered. He shouldered the rifle, aiming at the SUV's windshield.

Hayes crawled to the rear of the car while Smith covered the interior. Avoiding the taillights, he stayed low, then stepped into a squat. Lightning quick he took a peek into the rear compartment. Nothing.

"Clear," he called softly.

"Okay." Smith squatted, reached for the passenger door with one hand while aiming her Glock with the other. She yanked it open. Empty.

"Clear!" she called.

Inez slowly walked forward, lowering his rifle to low ready. Smith returned to comfort the terrified woman driver while Hayes began scanning the surrounding darkness for any sign of movement. The utter stillness was disconcerting after the violent action of the last thirty seconds. Sirens wailed in the distance, getting closer.

"What the hell?" Hayes snapped as his entire body began shaking. "What the hell?!"

• • • • •

Phil Ortega wiped sleep from his eyes, trying to make sense of the surreal chaos around him. The clouds were tinged with yellow, announcing the approaching dawn. Red-and-blue emergency lights flashed eerily, radios blared, and K-9s barked, eager to begin the chase. A state police helicopter overhead kicked up dust, the roar of the engine adding to the din. Thankfully it moved off toward the west, and the noise lessened a bit. Ortega approached a thin sergeant who was standing on the centerline of the highway, sketching on a pad. His black uniform was creased and neat. No matter what the situation, the New Mexico State Police always looked sharp, and Ortega grinned with pride.

"'Morning, Sarge."

"Hi." Sergeant John Phillips looked past Ortega. "Where's Mike?"

"Home with his sick baby."

The sergeant nodded.

"The officers okay?"

"Yeah, just shook up. They're at Tribal HQ with the captain."

"Thank God. I'll talk to them later. How's the search going?"

"Nothing so far. Found a shoeprint, but the ground's so hard, it's not useable. K-9 lost the scent after a few feet. Wanna take a look at the car?"

"Sure."

They walked to where the SUV had been abandoned. A technician was kneeling on the pavement, leaning inside the driver's door.

"Anything, Mick?" the sergeant asked the tech.

"Not a lot. Looks like someone's been using this awhile from all the trash in here. The plates are stolen from Oklahoma, but the trace of the VIN turned up negative."

Ortega walked to the rear of the car. "Okay if I take a look in the back?"

"Yeah, I've checked it once. I haven't dusted for prints."

"I'll be careful." Ortega donned rubber gloves and carefully opened the rear hatch. The compartment was surprisingly clean compared to the rest of the interior. There were a few blotches on the carpet and several fibers.

"These stains on the carpet. Blood?"

"Can't say. I'll luminol it when we get the car to the garage."

"There are some fibers stuck to the carpet. Make sure to take those."

"'Kay."

"We found two 9-mm casings just outside the door," the sergeant added. "We've collected them already."

"Good."

"Think this might be your murder suspect?"

Ortega shrugged. "Maybe." He turned and looked back toward the police units, getting a perspective while Phillips described the sequence of events. "Driver stopped here, leaned out, and fired. By the time they cleared the car, he was gone. No idea which way he went."

"Sure it's a male?" Ortega asked.

"Hayes says he thinks so. Smith and Inez didn't get a good look. There was another driver stopped at the time, but she couldn't tell us anything. Too scared."

"Yeah," Ortega mused. He felt confused and not just because he'd been roused from a deep sleep. Things didn't add up. Why would a murder suspect come back? Why leave a car that might yield a wealth of evidence? Whoever had dumped the body was very careful not to leave any clues. Why be so sloppy this way?

The police units had been left in place as if frozen in time. He walked toward them, trying to form a mental image of the shooting. Phillips's description of the incident fit the evidence. Why this had happened was a different matter.

· · · · ·

The Plaza, Santa Fe

"Taz, leave it," Tee ordered. Taz spit out the remnant of Navajo taco she'd retrieved from the sidewalk. "Good girl." Tee stroked her fur. The bichon wagged her tail, relieved at the praise — knowing it would end when another opportunity for scraps presented itself. Nose to the pavement, she continued her search. Tee and David were strolling the periphery of the Plaza. The day was warm with the promise of rain later on. The air was alive with the blended aromas of fry bread, chili, and caramel corn, blaring rock and roll, and squalling babies. The August Indian Market was in full swing, and throngs of curious shoppers crowded the sidewalks. Skirting around vendors, beggars, and tittering young folks, Tee and David drank in the atmosphere. The Plaza was a venue unrivaled for its tone and ambience, to be savored and relished in all circumstances.

"Let's grab a seat." David led the way toward the war memorial. They sat and watched the humanity flow around them. Taz lay down and splayed out her hind legs in the manner of all bichons.

"What did you think of La Vaca?" Tee asked. "You seemed a bit edgy with him."

David twisted his lips. "Was I that obvious? Hope I didn't spoil the tea party."

"No. Nobody noticed but me."

"He seemed to know a lot about me, my career. I had the distinct feeling he'd checked me out, and I didn't like that. I guess that's not surprising. I just... well give me a moment." David began. "What do you think about him?"

Tee laughed. "Okay, I'll take it. He's witty, smart, and enthusiastic about the arts. He appears to care about Anne. I didn't like the way he kept interrupting her, but it didn't faze her. I think she might care more for him than he does her."

"Why?"

"Just a feeling. He's charming, almost too charming. I suppose I'm not accustomed to all that formality. It just seemed a bit..."

"Put on?"

"Maybe. Not the sort of manners I expected. Too Old World. His affection seemed a little contrived. Does that make sense?"

"It does. Do you think Anne really loves him?"

"I do. I always could judge her feelings pretty well. It bothers me that she might be more committed to this than he is," she mused. "Some of the things he said about you he could have heard from Anne or from the news. They didn't seem suspicious to me."

"Maybe. But his comment about nearly losing my job more than once, that's not common knowledge. You ever mention any of my cases to Anne? Especially the ones when I got into trouble?"

"I could have. I don't remember. When we talk, it's usually about Anne and her daughters and her work. Just the things sisters talk about."

David pressed on. "I began to realize he asked more questions than he answered. Anne told us more about him than he did. He learned quite a bit about us. What do we really know about him? He sells olive oil, he's rich, and he raises money for an orphanage. Fine. What's underneath? My cop instincts tell me there's a lot he held back. I wonder if those phone calls were set up on purpose. Didn't the timing seem a little odd to you? Every time I started to ask about his background or family, the phone rang. He was in control; we weren't. Am I acting too much like a cop?" He rubbed the back of Tee's neck.

"No, although I don't think the phone calls were arranged. Anne warned us he's a very busy man. But you're right about one thing: Whenever we asked a question, he answered with one. I didn't pick up on it until now. Why did he do that? The conversation wasn't about him; it was about us."

"Pretty much. That's strange because he doesn't come across as one of those Type A personalities who always have to be in charge. On the surface, he seems to be an easygoing, nice guy. I want to know what's underneath. Think I'll check him out." He saw the look of concern in Tee's eyes. "Quietly. Okay?"

"This is supposed to be a vacation, remember?" She leaned up and kissed him.

"My love and my best friend."

"Mine too."

They sat in silence for a few moments while Taz alternately sniffed the air and poked her nose at every passerby, hoping for a handout or at least some attention.

"Look, isn't that Kate?" Tee asked, shielding her eyes against the sun. "Over by that jewelry stand?" She pointed.

David stared for a minute or two. "Don't think so."

"It is! She's talking to the man with the light hair and blue shirt." Tee stood. "Let's go say hello." David remained seated, shaking his head.

"Not now."

Tee glared at him, perplexed. "Why not?" she asked. Why ignore their good friend and David's former partner?

David looked up. "I'll tell you later. It's not a good time." He stood. "Come on, Taz. Let's check out the Market." He took the leash from Tee and walked away, leaving Tee standing alone, wondering. She glanced back toward Kate, who was still speaking to the man in blue. With a sigh of irritation, she followed David and Taz, who were picking their way through the hordes.

When they had left the environs of the Plaza, David found a shaded bench near a school, stopped, and sat down. A pickup basketball game was in progress on the playground — shouts and happy laughter drifted across the breeze. Taz leapt onto the bench and stretched out next to him. Tee stood before them, arms folded, irked at David's secretiveness.

"What's going on?" she demanded.

David stroked Taz's coat and looked directly into Tee's eyes, taking a serious posture.

"Remember I told you a while back that Kate was on special assignment?"

Tee nodded. "I remember you weren't happy about it. You picked up some of her cases on top of what you already were working."

"That was one reason but not the most important. She's working with a multistate, federal, counterterrorism task force. When she left for the assignment, it wasn't clear what her job would be, but John Stephenson is her boss. You remember, he moved on from CBI to work with the feds? He's with the same outfit she is."

"That's good, isn't it? John's a capable man."

"He is. It was CBI's loss, but it was probably a good career move for him. He specifically requested Kate as the CBI liaison, and I was okay with that. The director told me later Kate would be working as an undercover agent. That bothered me."

"Why?"

"She'll be dealing with some very dangerous people. I know John will take any precautions necessary, but this is another level from what she's used to. I worry about her. You know how impulsive she can be."

"You should have shared this with me sooner," she said quietly.

"I know. I'm sorry. I didn't want you worrying too."

"So today when we saw her, she was working, and you didn't want to compromise her."

David nodded. He reached up and squeezed Tee's hand. "Sorry I was so abrupt. We needed to get away from there before she saw us. If she reacted the wrong way..."

"That's all right. I hope she's okay. I wonder why she's in Santa Fe."

"We'll find out someday." He tickled Taz's flanks again. "Let's go, Taz." She jumped down and led them along the sidewalk, tail curled, prancing and sniffing the delicious air.

What David hadn't shared was that when they saw Kate, he saw someone else nearby. To his trained eye, it looked as if someone else was watching Kate too. And that added to his worry.

· · · · ·

NMSP Zone 1 Investigations Office

"Morning, Phil," Mike Charles said as he entered. He carried two coffees and a bag emanating the delectable aromas of cinnamon and apples — a rare treat, breakfast empanadas. "Sorry I couldn't be there last night. Mike's got a cough."

Ortega looked up from his desk, his face drawn and sunken with fatigue. The coffee was most welcome, and he gratefully he accepted it. "He okay?"

"Yeah, Kirsten's taking him to the doc this morning. You know how it is with these little guys — something's always going on."

Ortega took a hefty gulp. "Need this."

Charles sat down opposite. The bag rustled as he withdrew two empanadas and handed one to his partner. He unscrewed the lid from his coffee and sipped. "Hot."

"Um," Ortega mumbled. He sat back and closed his eyes, letting the delicious warm coffee roll across his tongue.

"Tell me about the shooting."

Ortega took another hearty drink and unwrapped his roll.

"Not much to tell. The trooper had a car stopped at the roadblock. This guy in an SUV comes down the road and stops when he sees the officers. Inez motions him to pull over. The guy leans out and cranks two rounds at Hayes. By the time they got to the car, it was empty. Suspect beat feet without a trace. Captain Villalva said he's calling off the search at nine."

"Damn! Close call. They find anything in the SUV?"

Ortega shrugged. "It's at the garage being processed. They lifted a couple of prints. There were some stains in the back compartment that could be blood and a few fibers. We'll know more later." Ortega sipped. "Strange thing. I guess you were right; it just doesn't make sense our suspect would come back to the scene. Why take the chance?"

"Like I told you, sometimes long shots pay off," Charles said, not quite believing himself.

"Maybe. The *good* news is the coroner called; he identified our victim. Her fingerprints were on file with DMV. He emailed the info to me a few minutes ago."

"Great. And?"

Ortega read from the computer screen on his desk.

"Mary Ellen Marston. Born in Las Cruces, February 11, 1954. Last known address 820½ East Water Street, Santa Fe. A couple of parking tickets, no other history. No next of kin listed on her driver's license application. One of the tickets shows the same address for business and home: a shop called The Sacred Way."

"Okay, I'll start working on a warrant."

Ortega bit off a healthy chunk of empanada. Detectives rarely ate small bites; in their work, there wasn't time. He chewed twice and swallowed. "Remind me, what county is Las Cruces in?"

"Dona Ana County. Check county records for all the usual stuff. But first finish your breakfast…and chew your food, detective!" Charles ordered in his best new-parent tone.

"Umm…yeth thir," Ortega said and chuckled through a mouthful of pastry at his partner's reproach. Charles typically inhaled his food; perhaps fatherhood was having a positive influence on his eating habits. He swallowed. "If there are no next of kin, why was she wearing the wedding ring?"

"No idea. Maybe she was a widow and wore it in memory of her husband. All we know is the inscription is in Latin. Maybe she was Catholic. That's the language of the church, right?"

Ortega swallowed more coffee. "I'm a Methodist. What do I know?"

"Well there's a priest at the diocese who's a friend of mine. He can find out if she was baptized a Catholic. I'll give him a call later. I'll start on the warrant." Charles signed on his computer, pulled up the warrant forms, and began typing.

· · · · ·

820½ East Water Street, Santa Fe, The Sacred Way

It was after midday by the time they arrived at Mary Marston's shop — finding a judge with a few minutes to look over the search warrant had proved troublesome. They parked next to a black-and-white Santa Fe PD cruiser in the rear of the shop. A patrolman slumped in the front seat gave them a bored stare.

"Sorry this took so long." Ortega waved the warrant at the officer.

"No problem." The officer got out, stretched, and yawned. "Last day of my week. Our lab unit is waiting for my call."

"Okay. I'll let you know."

Charles slowly walked the perimeter of the shop, peering through the dirty windows and getting an overall impression of the place. He discovered nothing of interest. A rusted, gray Dodge Dart squatted in the weeds at the back, dust-covered, one tire going flat, obviously unused for some time. He returned to find Ortega standing to one side of the rear door while the patrolman worked on the lock. Finally there was a soft click; he turned the knob and opened the door.

"That was slick," Charles said.

"Something I learned in my previous life. Better than breaking the lock." The officer chuckled. He pushed the door open and waved them in.

The shop smelled of dust and incense, thick and noxious in the heat. It was cramped and stuffy. In a minute, they had walked the three rooms — nothing obvious presented itself. A cubicle at the back, no more than a closet, held a tiny bed, chair, and small table.

"Phil, start at the front. I'll work here."

"'Kay."

It would be hyperbole to call the living quarters spartan. Charles searched the tiny cell in two minutes. The bed was rumpled, sheets twisted in an untidy mess. A plate sat on the table containing remnants of toast, molding and crumbling to crumbs in the heat. One tiny corner contained a toilet and sink. As he stepped out, he noticed a curtain hanging in one corner; it concealed an alcove used as a closet. A few blouses, skirts, and jeans hung neatly inside. On a shelf overhead was a small box. Inside were a few pieces of costume jewelry, a silver necklace, and two rings set with semiprecious stones. Neither was inscribed. There were half a dozen holy cards, which he read without interest. He closed the box and returned it to the shelf. Next to it was a faded, black prayer book, much worn with use. As he picked it up, a card dropped out. On the back in a small, cramped hand were written several Biblical references. He tucked it back inside. On the flyleaf of the prayer book was inscribed, "Mary Ellen-thank you for all you've taught me. God's beauty will follow you." The letter P was signed with an elegant, stylish hand, almost like calligraphy. A photo was taped below the inscription. It was a picture of Mary as a young girl, seated on a lawn with two other girls, all wearing silly smiles the way preteen girls do. Charles pulled it loose; on the back was written, "With cousins at county fair, 1965." He stuck the card back inside the book, set it aside, and turned to a box on the floor.

The contents were a jumble of shoes, pens, newspapers, and miscellany. He put the box on the table and returned to the closet, found nothing else, and returned to the box, working slowly through the tangled mess. Carefully as he could, he removed each item from the box, examined it, and put it aside. Beneath the shoes, he found a folio containing a sheaf of photographs. One photo startled him. In it Mary Marston appeared in the habit and frock of a nun, surrounded by young children, standing in a school yard.

"Phil," he called. When Ortega appeared, he pointed. "Look at this."

"A nun. But nuns don't marry! What's with the wedding ring?"

"I'll bet Father Dunleavy can explain it."

"Sure hope so." Ortega walked out.

Charles studied the photo. Sister Marston had a thin, kind face and a winning smile. At the thought of what had been done to her, bile rose in his throat.

"Why did this happen to you, Sister Mary?" he muttered. He set aside the photo and continued leafing through the album. One faded, creased photo was of Mary Marston as a small child, standing in front of two adults, probably her parents. The woman standing behind her could be her mother. In spite of the condition of the picture, he could see the resemblance: the same thin face, the same high cheekbones and kindly smile. The man was stern and thick, wearing the impatient look of someone clearly uncomfortable in a too-tight suit. On the back was a date: Birthday 1962. Charles sighed. Here he was once again, rummaging through the remnants of some poor soul's life, looking for clues amidst the fragments. The thought depressed him.

Most of the remaining photos were black-and-white landscapes or pictures of family pets. The newspapers were clippings from the Las Cruces *Sun-News*; Charles dropped them in the box to be examined later. What remained was a tangle of pens and pencils, rubber bands, paperclips, and bric-a-brac. He carried the box and the book into the main room, where Ortega stood at the sales counter, sorting through various papers.

"Anything?"

"Sales receipts, nothing since last Friday. A couple of bills. A few bucks and change in the cash drawer. Mail from last Saturday, unopened. Monday's mail was still in the box. A few prayer books, beads, cards with saints on them, incense sticks, stuff like that."

"The beads are called rosaries. She couldn't have made much of a living with this place," Charles said sadly. "All right. We know she was killed early Tuesday morning. Where was she between Saturday and Tuesday? We need to find out what time the mail was delivered Saturday and Monday. Since she collected the mail Saturday, that gives us a timeline. And take any bills you find; we need something with an address to match the warrant."

"We're assuming Mary collected the mail and not someone else," Ortega said.

"Let's go with that."

"You find anything besides that picture?" Ortega asked.

"One photo of her with her parents. A prayer book, signed by someone with the initial P. There was a picture of Mary with her cousins but no names. Old newspaper clippings." Charles began to feel sick; the airless cocktail of dust, incense, and mouse urine inside the shop was choking him. He thought he would pass out. "I'm going outside for a minute," he gasped.

"I'll join you. This place really stinks."

The scorching outside air was refreshing by comparison. Ortega walked to their car and returned with two bottles of water. "Sorry, it's hot."

"Never mind." Charles removed the cap and drank off half the bottle. "Whew! Nasty in there." He spat, then inhaled deeply several times. "That's better."

Ortega nodded. "Let's recap what we know. Mary Marston was born in Las Cruces and might have grown up around there. She became a nun. She ended up running a shop in Santa Fe selling beads and prayer books. Did she quit being a nun? How'd that happen? This couldn't have been a robbery — money's still in the drawer. No signs of any disturbance. Her car is still here — looks like it hasn't been driven for a while. If someone took her from here, I think it was somebody she knew. She was tortured before she was killed… why? None of this makes much sense."

"Phil, the other night at the scene you said she could have been killed by someone she knew. Let's assume the suspect *was* someone she knew, otherwise there'd be signs of a struggle, right?"

"True. So she left with the suspect or suspects. Voluntarily? Maybe. The torture happened someplace else, and she was killed someplace else. Then her body was dumped in *another* place. We need to find out where the torture and the murder happened. We'll only find out if we make an arrest *and* the suspect confesses. Otherwise it might be impossible."

"I agree. Okay, we need to find out who were her friends, people she associated with. We're looking for letters, diaries, anything personal. We know she had a friend with the initial P. That's all we have to go on unless the lab folks turn up anything." He turned to the SFPD officer who was sitting on the trunk of his unit, smoking a cigarette. "Call the lab tech, will ya?"

"Sure."

"After that check with the neighbors, see if they saw anything. Ask about friends or regular visitors. Especially anyone who drove a black SUV. Ask about people with a name beginning with the letter P. Anything they might know will help. Tell them that this is a missing person case, nothing else."

"You bet." The officer extinguished his smoke and began talking into his packset microphone.

"Maybe your priest friend knew her," Ortega said.

"Maybe. Talking to a priest right now isn't a bad idea; we need all the help we can get," Charles said and drained his bottle. "Okay, back at it." He gulped the rest of his water. They walked inside.

Five

Casa Diminuto Hotel, US Highway 85, south of Pojoaque

Eight people sat around a table, closely watching each other. The air in the room smelled musty; tiny speckles of dust drifted across the beams of sunlight, lending an atmosphere of untended dreariness to the proceedings. Air conditioning purred softly, and the room was cold, but no one paid attention; their focus was on a silver-maned man dressed entirely in black. Their restless anxiety was palpable.

After a brief interval, he spoke.

"Up four," he said firmly, rapping the table with his hand. Only one spectator reacted. The woman screwed her lips together into a frown. The bid was approaching her limit. She resumed her scrutiny of the figure at the center of the table, a scarred, chipped carving of St. Michael the Archangel.

"May I?" she asked, standing. Monje, the ninth member of the group, was standing quietly in a corner observing the bidding. He nodded. "Of course."

The woman leaned to examine the figure, sniffing; there was a hint of incense, the patina was faded, and the gilt was worn.

After a moment, Monje asked, "Yes?"

She shook her head. "No."

"The bid is sixty-four thousand," Monje announced, watching their faces.

47

A sturdily built man with protruding cheekbones wearing a tan shirt and jeans pursed his lips. "Up two," he said firmly.

Monje nodded. "Sixty-six."

A brunette woman wearing a mauve jacket leaned close to the man seated next to her, whispering. Ever so slightly, he shook his head. She whispered louder so that the others could hear her urging him. His face showed no emotion; his fingers curled and uncurled several times. Then he raised one finger.

"Up one," Monje said.

The woman smiled. Still stone-faced, the man sat back, idly stroking a thick, silver signet ring prominent on his right index finger. Monje scanned the room.

"The bid is sixty-seven thousand," he said evenly. Only the mechanical whirring of the air conditioner intruded on the silence. Monje checked his watch. "Any more? I'm selling for sixty-seven thousand." He glanced at each person in turn, hesitating a moment on the face of the black-clad bidder. The man opened his mouth, hesitated, stared at St. Michael thoughtfully, closed his mouth, and shook his head.

"Sold," Monje announced, slapping his hand on the table. The tension in the room vaporized. The crowd stood and quickly made its way out without conversation. Four people lingered: two men and two women. The successful buyers smiled at each other while Monje donned cotton gloves, retrieved the statue from the table, and carefully packed it in a box. He folded his hands in front of him and stood, waiting. The man produced a roll of bills and handed them to Monje, who carefully thumbed through the money, smiled, and handed over the box. "Well done," he said.

Cradling their new acquisition under one arm, he and his companion left. The other man who'd stayed behind watched them leave. He was tall and well-turned out in a mustard yellow, Western-cut jacket, bolo tie with a turquoise clasp, designer jeans spotted with silver studs, and snakeskin boots embossed with silver rosettes up both sides. He turned to Monje with a wide-eyed smile.

"That was all right," he said.

The woman who had asked to examine the St. Michael was the other lingerer. She was short and stocky, wearing a nice but not ostentatious gray blouse and navy blue slacks. "That was a fair price, but my client didn't want to go that high," she said and sighed.

"His loss." Monje grinned. "Now I have some business to take care of."

"Sure. Keep me in mind for next time," she said.

"I will." When she had left, Monje leisurely counted the money. "That's $60,300 to you," he said and handed the stack to the man who quickly thrust it into a pocket.

"I have a unique item for your next gathering," he said.

"Oh?" Monje was checking the room, ensuring nothing was left to betray their presence. One had to be careful in this business. "Another santo."

The man nodded. "A Virgin and Child. There's only one other like it, at the Loretto Chapel."

"Risky, selling another one so soon. People might catch on. Who's the artist supposed to be?"

"Someone prominent in Santa Fe. I haven't set a price, but in *this* market..." He winked. "I'll let you know."

Monje hesitated. "I want to know the artist's name first. What if a buyer shows up who's familiar with that particular artist's work? Could be tricky."

"Don't worry. My source only sells his work through me; no one will catch on. The real santeros has no way of knowing either. Slick, eh?" He laughed, then waved a hand around the room. "If these people really gave a damn about provenance, they wouldn't be here, right?"

"True. But I want a thousand up front," Monje said firmly.

"I know, you don't work on credit. Make it five hundred," he said, pulling an ornately engraved, gold money clip from a pocket and peeling off several bills. "That'll cover your expenses. I'll call you." Without another word, he left.

Monje stayed behind several minutes; it wouldn't be prudent for them to be seen together. He flipped open his phone and dialed.

"Hello?" a woman answered.

"It's me. Let's meet and settle up."

"I can't until later. How'd it go?" she asked.

"Sixty-five."

"Bring it. You'll get your cut when I see the cash. Not before." Monje knew better than to argue.

"Agreed."

"I'll call." She rang off.

"Stupid bitch," he snapped, smiling. He carefully separated two bills from the packet of money, tucking them into his left shoe. Lying about the price lessened the sting of working with such a partner; the two hundred was a nuisance fee. A little of this and a little of that added up. The remaining bills he thrust into an envelope brought for just this purpose. He sealed it, laid it in his briefcase, and walked out, taking care to use the rear exit of the hotel.

Out front the man in the Western jacket strolled toward his car. As he neared it, a voice called to him. He stopped, patting the .32 auto he had tucked on one hip.

"Got a minute?" The stocky woman approached him.

"Sure."

She produced a card. "Katrina Valverde." She smiled, extending a hand. "I deal in rare art."

"Oh?" the man studied the card. It bore only the name and a phone number. "You have a gallery?"

"No. I'm a personal representative of clients with cultured tastes." She appeared poised but deferential. In this avaricious game, a woman had to project subtle confidence or she'd quickly be cut up.

"So do I. Flavio Peralta." He took her hand.

"I know your work. Personalized jewelry. Exquisite!" Valverde said.

Peralta smiled broadly at the compliment. "Right. I also represent clients with certain tastes. What can I do for you?"

"I have a few clients who collect santos. The St. Michael you sold...any more like that?"

"Maybe. They'd be interested?"

"Definitely. Of course they require provenance."

"Of course. That will be provided."

Katrina smiled. "Particularly when a piece is, shall we say, doubtful?"

"Doubtful?" Peralta snapped.

Katrina shrugged. "Doubtful, dubious, fake, whatever you want to call it. It didn't seem quite right to me."

"You accuse me of selling fakes?"

Katrina held up a hand. "Caveat emptor — buyer beware. Don't mistake me, I approve. That St. Michael was the best I've seen. Whoever your source is does excellent work! How about an arrangement: If you provide the piece,

I provide the buyer. We can both make money by cutting the overhead." She nodded at the hotel.

Peralta stared at her. Without a word, he turned and got into the car. She jumped out of his path as he accelerated away.

"Guess I screwed that up," Kate Cordova muttered. She hurried to her own car and left, feeling distinctly discouraged at her mistake. These crooks were *so* touchy!

Twenty minutes later she arrived at the office of the federal task force, tucked into a scruffy strip mall. A paper cup rattled across the pavement, cigarette butts and refuse had collected in corners, and the pavement was cracked. The other stores were vacant; tattered sheets of paper were pasted across the windows. It was an ideal setting for their operation.

As she was stepping from the car, her phone jingled.

"Hello?"

"Ms. Valverde?" Peralta's voice.

"Yes."

"You still interested in santos?"

"Yes, I am."

"We can make some arrangement. I'll be in touch." Click.

Kate smiled at the phone. "You're a greedy SOB. That's good. *Very* good!" She walked inside.

. . . . .

NMSP Zone 1 Investigations Office
"Info from Dona Ana County?" Mike Charles asked when Ortega returned to the cubicle, carrying a sheaf of papers.

"Fax just came in." He sat and began reading. Charles resumed bagging the items they'd taken from The Sacred Way. While sorting through the photos, he stopped.

"Strange there's not many family pictures," he muttered.

"What's that?" Ortega looked up.

"Talking to myself."

Ortega turned the pages, squinting to read the blurry print. Finally he sat up. "Some good stuff here."

Charles sat down. "Tell me something good." He waved several sheets of paper at Ortega. "The neighbor canvass didn't turn up much. Not many customers. No black SUV. There's a woman who visits sometimes, but nobody knows her name. Brown hair, medium build. Not much to work with." He tossed the papers on the desk. "What do you have?"

"Mary Marston was born at the hospital in Las Cruces but actually grew up in Radium Springs. Parents were Al and Helen Marston. Dad was a uranium miner; mom was a housewife. It doesn't sound like her early life was very happy. She was orphaned at age twelve when her parents were killed in a car crash. Mary and one of her cousins were in the car at the time and were injured. Mary was briefly hospitalized. Her cousin was more seriously hurt. The accident report doesn't say if the cousin recovered."

"Go on," Charles grumped.

"Most of this is from the county social services office. Mary was placed in the St. Vincent de Paul orphanage after the accident and raised by the nuns there. Unfortunately the orphanage closed in 1984, so the records are incomplete."

"More?"

"Yeah." Ortega flipped through several pages. "This is the only info they could find from the orphanage. Mary entered a convent when she was eighteen. The convent was run by the same order of nuns who ran the orphanage school. Mary trained as a teacher and taught in the orphanage school until 1983. That same year she left the sisterhood. Not certain why. There's nothing about her after that; it's like she just dropped out of sight."

"Her tax records might give us an idea where she went. Too bad dealing with the revenue people is always a hassle. Dammit," Charles griped.

"There's some information about her cousins."

"Okay."

"They lived close by in La Mesa. The Van Houtens. Dad abandoned the family when the kids were little. Mom was an alcoholic. The county took the girls out of the home when they were seven and nine respectively. They bounced around several foster homes for a while. Mary's parents took them in and were considering adopting them about the time of the accident. In spite of all the turmoil in their lives, one cousin turned out to be an okay kid. Her name was Phyllis Van Houten." Ortega raised one eyebrow. "Could that be P?"

Charles nodded. "Maybe."

"Phyllis's sister, Vicky, was trouble — bad grades, fights in school, running away. Once she assaulted a teacher. Oh get this: Vicky Van Houten was the cousin who was hurt in the car crash. She had a severe head injury, went through several surgeries. While she was recovering, she disappeared from the hospital and was never heard from again. Phyllis ended up being raised by foster parents in Albuquerque."

"Maybe we can find the foster parents. I wonder if they adopted Phyllis. If she was adopted, she might have changed her name. The state should have record of that somewhere. We should try and find her."

"Okay."

"Anything else?"

"Nope."

"When you're finished, leave all of that for me. I want to show it to Father Dunleavy."

"What were you talking to yourself about?" Ortega chided him.

"I was thinking out loud, why aren't there more family pictures, personal stuff? There's the one photo of Mary with her parents, one of her as a nun, and one of the cousins. Seems to me there should be more. Does that seem strange to you?"

"Not especially. Maybe her family were camera shy. Maybe they didn't like taking pictures."

Charles shook his head. "No. What about all the others — pictures of pets, outdoor shots. There are only three with people in them. Something else: The photo of the cousins was tucked into Mary's prayer book, separate from the others. It means that photo was important to her. Maybe the good cousin, Phyllis, is P. Was she the woman who visited Mary sometimes? I wonder if someone went through the photos and got rid of any others connected with Mary's life. Whoever it was missed the one in the prayer book...ah, I'm frazzled. I'm reading too much into this." Charles stood. "Help me finish packing this stuff and let's go home."

"Right."

· · · · ·

The private residence of the archbishop of Santa Fe

"Your Eminence, it is good to see you again." Estefan La Vaca knelt to kiss the ring of Archbishop Octavio Pena. The archbishop stood six-feet-five and muscular — a testament to his days as a basketball player at College of Santa Fe — with deep brown hair graying at the temples. His size contrasted with his subdued manners and gentle voice. He stooped, clapping La Vaca's shoulder as he raised him to his feet.

"Estefan, how are you? Did you have a good trip?" He waved a hand, and the two of them settled into comfortable chairs that looked out over a cozy, lush courtyard. The private residence of the archbishop was simple yet comfortable. Pena enjoyed informally entertaining his friends here, for he was a gracious and likeable man who relished the company of people.

"The trip over was very comfortable, thank you."

"Would you like coffee, or would you prefer something stronger?" Pena asked.

"Coffee would be welcome."

Pena waved to his personal assistant, Alonzo Mana, who hurried to bring the drinks.

"How is Luis?"

"Fine. He regrets he couldn't be here, as he is very busy. This visit is not just for pleasure, and Luis is attending to some business."

"I hope to see him before you leave."

"I know he is looking forward to seeing you."

"Your engagement makes me very happy, Estefan. It's time you were married." Mana appeared with the coffee service, which he set on a side table. He stood quietly while Pena filled a cup and offered it to La Vaca.

"Thank you, Alonzo." The man nodded and left the room

La Vaca smiled. "You have been telling me that for years! I have finally found someone I can truly love."

"Have you set a date?" Pena asked, filling his cup, adding sugar, and stirring.

"Not yet. Next spring at my villa. I would be honored if you attend."

"You must let me know so I can arrange my schedule. It sounds as if Ms. Patrick is bright, gifted, and a lovely woman; the two of you will be very happy."

"I agree." La Vaca took in the simple warmth of the room and sighed. "I always enjoy the peace and quiet of your home."

"A retreat from the worries of the day. My garden brings me great joy." Pena leaned forward. "Let's talk about your happiness, Estefan. You still pursue your political ambitions?"

"Yes. I have a great vision for the future of Spain, as you know."

"Politics is a dirty business. You are successful, happy, soon-to-be married. Why involve yourself in such nasty affairs? Why not focus on your happiness with your wife instead?" Pena asked.

La Vaca carefully set his cup on the table and fixed his gaze on Pena.

"Spain must resume its rightful place as a power in Europe. Our culture, our history is important for the future of the European Union. If we do not approach this alliance from a position of strength, Spain can never hope to achieve true greatness again. That is my aim. I believe I am the person to lead us into a brighter future." La Vaca's voice had risen, his words had become fervent, and his eyes glowed from some inner flame. "Your support will lend credibility to my candidacy. Mother Church will greatly benefit if I am successful."

Pena smiled the fixed smile he'd acquired over the years when faced with political situations; it was the smile of someone concealing his true thoughts. "You know that I am only as political as is necessary. I will do what I can." Gently he changed the subject. "So how are things with your business? Good, I hope."

"Things are fine. The situation will be even better if I am able to put my plans into action." La Vaca seemingly ignored Pena's tepid response to his request for an endorsement. For the next ten minutes, he spoke about his goals as prime minister, detailing his thoughts on religion, politics, immigration, security, and economics. Pena listened politely. At last La Vaca stopped.

"I am monopolizing our chat. Please forgive me, Octavio!" La Vaca admonished himself. He picked up his cup and sipped.

"No apology necessary. Your passion is compelling."

"How is your dear mother?" La Vaca asked.

"She is well for eighty-seven. She walks to mass every morning, rain or shine."

La Vaca laughed. "You get your inner strength from her."

"I do." Pena nodded and stood. "Speaking of inner strength, I understand your sister is recovering from her cancer treatments. I pray for her at mass every morning."

"Thank you for your prayers. Yes, she is in remission and doing well. Before I left, she emailed a photo to me. Her hair is growing back." He chuckled. "Look." Scrolling through his phone, he selected a photo and handed the phone to Pena. The picture showed the top of someone's bald head; a hand was pulling a single strand of hair straight up. Pena laughed.

"That's wonderful! Elena always had a great sense of humor." He returned the phone to La Vaca. "Only someone of great strength would make jokes about such a ghastly ordeal. That's why she's a survivor." He set aside his cup and stood. "Sorry, but I have a late meeting. Our time together goes so quickly. Perhaps we can have dinner while you're here?"

"Possibly. My schedule is also very busy." La Vaca stood and offered his hand rather than stooping to kiss Pena's ring. Pena shook it, not failing to notice the breach of etiquette. Although his face betrayed nothing, La Vaca was clearly angered by Pena's prevarication over the endorsement. No matter — Pena raised a hand and gave La Vaca his blessing.

"God's blessing on you, Estefan."

"Thank you, Octavio." La Vaca smiled, but it was forced, and his voice was cool. He left.

A moment later, Alonzo Mana entered by a side door. "How'd it go?"

Pena twisted his lips. "He wasn't happy with me. As we expected, he asked for my endorsement of his candidacy for the ministership. I didn't agree. He's hinted before, but today he blatantly asked me. He said the Church would benefit when he succeeded."

"What an insult to the Church and to you. The arrogant fool!" Mana snapped.

Pena nodded. "I know. He's not as subtle as he thinks he is. In fact he's become rather a stupid man, blinded by ambition. That's one of several reasons such an endorsement would be problematic for the diocese. I truly can't see what difference it would make for La Vaca. Nevertheless he tried to convince me otherwise. I was treated to a monologue about his ambitions…he's become so full of himself, not like the humble merchant I met twenty years ago in Ascensione. Really, Alonzo, why a millionaire leaps to the conclusion that being rich qualifies him to lead a country, I'll never know! La Vaca should stick to peddling olive oil." The two of them laughed at that.

• • • • •

Casa Elegante, Agua Fria Street, Santa Fe

"Luis! Luis!" Estefan shouted, slamming the door as he entered. The noise bounced harshly off the walls of the luxury apartment. Luis Mirada quickly entered. Seeing that his employer was extremely upset, Mirada immediately shifted into "control" mode.

"What has happened to make you angry?" he asked, his voice calm and low. La Vaca smacked a fist into his palm.

"What progress have you made in acquiring the santo?" he barked.

"You must be patient. I have spoken with—" he began.

La Vaca cut him off. "I want this relic *soon!* No excuses. You hear me?"

"With respect, why such urgency?" Mirada asked.

"Archbishop Pena refuses to endorse me. The pious fool. Refuses." His voice trailed away in a stream of curses.

Mirada nodded. "I am sorry. What can be done?" he asked, concealing his amusement at La Vaca's tirade. *He reacts like a child who has been told he can't have his favorite toy*, he thought.

"I will demonstrate to him that I am serious. When he sees that I have discovered the Friar, he will understand. I will show him that withholding his support is a serious mistake." La Vaca's face was crimson with rage.

"I'm certain he will come around and offer his support. Now is the time for calm, rational thinking," Mirada said in a soothing tone. La Vaca was capable of the most ridiculous demands when angered and rarely had he been as angry as now.

"If Pena does not support me, he will pay. I will destroy him! He will learn the price of defiance," La Vaca ranted.

Mirada thought for a moment. He could demand, defy, or cajole La Vaca...which course best suited *his* ambitions? "If as the prime minister you were faced with the same situation, what would you do?" he asked.

La Vaca stopped, stared, inhaled deeply, and sighed. "I would..." He hesitated. "I would...?" He gave Mirada a quizzical look.

"Early in our association, you shared your political wisdom with me. Now I will reciprocate, if I may?"

"Yes."

"You told me, 'A doubtful friend is worse than a certain enemy.' Perhaps this applies to the situation with Pena?"

La Vaca's scowl turned to a smile. "Yes! I remember well enough. Treating him as a friend but considering him an enemy makes him vulnerable to me. Thank you for reminding me how important *our* association is, Luis." He walked across to the sideboard. "Will you share a glass of Oloroso?"

Mirada smiled. *Problem solved*, he thought. "Yes, thank you," he said.

Six

One Horse Dorp Gallery

Anne thrust her last parcel into a net bag and draped it across one shoulder. "Phyllis, I'm leaving. I'll be back late, so when you're finished with that frame, you can be done for the day," she called.

Phyllis Van Houten looked up from the workbench where she was sanding a strip of framing. "Where are you off to in case anyone asks?"

"Visiting a friend of mine: Roberto Artura."

"Oh you've mentioned him before. He does woodworking, something like that?"

"Something like that," Anne said, smiling at Phyllis's characterization. Describing Roberto as a woodcarver was like saying Paul McCartney was a musician. In his hands, simple cottonwood roots were transformed into santos whose faces radiated matchless, living beauty.

"Have fun," Phyllis called and resumed her sanding. Anne listened to the "whish, whish" of sandpaper against wood. It was a pleasing noise, calling to her mind how well things were going. She walked outside, got into her Honda, and drove away.

· · · · ·

The hills east of Nambe Pueblo

The afternoon clouds cast purple-black silhouettes across the sandy hills east of Nambe. Anne's hair whirled back and forth in the breeze as she drove along the unmarked tracks heading toward Roberto's cottage. John Denver's soft voice crooned a tale of lament from the stereo. Bumping slowly along the washboarded clay road, Anne's thoughts turned to Roberto.

"How long have I known him now? Six years, I guess. Wow," she mused aloud. "Seems longer somehow. I suppose because he's so unique. He doesn't have the egotistic disposition of most artists — he's a gentle soul." She laughed at Phyllis's description of Roberto. "Woodcarver. Ha, that's rich."

She drove several minutes in silence, reflecting on Roberto and his art. A man puts his soul into his work, so much that it becomes a part of him. If there was ever anyone who breathed life into art, it was Roberto. His santos were more than art; they were living faith depicted in wood. *I'm blessed to know him*, she thought.

Up ahead was the last turn to Roberto's, marked by a gnarled juniper post cloaked with a discarded tire. Slowing nearly to a stop, she eased the car across a deep, rain-carved rut. A quarter-mile beyond, she glimpsed the buff-colored adobe of his cottage. An unfamiliar King Ranch pickup was parked in front. Strange because Anne didn't recall anyone ever visiting Roberto; he was pretty much a recluse. She stopped and got out. A voice came from inside, but she couldn't make out the words, only the tenor — an angry voice. Retrieving her bag, she stepped toward the door, stopping to listen.

"You think about it!" the angry voice cried.

"There is nothing to think about. I said no." Roberto's voice was firm but with the same muted tone as always. Anne had never known him to be truly angry.

"You'll listen to your friends, but you won't listen to me. Well you'll change your mind soon. I'll make certain of that." The door burst open. A tall, dark-haired young man stomped out, drawing up short when he saw Anne.

"What's going on?" Anne asked indignantly. Who was this man to speak to her friend in such a fashion?

"Get out of my way, bitch!" he snarled and pushed past her to the truck, slamming it into gear and roaring off in a cloud of dust and gravel.

"Roberto?" Anne called, stepping inside. He was standing in the dark, his elfish face looking wounded and sad.

"My dear Anne. I'm sorry. My nephew had no right to talk to you like that."

"Are you all right?" Anne rushed across the room and hugged him. Roberto was easily six inches shorter than she; it was like embracing a child. He clung to her tightly.

"I'm okay." After a moment, they relaxed.

"What's happened?"

"I'll get us some tea and tell you about it. What have you brought?" he asked. Now that the tension had passed, his eyes twinkled as he eyed her bag, licking his lips with anticipation.

Anne grinned. "Banana bread, of course." She retrieved two packages from the bag. Roberto gratefully accepted them and held them to his face, inhaling deeply.

"Ah yes." He was euphoric. With reverent care, he placed the packages on a scarred, mahogany table that nearly filled his tiny kitchen. He produced two former jelly jars from a cupboard and a plastic pitcher brimming with tea from the refrigerator, filled them, and put them next to the parcels. He un-wrapped one, smiling as he licked crumbs from his fingers. A serrated knife appeared from somewhere, and he cut two thick slabs, which he served over paper napkins. The ceremony with which he served contrasted the rude sur-roundings and would have been worthy of a five-star Paris bistro. Such were the simple joys of a simple man.

"Thank you, mi amiga," he said and took a generous bite. He chewed hap-pily, eyes closed, relishing the layers of flavor. "Ah! Wonderful!"

Anne pinched off a morsel and popped it into her mouth. "It is good, if I say so myself." She smiled broadly. They ate quietly for a few minutes, enjoy-ing the shared pleasures of food and companionship. Anne broke the silence.

"Who was that man?"

Roberto frowned. "My nephew, Flavio Peralta. The jeweler. I've told you about him."

"A very angry man. What did he want?"

Roberto nodded. "The same as always. He tells me I should sell my santos so I can make a lot of money. Pah! Money." He sipped. "When I was in the army, I saw what money did to people. I saw young men with money in their pockets for the first time. I saw drunkenness, cruelty, sinfulness; it made me sad. I made a prayer then that I would never chase after money."

Anne shook her head. "You refused him, of course."

"Yes, and that makes him angry. He thinks money solves every problem. *He* has money, and now he has more problems than before. Divorce, God forgive him. He never sees his children, he calls his wife all sorts of bad names. He lives in a big house, he has nice clothes, and what does it do for him? He just wants more. He makes his jewelry for profit instead of love. Flavio is a lost soul. I try not to be angry at him, but what can I do? He won't listen."

"I heard him threaten you. Would he do something, hurt you?"

"No, it's just talk," Roberto said. But Anne sensed the fear behind the words.

"I'm worried for you."

"Every day is a gift from God. He blesses me with good health. This trouble will pass." Roberto smiled at her. "Enough about me. Your work goes well?"

"Very well. You remember I told you the portrait we did together was nominated for the Osgood Prize? We won! It's a very prestigious award. I owe you many thanks."

"I had little to do with it. I am happy for you."

"Also I am engaged."

"Really?" Roberto cried. "That makes me very happy! Who is the lucky man?"

"Estefan La Vaca. He's a Spanish businessman. He's a fine man, very kind. He's a patron of the arts here in New Mexico. I met him at a reception for a charity he supports."

"That's wonderful. I'll light a candle at mass for your happiness! When is the wedding?"

"Next spring. It will be in Spain. I know you hate to travel, but I would love for you to be there."

Roberto smiled thoughtfully. "We'll see."

"Tell me about your work. What are you doing?"

Roberto frowned. "It's difficult. This trouble with my nephew disturbs me and makes it difficult to concentrate."

"Have you finished your Santa Maria?"

Roberto shook his head. "No. I was working today when Flavio arrived."

"May I see?"

"Yes." Roberto disappeared into an adjacent room, returning with something wrapped in a ragged towel. He placed it on the table and carefully unwound the wrapping. Even though the work was still in progress, Anne could make out the features of the saint. The face appeared careworn and sad, yet there seemed to be an undercurrent of hope. Such was the artistry of Roberto.

"It's lovely!"

"I'm not sure. Her face should be more content perhaps. What do you think?" he asked.

Anne studied the figure closely. "Well…" And so they passed the afternoon in vigorous conversation, immersed in the art. Finally Anne checked her watch.

"I have to go. I've enjoyed this so much." She stood and embraced Roberto. He held her tightly.

"I am blessed with a good friend. Please take care. Via con Dios."

"I will. You too." They stepped into the twilight. The air was thin and warm, alive with the croaking of crickets and the lilting call of mourning doves. Anne got into her car, gave Roberto one last wave, and drove off, watching him in the rearview mirror. She sighed.

At the turn, she slowed. Without warning a truck appeared, blocking her path. She slammed on the brakes, and her car stalled; the resulting cloud of dust choked her. Suddenly a man was at her window. It was Roberto's nephew.

"I want to talk to you." He opened the door.

"What? Uh, uh…" She coughed and gasped. "What do you want?" she cried.

"Uncle trusts you. It would be to his benefit, and yours, if he starts working with me. You can convince him. You understand?" His voice sounded enticing, but his eyes had a terrifying sheen in them.

"I do, but you don't. I won't do it."

He leaned in the window. He reeked of stale cologne and tequila; Anne fought down the urge to retch. "I think you will," he said in a menacing undertone. With one hand, he lifted his shirt, revealing a pistol tucked into his waistband.

"Oh my God!" Anne shrieked and reached for the ignition. Flavio snatched at the keys. "Ah! Leave me alone!" she cried as she flailed at his hands. He grabbed her hair. "AHH!" she screamed.

He dragged her halfway out the door, thrusting his face close against her cheek.

"Now it's time for *you* to understand," he snarled as he yanked her head back.

At that instant, she jerked, wrenching free. He snatched at her again; she cranked the ignition, the engine started, and she slammed the car into reverse, backing without looking, desperate to escape. There was a sudden jolt, and the car stalled again. She pushed open the door, leapt out, and began running aimlessly. A scrubby juniper up ahead offered shelter; she ran behind it. After a minute, she peeped around the bole of the tree. A haze of dust lingered in the air. Her car was canted in the sand, door open. Peralta and the truck were gone; there was no sound but for the wind rustling the juniper. Her whole body began to shake and then tears started.

· · · · ·

One Horse Dorp Gallery

While Tee busied herself about dinner, David was on the phone to his friend and former boss, John Stephenson, who now was director of the Southwest Trafficking Task Force. He pressed his cheek close to his cell phone to muffle the sound. "John, we need to meet — soon. I have some information to do with Kate's assignment."

On the other end of the call, John sat forward in his chair.

"What about Kate? Can't tell me now? Why so secretive?"

"Better if I tell you in person. If Tee overheard, she'd worry."

"Tee knows about this too?"

"She was with me at the Plaza, and we saw Kate. She wanted to approach her, but I said no. I had to tell her what Kate was doing, but I didn't tell her anything else. I wanna keep it that way."

"All right. Kate's checking in tomorrow at ten. Why don't you come at the same time?"

"That works. Where's your office?" David scribbled the directions and thrust the paper into a pocket. "Thanks, John. See you at ten." He rang off.

At the sound of voices, he walked through. Anne was coming in.

"Good, you're back," Tee said when Anne came in to the kitchen. "We have a controversy and need your wisdom and wit to solve it." She laughed. She got an anemic smile in return. "Are you okay?"

Anne nodded and walked toward the living area; Tee followed. "Anne?"

"I need the bathroom." Anne deposited her bag on the kitchen table and disappeared.

Tee shrugged and turned her attention to a recipe book laid open on the table. After a moment, Anne returned. "Feeling better?" Tee asked.

"Much," Anne answered. Even so Tee sensed a certain apprehension in her sister, hovering just below the surface of consciousness.

"Is something wrong?" she persisted. Anne poured herself a glass of water and drained it. She turned.

"No, I'm all right. I had a close call with a drunk on the way home. I ran off the road avoiding him. Just a bit unnerving, that's all."

"Oh, Anne. Thank God you're not hurt!" Tee exclaimed. "Sure you're all right?" Anne nodded.

David appeared in the doorway. "What's happened?"

"Anne was almost hit by a drunk on the drive back. She went off the road," Tee said.

"Damn drunks. Did you call him in?"

"No, all I saw was a dark-colored pickup. I couldn't get the license number." Anne shook her head. Obviously she didn't want to talk about the encounter.

"I'd better check your car." David walked out.

"Want something stronger?" Tee asked with raised eyebrows.

Anne shook her head. "Maybe later. I just want to sit down and relax." She pulled over a chair and flopped onto the seat. "Now what's this big controversy?" she said and smiled.

"Dinner. I surveyed the fridge and came up with an idea for a frittata. David says it sounds boring."

"He have a better suggestion?"

"Of course not. That's where you come in."

"I have the decisive vote? Good. Tell me your idea."

David returned and announced the car was undamaged. Tee greeted him with the news: Anne liked her idea, so dinner was to be a frittata. "You can choose the wine," Tee said soothingly.

"Oh fine," David answered, feigning annoyance. "Hope my choice meets your approval," he said, laughing and bowing to Anne, who returned the bow with a regal nod of her head.

Anne was quiet and distracted through dinner. Tee considered asking about the incident with the drunk driver again but rejected the thought. Both Anne and Tee sported a healthy stubbornness inherited from their mother. If Tee pushed the subject, Anne would shut down altogether. So she let it pass.

The evening was cool after the day's heat, and after dinner the three of them lounged on the patio, enjoying a last glass of wine.

"Things with the gallery going well?" Tee asked. Anne couldn't resist a conversation about the Santa Fe art community.

"Yes. I may have the best year yet. I'm one of the rare ones who's making a profit."

"Tough making a living in the art business, isn't it?" David offered.

"Very tough. The average gallery in Santa Fe closes in eighteen months," she said with a shake of her head. "Too much competition."

"You've found your niche?" Tee asked.

"Yes. But it's more than just the competition. There's always been an underground market for art. You know — you've heard the news stories over the years. People with lots of money and no scruples come here, looking for 'bargains.'" She emphasized the word by making quotation marks with both hands. "That stimulates art theft, as well as art fakery. The legitimate dealers can't compete with those prices."

David sat forward. "The thefts that make the news are world-famous pieces like when the *Mona Lisa* was stolen. They're priceless, difficult to move. It seems a black market in art would drive prices up, not down."

"Sometimes. If you're a buyer looking for a specific piece, you're at the mercy of the seller, more or less. I don't know much about it, but one hears rumors, you know?"

"Art fakery? I thought that was something that happened in the movies," David said.

"You'd be surprised. And it's terrible because it not only undercuts the artist, it's like an affront to them. Like slashing a picture to get at the artist. It's like stealing their soul." She sipped, studied her glass for a minute, and continued.

"For example in New Mexican folk art, there are carved figures of venerated saints called santos. Their origins go back a couple of centuries. People began creating them as a visible representation of their faith."

"Like statues in churches or prayer cards? The nuns used to give us cards with our patron saint on them. We used them at prayer time. Supposedly the saint would act as an intercessor for us," David said.

Anne took a sip. "In a way. Santos have special significance. Some celebrate events, like the birth of a baby into a family. Others represent protection from evil. It's all rooted in people's beliefs. Thing is, they've become a recognized art form. The old believers would never consider selling them. Now there are artists who work in them solely for profit."

"I had no idea," Tee said. "Didn't I read somewhere that when churches are closed, the statuary sometimes are sold off?"

"That happens rarely. Most of the time they're sent to other churches. But sometimes they end up on the black market, particularly if they can be considered antique. Antique santos are worth a lot of money. A *lot* of money."

David shook his head. "Anything for a buck."

Anne nodded in agreement. "Yes. For instance there is a legend about a special santo that dates back to the Spanish colonial period. It's called The Weeping Friar of Chimayo. The story goes that it has mystical powers. Every so often a buyer shows up, usually during the Fall Market, asking about it, flashing a lot of money. A few years ago, a wealthy buyer from Brazil was beaten and robbed by two men who claimed they could get him the Friar. I have a friend who is a santeros, as they're called. He was terribly upset over the incident, not only because of the violence but because he believes a santo is like your prayer cards, David: a bridge to God. Thing is, that santo is only a legend; it doesn't exist."

"That's amazing," Tee said.

Anne drained her glass and stood. "I'm beat. Night, you two." She hugged each of them in turn and walked out. Both of them watched her closely as she left.

"I'm glad you got her talking. It's not just the drunk driver — something's on her mind," David said and turned to Tee. "What do you think?"

Tee nodded. "You're right. Whatever it is, she'll tell us when she's ready, not before." She took David's hand. "Let's go to bed." But their sleep was fitful.

· · · · ·

7-Eleven store, Paseo de Onate (Highway 285), Espanola, New Mexico
The shoes were what caught Officer Sam Vincentes's attention. Typical footwear for gang bangers in Espanola were red Nike trainers. With the sagging pants and the Arizona Cardinals jersey, this guy looked the part, *except*

for the shoes. His were some type of gray-green trail shoe with purple designer laces, and they looked too small; he walked tiptoe like his feet hurt. Watching the man closely, Vincentes pulled in, parked, and cautiously got out of his unit.

"Dude, come here," he ordered. The man gave him a sideways glance... and took off.

"202 foot pursuit! East from 7-11. Male wearing a Cardinals jersey and jeans!" Vincente shouted into his radio. The emergency alert warbled over the radio. "All units, 202 in pursuit east from 7-11 on foot." The dispatcher aired the man's description.

Vincentes raced around the side of the store. Up ahead he could see the man limping and stumbling as he ran. A fence blocked his path; awkwardly he leapt and fell across the wire. Something dropped as he did so. Vincentes was up and over in a flash; he grabbed the back of the jersey and yanked. The man fell backwards on top of him. Vincentes pushed the man off him, leapt to his feet, and grabbed his Taser.

"Stop or I'll tase you!" The man stumbled to his feet, scrabbling at his waist. His shoulders sagged, and he raised his hands. Vincentes had just finished cuffing him when two other officers ran up.

"Got him?" one shouted. "You okay?"

"Yeah. He dropped something when he jumped the fence. Look around." Vincente searched the man carefully. "What's your name?" he asked. The man lowered his head. "Name?" Vincente ordered. Nothing.

"Hey look at this," one of the officers yelled to Vincente; he turned around to see the officer holding a 9-mm pistol. "It was right here." He pointed to the spot where the man had crossed the fence. He pulled open the slide. "One in the chamber, ready to go." Vincente grabbed the man by the cuffs. "You're in a lot of trouble, dude," he snapped. The man stared at him but said nothing.

"Come on." Vincente escorted him to his unit, being none too gentle.

Espanola PD headquarters, 411 North Paseo de Onate

"Good job, guys," Mike Charles announced as he walked in. He shook the hands of Officer Vincentes and the two others. "We're pretty sure he's the shooter from the other night. Glad no one was hurt."

"Thanks. We got an AFIS (Automated Fingerprint Identification System) hit half an hour ago," Vincentes said as he led Charles and Ortega along a hallway. "His name is Thomas Steven Porter. He has warrants in Texas and Oklahoma for armed robbery. Got a history like a book. Been in the system a long time."

"We'll add a page or two to his history," Ortega snorted. They walked into the interview room to be greeted by a scruffy, thin-faced man; he looked up as they entered, eyeballing them with the hateful stare of all cons. One hand was cuffed to the table. The other held a lit cigarette. An ashtray and a bottle of water were the only things on the table. The air was sour with smoke and body odor. They sat; Charles could feel the man sizing them up.

"Put that out," he ordered. Thomas Porter took a deep drag, lingering over the smoke. Charles fixed his eyes on the man. Finally Porter snorted and stubbed it out.

"What's the charge, man?" he asked in raspy, south Texas drawl.

Ortega opened a file folder. "You're in a shitload of trouble, Thomas."

Porter shrugged. Charles kept staring at him. Porter shifted in his chair, reached for the water, and took a swig, staring back at Charles. "What's your problem?" he mumbled.

"I got no problem," Charles said. Porter glared at him for minute. "You're the one with problems. Let's talk about them."

"Ain't you gonna read my rights?" Porter said and smirked, slumping in his chair with total indifference.

"Sure. We want to make sure everything's legal. That way there won't be any stupid tricks in court," Charles said. He nodded at Ortega, who read from a standard advisement-of-rights form. Finished he pushed it across the table. Porter stared at it.

"What's the charge, man?" he asked again.

"Lots of charges. Murder, attempted murder, felony assault..." Ortega began. Porter bolted upright.

"Murder? I ain't killed nobody!" he snapped.

"I'll take it from that you want to talk with us," Charles said. He leaned forward. "Is that right?"

"Don't know nothin' about no murder."

"Well sign the form and let's clear this up." Porter hesitated, then accepted the pen Ortega offered and slowly wrote his name. "Good." Ortega retrieved the pen and the form.

"We're investigating a murder that occurred last week. Not far from here. Near the Okay Owinge Pueblo. You know it?"

Porter sat silent. Charles took a paper from the file. "It says here you were married to a pueblo woman, by a JP right here in Espanola. Come on, Thomas, we know you're familiar with the area." Charles leaned forward. "Thomas?"

Porter leaned forward. "Can I have a cigarette?"

Ortega nodded, but Charles held up a hand. "You talk to us, you can have the smoke."

Porter thought for a minute. "Okay. Look, I'll cop to the gun and shooting at the cops. I ain't goin' down for no murder though."

"Tell us everything, Thomas."

For forty-five minutes Porter detailed his exploits, readily admitting buying the gun, a string of robberies across north Texas and southern New Mexico, and his encounter with Officer Hayes.

"I got scared, man. I was so close, *SO* close and then come around the corner, here's these pigs. I was scared. They had their guns out; it was like self-defense. I didn't want to kill anybody!" He was adamant. "Really."

"Gimme a break! Self-defense? Try another line," Charles snapped. Porter shrugged. "What were you doing on that road?"

"Trying to find my ex-wife's house; I f—cking got lost! I figured she could put me up for the night. Give me time to figure things out. I was gonna dump the car and get another one." Porter took a sip of water.

Ortega scribbled while Charles read the papers before him. Then Charles opened a thick folder he'd brought along.

"Okay, Thomas. Let's talk about the woman."

"What woman?"

"Mary. Mary Marston. The woman you killed and dumped on the road, right where you ran into the police."

Porter's demeanor changed from dejected resignation to intense anger.

"I don't know anybody named Mary. What you talkin' about?" he blurted.

"Don't start lying now," Charles said.

"I been telling the truth the whole time. I'm tellin' you I didn't kill no woman!" Porter snapped. He squirmed in the chair. "Man, lemme have the cigarette."

"Not until we're finished. That's the deal," Charles said.

"You got the wrong guy," Porter snapped. He sat quietly for a minute, then his eyes flickered. "What night was that?" he asked. *Now we're getting to it*, Charles thought.

"Monday night," Ortega answered. At that Porter grinned through his crooked, yellow-stained teeth.

"I got a alibi," he said, obviously pleased.

"Aw come on, Thomas. You were there," Charles snapped loudly, pounding one finger on the table. "We know you were."

Porter shook his head. "I was in Roswell."

"Prove it," Ortega chirped. "You got no proof."

Porter pushed his tongue against his foul teeth in a broad grin. "You call the Roswell cops. Ask 'em about the robbery at the Giant station last Monday night."

"That's your alibi?" Charles asked, incredulous.

Porter nodded. "Check it out. I'll wait." He chuckled softly.

Ortega left the room. Charles made notes, trying to ignoring the man's arrogance while his mind raced. What if this were true? Criminals lied all the time, but why make up such a lie? Only an idiot or a desperate man would admit to committing a felony to establish an alibi for another crime…which was Porter? Well criminals' minds run on different paths. He kept writing.

A few minutes later, Ortega returned. He gave Charles a slight nod. At this Porter laughed.

"How 'bout the smoke now, *detectives*," he said mockingly.

Charles stood. "Smoking's bad for your health."

They walked out, ignoring the stream of curses Porter threw after them. Ortega stopped outside the door. "I think his alibi's gonna stick. They've got video from the robbery. The suspect was wearing the same clothes Porter was when he was arrested. We sent them Porter's booking photo, and they're gonna show a photo spread to the clerk." He sighed. "What now?"

Charles scowled. "Oh hell, Phil, I have no idea. We're back to the beginning. I hope Father Dunleavy can tell me something I don't already know." He stomped out.

Seven

Southwest Trafficking Task Force office, Industrial Way, Santa Fe
John Stephenson was short and blocky with a deep, rumbling voice that filled the room when he spoke. He wore the perpetual wide-eyed look of a man who might run over you at any second. The dramatic blue tint of his eyes reinforced his intensity. Whenever they met, Tee nagged him to lighten up and bring out his mischievous smile more often. At the moment, sitting across from David, the smile was nowhere in sight; the blue in his eyes deepened, and there was worry in his voice.

"Countersurveillance? You sure?" he asked.

David nodded.

"You watched Kate for how long?"

"About five, ten minutes. Kate was talking to a man. Every time either of them shifted or moved, the other guy moved too, like he was keeping them in his line of sight."

Stephenson checked his watch. "She should've been here by now."

"Kate's always been punctual. Maybe working on her own she's slipping a little."

"Could be." Just then the door opened, and Kate walked in. David hardly recognized her. He was accustomed to seeing her in jeans and sweatshirts with her hair in a tangle. She was dressed in a pale blue business suit and gray,

73

slingback heels. Her hair was curled, and her bangs brushed to each side, framing her olive-hued cheeks. He liked the different, smartened-up version of his friend.

"Hello, Kate," David said, standing.

"Hey, Sarge! What are you doing here?" Kate rushed over and hugged her former partner. "I wasn't expecting to see you until Christmas."

David gave John an amused look. "Still calls me Sarge after how many years?" He laughed, releasing her from his embrace. "We're here visiting Tee's sister. Thought I'd look you two up and see what's going on."

Kate and David had worked together at Littleton PD for five years; he'd been her sergeant in investigations. While Kate was deployed to the gulf during the first Iraq war, David accepted a job at the CBI. When she returned, she'd followed. Kate had never stopped calling him Sarge even though the rank didn't exist at CBI. It was a habit that always charmed David.

Kate waved to John and sat down. "It's all secret; I can't tell you!" she said, laughing. She turned to Stephenson; seeing the look on his face, her voice turned serious. "What's up?"

"We saw you at the Plaza day before yesterday," David said. "You were talking to someone, and I realized you were working, so we left. But I had to explain to Tee what you were doing."

"That's okay, isn't it?" Kate looked at John.

"Too late to matter now," he answered.

"Something wrong?" Kate asked. She'd worked enough with John at CBI so that she could read his moods; he was obviously troubled.

"Kate, someone's doing countersurveillance on you. I saw him," David said. It was better to be straightforward with her.

"Seen anyone, noticed anyone following you?" John asked.

Kate thought for a moment. "No. I've been careful. Think I'm burned?"

Stephenson shook his head. "No way to know unless something happens. Keep on your toes, okay? If you hear anything, you need to let me know right away. If someone makes you, we'll have to pull you out."

"I'm always careful." Kate gave him her most innocent smile, trying to dispel his anxieties. Stephenson wasn't convinced but let it go. He switched gears.

"You went to another auction last night...how'd it go?" he asked.

"Really good. This guy Peralta showed up with another santo. This one was a fake too, not as good as the one he had the other day. I wrote down the description…shit, left my notes in the car. Be right back."

Stephenson nodded. While she was out, he stared down at the desk, thinking.

"She telling the truth, David? You know she always thinks she can take care of herself," he said without looking up.

"Yeah, I do. She learned her lesson after Ron Ramsey," he replied. Several years before, Kate went undercover with a con man named Ron Ramsey. She and David both assumed it was a relatively safe operation because Ramsey had no history of violence. However, when Kate was inadvertently exposed as a CBI agent, Ramsey flashed a gun and took her hostage. In the course of wrestling over it, Kate shot and killed him.

"I hope she did. She's just as headstrong as ever. I've had to sit on her a couple of times."

"She can be high maintenance," David agreed. Stephenson looked up as Kate returned, carrying a notebook and a camera.

"I got some photos too when people were leaving. We might be able to ID some of them."

The electronic lock on the entry door clicked, and an incredibly large man walked in. "Oh sorry."

Stephenson shook his head. "No problem."

"Hi, Art," Kate said. "This is a friend of mine from Colorado: David Harrowsen. David, meet Art Smart, art dealer."

David stood. "Nice to meet you, Mr. Smart. You should change your first name to Real." David chuckled and smiled. "Suppose you hear that all the time."

"Yeah, I'm used to it," Smart answered without rancor.

David turned to Stephenson. "I'd better go. You have work to do."

"You sure?" Kate asked. "Maybe we can get together while you're here." She gave Stephenson a sideways glance.

"We'll see. You take care." David squeezed Kate's shoulder and left.

"What's up?" Stephenson asked Smart, who squeezed himself onto a chair. Describing him as large was like saying the Rocky Mountains are high. Smart stood 6'6" and was easily 350 pounds with a frame sturdy enough to carry the load, little of which was fat. He wasn't at all handsome; his head was shaped like a lumpy egg, accentuated by his spreading baldness. His smile revealed a row of silver-capped teeth, giving the impression of the chrome grill on a 1959 Buick. His voice was surprisingly soft, almost a whisper. Smart countered his intimidating presence with a kind gentility. He had three passions: art, dancing (he was amazingly light on his size-fourteen feet), and barbecue.

Months before Smart had approached the task force and offered to work with them simply because he was an honest dealer disgusted with the greed and dishonesty engulfing the art community. After a background check, Stephenson had agreed, which proved to be a wise decision. Smart was a straightforward man, not given to embellishment. He knew the art community extremely well; he had introduced Kate to several "players" without arousing suspicion. If he had one weakness, it was his enthusiasm for his work with the task force. Kate and John had to continually hold him back.

"How's everything, Art?" Stephenson asked.

Smart flashed his gleaming smile.

"Everything's great! I'm selling a lot of prints, the Market is in full swing, and no one suspects I'm working with you."

"Good."

"There's some talk about the ring this fellow Monk is running. A guy I know from Taos mentioned it to me. He says the two of us should try and wangle an invite."

"What's his name?"

"Donald Levinson. He runs a secondhand store in Taos, deals a little weed, likes to work in acrylics, fancies himself as a painter. I've seen his stuff; I wouldn't let him paint my garage." Smart laughed. "He didn't tell me how he heard about Monk. I'll see if I can find out. But he's not into anything except the pot as far as I know."

Stephenson chuckled. "Anything else?"

"Yeah. Ever heard of a woman named Scott?"

Stephenson frowned. "Her name came up somewhere, but I don't remember why."

"She's been around Santa Fe for a while. Nobody knows much about her, except she moves a lot of merchandise. She was asking a vendor I know from the Taos pueblo about santos, Anasazi relics, and a lot of other stuff. He played dumb and didn't tell her anything. Said she had a bad aura around her."

"A bad aura?"

Smart raised his eyebrows. "Some Native Americans claim they can feel the aura around a person, that they can tell whether the person has good or bad intentions. Who am I to question? Anyway, he said she was an evil spirit, and he was glad when she left."

"Okay. She didn't tell him her first name, leave a card, or anything like that?"

"Nope." He turned to Kate. "You think you could get me into that ring?"

"No way, Art. You're too well-known and too easily recognized. I need you doing what you're doing," Stephenson interjected. He knew Kate would invite him along if given the chance.

"Just thought I'd ask," Smart replied, checking his watch. "Oops, I need to go. There's an exhibition at a new gallery out near Ojo Caliente I want to check out."

"Thanks, Art," they said. He left.

"Let's take a look at those photos," Stephenson said.

"Okay." Kate began the process of loading the photos into her laptop.

"So what's new with Monje?" Stephenson asked.

"The DEA was right about him — what a snake. When this is over, let's send him back to them in cuffs. That oily grin of his gives me the creeps."

"Find out who he's working for?"

"Still don't know. He likes to talk like he's connected, you know? All secrets and bullshit. I've tried tailing him a couple of times but no luck; he's tough. He's got something going with Flavio Peralta. I'm not sure what — maybe they're partners, maybe not. I'm sure that santo Peralta sold last night was a fake, just like the one he sold last week. He only shows up when he's got something to sell — never buys. He and Monje are working together when it suits them, but my instincts tell me Monje's being bankrolled by someone else. I don't think he's smart enough to do this on his own. Someone else's calling the shots."

"Watch yourself with him. Remember, he's a very experienced crook. DEA says a few years ago he was tied up with some real nasty guys with one of the Mexican cartels."

"It ever occur to you DEA loaned him to us because they got sick of him?"

"I'm sure they were. He's like a lot of snitches — plays both ends against the middle. Makes it hard to work him. Our hammer is that he's got a lot of charges to work off. If he screws up, he'll serve some serious federal time."

"He'll screw up sometime. He's too greedy not to."

"Greed gets you killed in his business. So what's the story with the man you met at the Plaza?"

Kate opened her notebook, flipped through several pages, and began reading.

"I was doing a walkaround, and we started talking. Name's Luis Mirada, age late forties or early fifties. Spanish. Works for some rich businessman who's also from Spain. He says his boss is looking for a particular santo called the Weeping Friar of Chimayo. I've heard about this piece. It's supposed to be a relic from Spanish colonial days. What I've read, no one knows if it even exists. I told him that. He didn't seem to care. I also said I could do some checking around and represent them if he wanted. At first he seemed hesitant, but I could tell he was interested." She handed Stephenson her notes.

"A new player? I'll check him out. How'd you leave it?"

"Told him if I found the Friar it would probably cost a lot. That didn't faze him. He didn't look like a guy with a lot of cash himself — he's spending his boss's money. Something else though. He acts like he's looking to *make* a lot of cash. He might be cheating his boss by feeding him a line of bullshit. Or he could be into something else. Anyway, he's a player."

"This rich guy from Spain, the one Mirada's supposed to work for? Suppose he didn't give you his name?"

Kate shook her head. "No, and I didn't ask. Didn't want to scare him off with too many questions."

"Good work, Kate. You going back to the Market today?"

"Yeah, I thought I'd ask around about the Friar. See if anyone knows anything about it. Subtle, you know."

"Just be careful. Careful, careful, careful. Keep your eyes open. People only do countersurveillance if they think something's wrong. Okay?"

"Yes sir." She hated obeying orders, and this was definitely an order. "What do you have on today?"

"Paperwork. But tomorrow I'm cold-hitting that photographer, Anne Patrick. Remember her? Her name has come up a couple of times, and it's time to check her out. I'll be interested to hear what she has to say."

"Well good luck." Kate walked to her cubicle and got on the computer. She hated being nagged, and John was nagging her.

Stephenson knew how stubborn Kate could be when pushed. But this was important enough to get after her, and he was glad he had.

· · · · ·

Diocese of Santa Fe Catholic Center Offices, 4000 Saint Joseph's Place NW
If one were to envision the typical Irish priest of Hollywood creations, Father Robert Dunleavy, "Father Bob," wouldn't fit the image. While his mop of gray-white hair hinted at his age, he had the round face, smooth cheeks, and sparkling brown eyes of a much younger man, with the energy to match. Dressed in jeans, a burnt orange Polo shirt, and deck shoes worn over bare feet, he might have been a student intern or perhaps a retail associate at an upscale boutique. His voice was high-pitched with the crisp accent of Michigan's Upper Peninsula, where he'd grown up. He had an easygoing manner that made him someone who could make anyone comfortable. Right now he was standing in the portico attached to the diocese offices, smoking a rancid-smelling cigar. When he saw Mike Charles approach, his face lit up.

"Hello, Mike. Good to see you. How are Kristen and Mike Jr.?" He pumped Charles's hand while clapping him on the shoulder.

"They're fine. You're looking casual today."

Dunleavy laughed. "People expect a priest to be in uniform, don't they? I want 'em to know I'm just like everyone else, just a guy getting on with life."

"It suits you."

Dunleavy pushed the cigar into a pyramid-shaped receptacle and steered Charles to a nearby bench. They sat down together. Father Bob spread his arms and let out a contented sigh.

"What a day. I should be out on a boat on a BIG lake — not the puddles they call lakes in New Mexico — going after Northerns. No matter — what can I do for you?" he asked, contemplating the folder Charles carried.

Charles took out several papers. "Like I said on the phone, I'm working a homicide and need help. You'll have to be patient; I'm developing some background information, so my questions might seem strange."

"No problem. I work with strange people asking strange questions every day." Dunleavy chuckled, as did Charles.

"Good. To begin with, why do nuns wear wedding bands?"

"Not all orders do today. It's an anachronism, a throwback to earlier times. Wearing the wedding band signifies complete dedication to God, being 'wedded' to God so to speak. Some people consider that sexist nowadays."

"I suppose. Is it customary for the ring to be inscribed with a date?"

"Certainly. The inscription is the date of the sister's final vows." Father Bob's jovial mood turned serious. "Tell me what this is about."

Charles selected a photo and turned it face up. He handed it to his friend. "Do you know this woman?"

"Sister Mary Marston! Oh no. Is she the victim?" Dunleavy exclaimed instantly. Then his cheeks sagged, and his eyes teared up.

Charles nodded.

"Father, have mercy," Dunleavy whispered.

"I'm sorry. She was a friend, wasn't she?" Charles said.

Dunleavy waved a hand. "It's just a shock. Give me a minute." He took several deep breaths to compose himself. "I've been a priest thirty-three years, and death still affects me like this." His voice was pinched with sorrow.

"I know. Every time I go to a scene, I have to screw myself up and remember I'm there to work a case. I've been to hundreds, and each one still bothers me."

Father Bob sat quietly for a few minutes, staring down at the image. Then he handed it back to Charles. "I knew her a long time ago. She was one of those rare people who are born for holy orders. She was a wonderful teacher. Fantastic with kids."

"Tell me about her."

"I worked at St. Vincent de Paul orphanage in Las Cruces. We took Mary in after her parents died in an automobile accident. She was about eleven or twelve at the time. She lived there until she was eighteen. I was her catechism teacher, and we got to be good friends. She started asking me about the religious life, the kind of questions any young person might ask. Then our conversations became deeper, more exploratory. After a time, she told me she was moved to become a nun. I encouraged her; I could see the depth of her faith. The day she told Mother Superior of her decision, Mary was so happy! No, more than that. She was radiant with joy. I could see God's hand had touched her heart."

"So she became a nun. Did you stay in touch?"

"We did. She wrote to me occasionally while she was a novitiate, even though outside contacts are severely limited during that time. I was honored to attend her final vows. She joined the Dominicans, an order of teaching nuns, and trained as an elementary grade teacher. Eventually she was assigned to the school that was associated with St. Vincent's."

"In 1983 she quit or resigned or whatever it's called. I didn't know nuns could do that."

"Anyone can leave a religious order although there's a possibility of excommunication. However, leaving doesn't mean they have given up their vows. Renouncing one's vows is an extreme step. It doesn't happen often. Mary resigned, but she didn't renounce her vows."

"Do you know why she resigned?"

Father Bob's countenance changed; the recollection produced a profound melancholy in him. "She was accused of improper sexual contact by one of the students, a young boy. The complaint was investigated by a priest from the diocese; no evidence of misconduct was found. Turned out Mary had given the boy failing grades in two classes, and he was upset, so he accused Mary as a way of explaining his bad grades to his parents. Problem was, they were prominent members of the parish, and, of course, they sided with their son and demanded the diocese do something. The diocese wanted to keep things quiet, so Mary was to be transferred somewhere out of state, to an assignment where she'd have no contact with children. That broke her spirit. She resigned and left her order. We lost contact with each other after that."

"What happened to her?"

"For a long time I never knew. The year after Mary left, the orphanage closed. I moved on to several parishes around the States, was sent to the Holy See for two years. Then I was transferred to the Santa Fe diocese. Archbishop Pena and I are old friends, and he asked for me. I've been here ever since. Anyway, one day quite unexpectedly, maybe eight or nine years ago, I got a phone call from Mary. She wanted to see me. I couldn't have been more surprised to hear from her. She wanted to see me; we met right here at the center offices."

"And?"

"We talked for hours. After she left Las Cruces, she went through a terrible crisis of faith, as you can imagine. Got mixed up in drugs and alcohol, lived in a commune, was arrested for drunk driving, was homeless for a time.

But she recovered herself and her faith, although she never completely shook her problems with alcohol."

"Was she looking for a handout? Was she interested in rejoining her order?"

Father Bob shook his head. "No to either of your questions. She wanted me to hear her confession, which I did. When she found sobriety, she was able to get work, cleaning hotel rooms, working in restaurants. She'd saved a little money and wanted to open a shop selling religious stock, prayer cards, missals, figures of the saints, that sort of thing. She wanted my blessing, and I happily obliged. I offered her money, but she refused."

"The shop was called The Sacred Way."

"That's right. I visited once or twice. I used to see Mary at mass sometimes. Occasionally I'd call her to check up on her. We weren't as close as we had been, but we stayed in touch."

"What about relatives or friends?"

Father Bob thought a moment. "She never mentioned anyone in particular. I think she kept to herself mostly."

"At her shop, I found a prayer book with an inscription signed by P. The note was very kind, the sort of thing a close friend would write. Did she ever mention someone with a name beginning with P?"

"No one comes to mind."

Charles shifted uneasily. "Did anyone work for her at the shop?"

Dunleavy shook his head. "She could barely make ends meet. She couldn't have afforded to hire anyone."

Charles dug into the file and pulled out several newspaper clippings.

"Going back a little, we found these at the shop. One article talks about Mary. It says, 'Popular nun leaving St. Vincent's.' It also mentions rumors there was some sort of problem and that's why she was leaving, but, of course, there aren't any details." He handed the clipping to Father Bob.

The priest read it slowly. "The diocese went to some lengths to keep the lid on things, hence the lack of detail. I'm surprised the reporter got any information at all." He handed the clipping back.

"Think back; do you remember the name of the boy who accused her?"

"I don't. The family had an unusual name…Vickery. It was Vickery. I remember because it sounded like vicar." He smiled and tapped his temple. "The ol' brain still works pretty well, eh?"

"Would there be anything in the diocese files about the case?"

Father Bob shrugged. "If the file still exists, it's buried in the diocesan archives. Might even have been destroyed. You read the papers; that sort of thing still goes on — to the everlasting shame of the Church."

"How would I get a look at it?"

"They'd never allow it."

"Could you? This could be an important lead."

"Why?" Father Bob asked. Realization spread across his face. "You think the boy might have murdered Mary? After all these years? Really?"

"It's possible. Revenge is a powerful motive. Right now we don't have many leads. The way..." Charles hesitated. He liked Father Bob a lot; the man had been Mary's friend and confidant. Sharing the details of Mary's death would be terribly upsetting to him. "The way she was killed makes me think it was a revenge murder. I won't go into specifics."

The priest nodded. "I'm worldly enough to imagine, but thank you for your kindness. As for the archives, I'll see what I can do."

Charles closed the file. "Thanks, Father. Look, if you find anything in the archives, great. But don't put yourself at risk. There may be people in Las Cruces who remember and can help us out. We'll check around." He stood and offered his hand. Father Bob took it with both of his.

"Mary was my friend, a gentle and good woman. I'll do whatever it takes to help you find her killer."

"Thanks. When this is over, let's get together and have a beer." Charles waved good-bye.

"Make it soon," Father Bob called after him. After he was gone, the priest took a rosary from his pocket and began, "In the name of the Father..."

Eight

One Horse Dorp gallery

There are mornings that are commonplace. And there are mornings when the air is particularly crisp, the sun particularly comfortable, and the coffee particularly toothsome so that the day tingles with opportunity. Anne was enjoying just such a morning. Her camera bags were arrayed on a table in the rear of the workshop, ready for duty. She hummed the opening lines from the Third Movement of Beethoven's *Violin Concerto in D* as she hurried about, placing several rolls of film in one of the bags and checking her cameras. The bells hanging over the gallery door tinkled. A visitor.

"Oh not now. Phyllis!" she called. "Phyllis, would you see who that is."

"Sure." Phyllis entered the gallery's main showroom to find a man carefully examining one of Anne's favorite works, a black-and-white image of broken pottery overlaid by the open doors to the Santuario de Chimayo. "Hi, may I help you?" she greeted him, trying not to sound impatient.

"This is very nice," the man commented. "Are you Anne Patrick?"

"No. She's busy right now. Can I help?"

"I need to talk with her if it's possible."

"I'll see, but like I said, she's very busy. What's this about?"

He produced a small wallet and displayed his badge and identification. "John Stephenson. I'm a federal law enforcement officer. Official business."

His voice rumbled around the walls like far-off thunder.

Phyllis's eyes grew wide with surprise. "Wait here," she said. *Officious jerk,* she thought as she walked through to the workshop.

"Anne, there's a man here to see you," she said.

"I don't have time right now! Tell him…"

"He's a cop. Says it's official business."

Anne scowled. "What in the world…?" she muttered. "All right." Phyllis followed her into the showroom, where Stephenson was studying the prints and photos displayed there. He handed her the ID wallet.

"Ms. Patrick? I'm Agent Stephenson. I'm part of a special federal task force investigating smuggling and trafficking in artwork and relics. I believe you might be able to help me. Is there someplace where we could talk?"

"I'm sorry, but I have an urgent appointment. Could we do this another time?"

"The information I need is very time-sensitive. It would be better to do this now," he said evenly, making no move to leave.

Anne glared at him. "All right, if it doesn't take too long."

"Thank you."

"Thanks, Phyllis," Anne said. With a final glare at Stephenson, Phyllis disappeared into the workshop.

Anne led him to her office just off the main gallery. "I don't suppose I could have a cup of coffee?" Stephenson asked. Anne ignored the request. "Never mind." He closed the door, sat down opposite her, and opened a notebook. She sat down and folded her hands in front of her, making a great show of impatience.

"I don't know what information you think I may have," Anne snipped. This would be a contest of wills, one she was determined to win. She clenched her hands together tightly, fighting the tension rising in her.

Stephenson was secretly pleased; her apprehension suited his purposes.

"To begin with, you're a prominent artist here. You know a lot of people in the art community. You know a lot of what goes on. Have you heard about stolen or fake works of art being sold?"

"No."

"Do you ever take in works to sell on consignment?"

"No."

"What about private auctions? Do you attend these gatherings or sell your works at them?"

"No."

"You're certain?"

"I do just fine selling my works here at my gallery."

Stephenson nodded. "Good for you. What do you know about santos?"

"They have deep religious significance to many people."

Stephenson nodded. "They're also considered works of art by collectors. Some are sold for huge amounts of money."

"Yes, I've heard that."

"Do you know anyone who buys and sells santos?"

"No."

"Know anyone who makes them? Woodworkers or woodcarvers?" The flesh of Anne's cheeks tightened ever so slightly; Stephenson noticed but didn't react.

"No."

"Has any of your work ever been stolen from the gallery?"

"No."

He'd had enough of her singular responses. "Ms. Patrick, I'd hoped you would be cooperative. Instead you give me one-word answers that really aren't answers at all! That makes me very suspicious."

"Cops are always suspicious; it's their nature," she snapped.

"We have to be suspicious. A lot of people lie to us. They withhold information when what they should do is be good citizens, cooperate, and help us out."

"I'm not withholding anything! You ask questions, and I answer. I'm cooperating."

"One-word answers are hardly what I'd call cooperation."

"That's your opinion."

Stephenson plunged ahead. "Do you know a man called Monk?"

Anne snickered. "Monk? This sounds like a B-grade film noir. I really don't have time for this nonsense."

"Well? Do you?"

"No, I don't know someone called Monk. This is ridiculous!"

"I think you're hiding something, Ms. Patrick."

"I don't care what you think. Why don't you just leave?"

"Because I'm not finished. Because I think you know a lot more than you're telling."

"Maybe I should call my lawyer before I talk with you anymore."

"That's your choice. I'm not accusing you of anything — not yet. I'm simply trying to establish who and what you know about the underground market in art and relics."

"I told you, I don't know anything about all of this," she snapped. She stood up. "I'm done," she announced and wrenched open the door...to find Tee, David, and Taz standing there. Taz immediately stood on her hind legs and pawed at Anne, begging to be picked up. Anne ignored her.

"Oh! Um, hi. I..." Anne began, flummoxed.

"Good morning, Anne," Tee said, puzzled but unruffled by Anne's visible perplexity. "We wanted to...hello, John!" she exclaimed when she caught sight of Stephenson. "What are you doing here?" She stepped forward and hugged him.

"Working," Stephenson said evenly while staring at David over Tee's shoulder.

"Oh it's good to see you," Tee replied.

"And you," he said. "Hello, David." He extended a hand, which David accepted.

"Hi, John. Wasn't expecting to see you here."

"You know each other?" Anne asked, shocked.

"Yes we do. John and I worked together at CBI for a lotta years," David said.

"Really. Well Mr. Stephens was just leaving," Anne announced.

"Stephenson," John said. "It's Stephenson."

"Okay," Anne snapped.

Her peculiar manner puzzled Tee. "Not because of us?" she asked, searching her sister's face. "We didn't mean to interrupt."

"No problem. Actually Ms. Patrick and I still have a few things to talk about," Stephenson said. He fixed his purposeful stare on Anne. "It won't take too long," he added.

"No problem. Anne, we thought we'd take you to brunch. Maybe tomorrow," David said.

"Tomorrow," Anne mumbled.

"John, maybe you'd like to join us?" Tee asked.

"Afraid not. I'll give you a call before you head back to Colorado." He nodded at David, who took Tee by the arm.

"Later. See ya," he said and ushered Tee and Taz out of the gallery.

Stephenson turned to Anne. "Shall we resume?" he said in a low voice, his tone more like an order than a question.

Anne stood quietly, trapped by her own emotions as well as her in-laws's expectations. If Tee and David knew Stephenson, what would be the harm in answering his questions? But she resented being ordered about by anyone. Finally she relented. "All right." They re-entered the office. This time Anne closed the door. Stephenson sat down.

"Do you still want to talk to your lawyer?" he said.

"I don't like the way you're talking to me," she complained, with less rancor than before.

"Yeah, people tend to respond to me that way. I get results though," Stephenson said. "Ms. Patrick, I'm really not accusing you of anything. I think you could offer me a lot of information if you're willing to help."

"You may call me Anne," she said rather formally. "You still want that cup of coffee, Mister Stephenson?"

"Sure do," he said. Progress at last! "And you can call me John," he added.

"Thanks." Anne knew she deserved the jab and let it go. With a wry frown, she stood and busied herself with the coffee things. Stephenson divided his attention between his notes and watching her; he forced himself to concentrate. When the coffeemaker began to puff and burble, Anne sat. "What do you want to know?"

Stephenson had a peculiar habit of screwing his lips together while he was conducting an interview, and he did so now. "Let's talk about santos. Tell me what you know about them."

"To begin with, I don't deal in them because they're religious artifacts. They represent people's spiritual beliefs, and I believe selling them is sacrilegious. People may admire their artistic character, and that's why they collect them as works of art. Even so I think it's wrong to collect them."

"Interesting perspective. Unfortunately there are people who don't agree with you. They pay serious money for these pieces, particularly if they're considered antiques. Earlier you said you don't know any artists who create santos. Is that really true?"

"I don't know anyone who sells them."

Stephenson eyed her closely; her expression was blank, and her hands were clasped together in front of her. She was trying too hard to look relaxed.

"That's not what I asked you. I take it that you *do* know someone who makes santos, Anne. Is that true?"

She nodded.

"You're protecting someone. Why?"

"I don't want to say."

Stephenson leaned across the desk. "Are you caught up in something and don't know how to handle it? If you tell me, I can help you." He laid one hand on top of hers; it was trembling.

"I'm not involved in anything. I just want to keep him out of this."

"If he's not doing anything wrong, what harm is there in talking about him?"

Anne's head sank. "He's a dear friend. A kind and gentle soul. I tend to be protective of him."

"Nothing wrong in that. He's a santero?"

Anne looked up, surprised and pleased. "Yes, that's correct. You say the word with a certain respect — that's unusual."

Stephenson smiled. "Thanks. I've done a little research on the subject. The artists who create santos are special people and worthy of respect. So will you tell me who this person is?"

"His name is Roberto Arturo. His work is in a class by itself. His art is an extension of himself, of his soul, and his creations reflect that."

"He doesn't sell his work?"

"Never. Sometimes he gives pieces away to close friends. I'm honored to be part of that group."

"May I see the piece he gave you?"

Anne shook her head. "It's in my bedroom. It's not something I put on display, you understand."

"I do. What about other people? Do you know people who buy and sell santos?"

Anne hesitated. Should she tell Stephenson about Flavio Peralta's threats? Unconsciously she nodded. It was the kind of response he'd hoped for.

"Anne?"

"There's a man I know of who's the complete opposite of Roberto Arturo. He's interested in art only for its commercial value. For him art is all about money. His name is Flavio Peralta."

"Okay. How do you know him?"

"He's Roberto's nephew. Roberto told me about him."

"Interesting. What else can you tell me about him?"

"Not much. I've only met him once. I don't like him."

"I have a list of names here I'd like you to look at. Peralta's name is on it." The nutlike aroma of coffee filled the room, and he sniffed appreciatively. "Mmmm. Why don't we share some coffee while you go through this?"

Anne unclasped her hands and smiled. "Sure."

"That's the first time you've smiled at me. See, we're getting along. I'm not a bad guy, right?" Stephenson sat back.

"I guess not," she answered. Forty minutes later the coffee was drunk and the list nearly exhausted. Most of the names were unfamiliar to her. She'd been able to eliminate three as honest dealers. She hesitated over one name, surprised to see it.

"I know this name: Luis Mirada. He works for my fiancé. May I ask why his name is here?" She sounded troubled.

"It came up a few days ago. That bothers you?"

"Only because he works for my fiancé. I don't want him to have any trouble."

"Well Mirada's been asking around the Indian Market about a particular santos. It's called the Weeping Friar of Chimayo. You've heard of it?"

"Yes. It's a myth. Anyone who knows New Mexico would know that."

"What does Mr. Mirada do for your fiancé?"

"He's his private secretary and bodyguard."

"Well maybe he heard about the legend and was just curious about it. I wouldn't make much of it. This probably isn't worth mentioning to your fiancé. Congratulations on your engagement."

"Thank you."

Stephenson glanced at the list. "How about the last name on the list? Kind of a mystery woman."

Anne looked at the name, then shook her head.

"I've heard the name once or twice, but I've never met her. People say she can move almost anything, but I don't know what they mean by that. Actually I don't know anyone who's actually met her. Unfortunately I've never heard anyone call her anything but Mrs. Scott. Sorry." She pushed the list across the desk.

"Thank you. This took a lot of your time, and I appreciate it."

"That's all right. Is there anything else?"

"Nope." Stephenson folded the list and tucked it into his notebook. "I'm sorry we got started off on the wrong foot. I really appreciate your help," he said evenly.

A thought occurred to Anne, and she chose to voice it. "I'd like to be of more help. Is that possible?" The same thought had occurred to John, but he'd hesitated to ask; her question surprised and pleased him.

"Would you? Let us know what you hear or people you run into who are doing shady deals? That would be terrific! You'd not only be helping us, you'd be helping the legitimate artists here, people like you. If we can shut down the trafficking in stolen art, fake art, and stolen relics and the like, it will benefit everyone."

"That's what I think too."

"But there's a downside," Stephenson said.

"Yes?"

"You'd be passing on information about people you know and work with. That can be an uncomfortable place to be. You're established here; you have a future here. These people trust you. You'd be putting all of that at risk. You might find out things about them you'd rather not know."

"You're right. What would happen if someone found out I was a police informant?"

"Not an informant. You're a cooperative citizen, nothing more."

"That's just semantics. If people think I've violated their trust, saying I'm a cooperative citizen won't matter."

"True. You'd have to be very careful. Take some time to think this through."

"I will. I want to talk this over with David and Tee. They'll ask why you were here anyway. They're my family; I trust their judgement."

"Good. If you decide against this, I'll understand. No matter what, call me." Stephenson produced a business card.

"I will."

As they walked out together, Phyllis came out of the workshop. "Oh you're still here." she said to Stephenson with obvious disdain. "Is everything all right, Anne?"

"Everything's fine," Anne replied. She stood on the porch and watched him drive off, wondering at the turn this morning had taken. More than anything else right now, she wanted to be with Estefan, to hold him close and talk about their future together…and about Luis Mirada.

As he drove away, Stephenson mentally played back his interview with Anne. He wanted to trust her, yet part of him urged caution. He couldn't let her relationship with David and Tee influence him; in these circumstances, he wouldn't let it influence him. Anne would have to prove herself trustworthy, and that would happen when she produced viable information. On the other hand, he'd know she couldn't be trusted if he caught her in a lie. And he hated that thought because he found her very attractive and extremely interesting. "Forget it, John," he said aloud. "She's engaged. You've got a job to do."

Nine

595 Dyne Ave., Las Cruces

"Hope this turns out. If not, we're sunk," Mike Charles said to his partner. He was in a sour mood. Father Bob had called; the file on Mary Marston had been purged several years ago. Their visit to the diocese offices in Las Cruces had been a washout; a ruddy-faced, stumplike priest had refused their request to examine the records in a most unpriestly way. At the Cathedral of the Immaculate Conception offices, they'd fared no better. At least the secretary had been cordial, if not helpful. This was their last option; DMV records showed Ellen Vickery lived here. But the record was more than four years old, and the copy of her driver's license was so dark it was virtually illegible.

The house they sought was a nice, tan, brick ranch with neatly trimmed maple trees and flower beds filled with marigolds fading to brown in the summer heat. At their knock, a tiny, stooped elderly woman opened the door a few inches, glaring at them through the screen. Her hair was wispy gray, her face deep brown and sun-spotted — testament to a hardy life — but her voice resonated in the stifling air. Charles sensed she'd been watching them approach the place.

"What do you want? No solicitors." She pointed to a prominently displayed sign screwed onto the door frame. It was a command, not a comment.

"We're state police officers, ma'am," Ortega said. Each in turn opened their wallets and held them close to the screen. "Are you Ellen Vickery?"

She squinted at the documents "More police? You find him yet?" she snapped.

"Find who?" Ortega asked.

"Jim! Her son."

Ortega glanced at Charles as if to say, *Play along?*. Charles nodded. "It would help us find him if we could talk to Ellen," he said. Cool air wafted through the screen from the interior. A single stream of sweat made its slow path around his left eyebrow and into his eye. Irritably he wiped it away.

"She can't talk right now." The woman began closing the door.

"Wait. We're here to help her. Why can't she talk?" Ortega asked.

"Things go a lot smoother when we know who we're talking to. Mind telling us your name?" Charles asked.

"Millie."

"Is that your last name?" Charles asked impatiently, swatting at black gnats that had begun clustering around his face. The heat, the gnats, and the woman's irksome stubbornness were getting to him.

"First name," she answered. "Last name's Schwartz."

"That's better. Ms. Schwartz, we really need Ellen to help us. We're investigating a murder, and there's a chance her son is involved," Ortega said calmly. Stinging insects seldom bothered him. He opened his notebook.

"Murder? There was almost a murder here the other night! He damn near killed Ellen," Millie cried. "He's nothin' but scum."

"Could we come in and talk?" Charles asked. Millie hesitated. *We're done,* Charles thought. Then she pushed open the screen door.

"Okay, but Ellen won't talk to you." They stepped into a comfortable, livable family room. The furniture was undistinguished — a bit careworn but presentable. The room needed painting, and the curtains were sun-faded and drooped from their rods. Family pictures filled the walls. There was a hint of Lysol in the air. The two detectives sat down on the couch.

"Thanks. Now—" Ortega began.

"Shhh! Be quiet! Don't want her to hear. She's asleep."

Charles looked at Ortega with raised eyebrows. "All right. Tell us what happened," he said in a hushed voice.

Millie sat down; it was easy to see she was tired, angry, and worried about Ellen. "Jim come here three nights ago. I was in the back bedroom. Ellen was in the kitchen. I heard a noise, like something banging. Then I heard Ellen say, 'No, you go away. You're hurting me.' Then I heard her cry; it was a yelp, sort of like you hear when someone's hitting a dog, you know? I came runnin' in and saw Jim goin' out the door. Ellen was lyin' on the floor, all bloody. I ran outside, but he was gone. I came back, and she was hardly breathing. Her pulse was real weak. So I called an ambulance. I was afraid this might happen."

"Is she going to be all right?" Ortega asked. He wanted to get his hands on Jim Vickery *right now*!

"Don't know. They said at the hospital she has a concussion. I just got her home this morning. I'm supposed to keep her quiet and keep an eye on her. They said she could take a turn any time, so she has to stay real quiet and rest."

"It's kind of you to take care of her like this. You're a good friend."

"I'm probably the only friend she's got now."

"You live here with her, or are you just staying here?" Charles asked.

"I live with her. Goin' on two years. Moved in after her husband died. We've been best friends since we were at school."

"You said you were afraid this might happen. Why? Jim's done this before?" Charles asked even though he knew the answer.

Millie nodded. "He's knocked her around a few times, threatened her lots of times. After Alan died, that was her husband, things got worse. Last time she wouldn't call the cops even though I begged her to."

"Why'd he do this?" Charles asked.

"Money to buy drugs, I expect. He's always botherin' her about money. Been that way ever since I remember. He's always been in trouble."

"We know there was some trouble with a teacher when he was in school. Do you know anything about that?" Ortega asked.

"That was a bad thing. Ellen never talked about it, not for years."

"Did she ever tell you about it?"

"Why's that so important? You should be out lookin' for Jim, not here askin' me 'bout things that happened a long time ago."

"I said earlier we're investigating a murder. This might have something to do with the case," Charles said. He forged ahead, not giving Millie time to object. "Jim had some trouble with one of the nuns at school, right?"

"Yeah. He claimed a nun tried to molest him. Ellen didn't believe his story, but Alan did. She told me Jim did it because the nun gave him an F in two classes. She said there wasn't nothin' to it, but Alan raised hell with the school about it. He always took Jim's side of things. Well I think somebody from the church looked into it. After that the nun left the school. That was pretty much the end of it."

"So we understand. Was that when Jim started getting into trouble?"

Millie nodded. "He was already trouble by then. He weren't ever good in school, but he got worse and worse — finally was kicked out. Ellen told me he got started on the drugs about then. He's been in jail lots of times. 'Bout nine years ago he went to prison, up in Santa Fe. When he got out, he went back to the drugs, only this time he was sellin' 'em too."

"Do you know what he went to prison for?" Ortega asked.

"Had somethin' to do with killin' someone. He was only in prison for about five years. That's not much for a murder!" Millie snapped. "That important?"

Charles shook his head. "Don't know. It could be. Anything else you can tell us about Jim? Any idea where he might be?"

"He could be anywhere. He better not come back here. I got a pistol, and I'll use it if I see him."

Charles nodded. "I understand how you feel." He looked over at Ortega, who shook his head. They stood; each handed her a card.

"You've been a great help. Thank you. Promise me you'll call and let us know how Ellen is doing, okay?" Charles said. He hoped Millie would call and not just because he wanted to talk with Ellen; he really wanted to know how she was.

"All right," she said. They walked out.

"That was worth the drive," Ortega said. "Sounds like Jim Vickery might be our guy."

Charles nodded as he retrieved his cell phone from his belt. "Callin' Las Cruces PD. They should have a warrant for him by now. I want it flagged if he's picked up; we need to talk to him. While I'm doing this, you check his history, see what he was in prison for and if he's on parole. If it was a homicide and he only served five years, I'll bet he cut a deal and testified against someone else."

There were three problems with these plea bargains. First, the only way someone could offer significant information was if they were a participant in the crime. So a guilty criminal was getting off cheap. Second, their testimony was never completely trustworthy because they had incentive to embellish the truth for their own benefits. Third, they *always* kept something back. It was part of the game. These deals were necessary sometimes, the old "serve the greater good" routine. But Charles hated every bit of it.

. . . . .

Casa Elegante, Agua Fria Street
"I think you'll enjoy this." Anne handed a glass filled with wine to Estefan and Mirada in turn. "A friend of mine at my liquor store is a sommelier; he recommended this particular vintage. He says it's comparable to Clos Erasmus or Muga Torre Muga even though it's from California. It should have breathed properly by now."

Estefan raised his and inhaled deeply, nodding his approval. "A hearty bouquet with hints of oak and blackberries." He sipped, rolled the liquor around his mouth, and swallowed. "Ah. Your friend was correct. Thank you." He smiled at Anne over the rim as he drank. "May good fortune smile always on our marriage." She mouthed, "I love you."

Mirada toasted each of them. "To your good health and success."

"Thank you, Luis. I'm happy you joined us tonight," Anne said, tilting her glass to him.

"So am I," he replied.

The three of them sat, Anne next to Estefan on a love seat while Luis occupied the sofa opposite. Dinner had been an excellent pollo pibil followed by polvorones and coffee; now they enjoyed the wine quietly, allowing the evening to settle around them. After a few minutes, Estefan spoke.

"You seemed tense earlier; I was concerned. You're more yourself now. Is everything all right?"

Anne looked down at her glass and nodded. "I'm sorry. I had a difficult day at work, that's all. I'm fine now." Estefan squeezed her hand in reply.

The dinner invitation couldn't have been timelier. After John Stephenson left, Anne found herself worrying about their encounter. She desperately wanted to tell Estefan about Stephenson's interest in Mirada. The more she thought it over, the more vexed she became. If Mirada was involved in something illegal, she felt compelled to tell Estefan so he could distance himself from any trouble. However, if Mirada wasn't in the wrong, mention of this might compromise Estefan's relationship with the man, and that would be unfortunate. It was evident Mirada had Estefan's confidence in most matters; if she created a wedge between them, it might seem like petty jealousy on her part. She'd settled on a risky compromise: Given the opportunity, she'd subtly quiz Mirada herself. His responses would decide whether she told La Vaca anything. She hated all of this and right now heartily wished she'd never made her offer to Stephenson.

"How is your work?" Mirada asked. "I have been told your gallery is very successful."

Anne took another sip. "This is a particularly busy time with the Indian Market going on." She watched Mirada to see if mention of the Market provoked a reaction; it didn't. "Fall tourist season begins in another ten days. I have a lot to do."

Mirada sat listening politely. Anne didn't know Mirada well; she felt awkward around him, not only because she was the newcomer in Estefan's life but also with Mirada's manner and the way he smiled. There was a hard edge to the man that unnerved her. As for his smile, it seemed contrived, a reflective mask offering nothing to the observer but his or her own image. What was behind it? She felt compelled to explore the man further.

"Are you enjoying Santa Fe? What have you been doing?" Anne asked.

"Luis has been taking care of some business for me," Estefan interjected. "Unfortunately that leaves little time for sightseeing."

"Yes. I had hoped to visit your famous Plaza and see this Indian Market myself. There's been no time," Mirada answered.

Anne's face betrayed nothing even as her pulse rose. *He's lying.* Stephenson said he'd been around the Plaza, asking questions. Why lie about that? There *is* something going on.

"That's a shame. The Market is always special. If you want to sample the artistic culture of New Mexico, the Market is the place. There's everything: jewelry, pottery, beadwork, santos. Oh you probably don't know what a santo is. It's a carving of a religious figure or a saint, like St. Francis or the Virgin. They're incredible." Anne laughed; Mirada's face tightened just slightly at the mention of santos. She shifted her eyes from Mirada to Estefan. He seemed his usual handsome self. She'd missed the look of caution that had passed between them.

"You know Archbishop Pena is a good friend of mine. He has a number of these figures in his private chapel. You're right, they are wonderful, even to a non-artist like myself," Estefan offered. "I had no idea people sell them. It seems sacrilegious."

"I feel that way too. Their religious significance should not be overshadowed by their commercial value. What do you think, Luis?" Anne asked. Mirada's eyes were fixed and cold.

"Not everyone would agree with you. Many people are driven by money."

His answer intrigued Anne. *That's a cynical view; what about you, Luis? What does money mean to you?* She continued.

"Unfortunately you're right. Some artists compromise their ethics to make a living," she said. "There are people who will sell fake art or stolen art. Some pieces are worth hundreds of thousands of dollars. People who regard artworks as no more than commodities will do anything for that kind of money. It's very risky. And sad."

"Life is full of risks. Some people are better suited to taking chances than others," Luis said firmly. Anne felt anxiety begin to rise in her. Did he know what she was up to? Was she pushing things too far?

"Art should rise above such nefarious motives. It inspires people, teaches them to appreciate what is fine and beautiful in life." Estefan took Anne's hand and kissed it. "Just as I appreciate your beauty."

"Mi cariño," Anne said softly.

Estefan stood. "Please excuse me for a minute."

While he was gone, Anne drank her wine in silence, giving thought to her next move.

After a few minutes of silence, Mirada spoke up. "Earlier when you were talking about santos, you said they represent different saints, like St. Francis. You must know quite a bit about them and the people who make them." She felt a surge of confidence; he *was* interested, and he *was* involved in something.

"Not really. I have seen several examples in museums. Some of them date back to Spanish colonial times. The artists are called santeros; I don't think I've ever met one. Their work is unique to the art world because they don't advertise or exhibit it. They're very secretive."

"That seems strange to me. Why the secrecy?"

He's pumping me for information. Better to play dumb. "I really don't know. Perhaps because their art has a personal connection. I've been told that creating a santo is an act of faith. Sadly not everyone believes this to be the case. There's even a special market for santos every fall. It's a shame for art to become just another commodity." *Don't dwell on this too much. Best to move on.* "Your business here must be very important to keep you from exploring Santa Fe," she said.

"Señor La Vaca is exploring several business opportunities here. This visit allows me to investigate them firsthand. People say New Mexico is the land of enchantment. Next trip you could act as my guide. Perhaps I will become enchanted." His tone was less forceful than before, almost patronizing, as if he were trying to put her at ease. It didn't work.

"Certainly. I am curious about these business opportunities though. Perhaps you would share them with me? My accountant has been nagging me to make some investments. 'Diversify,' he told me."

"They might not be the sort of opportunities that would suit you. Besides, nothing has been decided yet. It would be better to talk with Señor La Vaca about them. "

"You're probably right. I'm hopelessly lost when it comes to such things," she said.

Mirada nodded. "You can never be too careful. People are quick to notice if you're in over your head." The cautionary reply sent a frosty wind across her heart. *He's warning me off*, she thought. Thankfully Estefan returned and resumed his seat next to Anne.

"What have you been talking about in my absence?" he asked with airy good humor.

"I told Luis it was a shame he's not been able to explore Santa Fe this trip. He asked me to be his tour guide on your next visit," she said. "He wants to experience the enchantment of New Mexico." She smiled.

At this Estefan gave out with a gusty laugh. "Luis, enchanted? I look forward to seeing that!" The idea obviously amused him. "Yes, I look forward to that."

Mirada placed his glass on the side table and stood. "I have some things to attend to." He turned to Anne. "Our talk was most enlightening. Thank you, señora." With a slight bow to Estefan, he walked out. Anne mentally sighed with relief. Fatigue was beginning to sink in, born of the emotional yo-yoing she'd just been through, coupled with the heady vintage she'd consumed.

"I think you hurt his feelings."

Estefan shrugged. "Luis isn't thin-skinned. That's why he's so valuable to me." He leaned and kissed Anne on the neck. "Stay with me," he breathed.

Longing mixed with anxiety surged through her. She wanted so much to stay and be with Estefan, but the conversation with Mirada discomforted her. She turned and kissed Estefan.

"I can't," she said. "I must go."

His shoulders sagged with disappointment. "Are you sure?" He took her hand and stood, pulling her so close she could feel his heart beating. His eyes were bright, expectant. She nodded.

"I am. Thank you, mi cariño."

With arms wrapped around one another, they slowly walked to the door. As he opened it, he turned to her one last time. "I can promise you a night of bliss. Please?" he pleaded. Anne felt embarrassed.

"Not yet. Soon," she said, squeezing his hand. "Good night."

She felt his eyes on her as she walked to her car, fought down the urge to return to him, and drove away. The sweet, crisp, night air washed over her as she drove; she hoped it would clear her mind from the wine and her emotions. Her feelings were an unsettling blend of sad yearning, chagrin at Estefan's pleading, agitation at Mirada's subtle warnings, and anger that she'd compromised herself with her offer to John Stephenson.

During the drive home, she'd convinced herself that now was the time to open up to Tee and David about her offer to work for Stephenson. She imagined they'd not be happy about it. But when she arrived, everything was dark — they'd gone to bed. Anne took this as a sign; it wasn't important for them to know, at least not yet.

"I'll think about that tomorrow," she said aloud.

Ten

Ojo Agua Gallery, near Ojo Caliente

One of Art Smart's pleasures was scoping out new galleries, the small, unobtrusive places where obscure artists exhibited their works, places where new talent might be lurking, waiting to be discovered. He knew the owner of Ojo Agua as a woman with a discerning eye, and today's exhibition was up to her usual standards. The best pieces were prominently displayed while the "art-school grade" works were few and cleverly tucked away in corners.

One item caught his attention immediately. It was a large, metal etching of San Juan Pueblo pottery surrounded by cornstalks and squash, shaded gold, cinnamon red, and jade green. He recognized the work as an Anne Patrick titled "Golden Harvest" and bent closer to examine it. After a moment's inspection, he removed a small magnifying glass from a pocket and peered through it at the piece.

"The jewel of my exhibition. An Anne Patrick photogravure," a voice said behind him. Turning around he saw the full-figured blond owner of Ojo Agua, Jaime Estes. "I'm glad you came by, Art."

He straightened himself. "Umph. Hold that thought, Jaime. Where'd you get this?"

"It's on consignment. The owner took it in trade for some jewelry he made for a customer. He asked me to sell it for him. I don't usually take consignments, but an Anne Patrick! I'm so excited. Of course it's drawn lots of interest."

"Good provenance?"

"The seller's well-known. Flavio Peralta, the custom jeweler? He showed me the receipt for the trade. I had no reason to question its authenticity."

Art's face screwed itself into a scowl. "Let's talk somewhere."

"Okay." Puzzled, Jaime led him to a cramped, cluttered office off the main showroom. Art closed the door behind them. The room smelled of oil paints and patchouli. They sat.

"What's up?" Jaime asked.

"I know Anne Patrick's works intimately. Each piece comes with a numbered certificate of authenticity signed by her. Did Peralta give you a certificate?"

"He didn't say anything about it."

"I'm not surprised. I'm sorry to say it's a fake."

"What?!"

"I'm certain of it. You can tell by closely examining the depth of the tones where the image transitions from, say, a curve to a straight line. In the photogravure process, the copper plates are deeply etched; the tonal variations will be darker and richer. Each print is made by hand. That's the process Anne uses for her engravings; it's one of the reasons they're so pricey. Counterfeiters use a rotating plate like you see in large print shops because they're readily available and can be reused for other purposes without much difficulty. The process is called rotogravure. The rotating plate is lightly etched, so the image isn't as sharp in the transitions. If you look closely, you'll notice the difference." He handed her the glass and pointed. "See? Here. And here." Jaime squinted and then sat up.

"Oh no! There's been a lot of folks looking at it too. A really nice couple from South Dakota came in earlier, and they loved it. They're coming back this afternoon and probably will buy it."

"Sorry. How much is Peralta asking?"

"Eight thousand. It's a good price; he just wants to move it. Art, you're really sure about this?" she asked, her voice colored with desperation. She'd worked hard to open the gallery; what would happen when word of this got around?

"I'm sure. That price cinches it…too low. This is a limited edition — a run of only five. They sold for twelve thousand each."

Her shoulders sagged. "It's been such a good day too."

Art reached over and nudged her under her chin. "Let me help. Anne Patrick's a friend. I'll take the etching to her so she can look it over. She'll be able to confirm my evaluation. Okay?"

"What'll I tell those nice people?"

"Tell 'em you're having an expert evaluate the print, and it'll be returned by tomorrow. It's your way of guaranteeing their satisfaction. Okay?"

Jaime nodded. Art followed Jaime to the showroom and carefully collected the photogravure. "I'll be in touch. Jaime, if it's genuine, I'll make sure you make the sale. I might even buy it myself. In any case, don't let Mr. Peralta know just yet. Wait until I confirm this. Maybe I'm wrong," he said, trying to sound reassuring. Jaime's face told him the effort was wasted. He walked to his car, got in, and punched numbers into his car phone.

"Kate? I'm onto something. Can you meet me at the Anne Patrick gallery on Delgado Street? About an hour? Call your friends and tell 'em you're coming. See if they'll leave for an hour or so. Okay good." He rang off.

When it comes to fakes, Art Smart isn't stupid, he said to himself.

• • • • •

One Horse Dorp gallery
Kate Cordova had been parked at the gallery for ten minutes. True to her nature, after nearly one minute, she'd begun fidgeting with her hair, scrolling through her phone, and moving around with boundless, albeit random, energy. It was the kind of thing that drove her coworkers crazy. All this stopped when Art drove in. She waved in greeting, stepped out of her car, and strolled over to him.

"Hi, Art. What's up?"

Art held up one finger. "Patience, dear girl." He grinned at her as he pulled up. He got out carrying the etching. "I need to have Anne Patrick look this over. You call your friends?"

"Yeah. They went to the Plaza."

"Good. Just play along with me, okay?"

"Yep." She followed him inside.

"Shop?" Art called. Phyllis appeared from a side door.

"Can I help you?" she asked.

"I'm Art Smart. My client, Katrina Valverde." Kate nodded at Phyllis.

"This is a nice gallery. I must come back," Kate said. Somewhere a dog began barking — a shrill, excited yelp of recognition. "Oh a puppy somewhere," she said airily. She'd forgotten about Taz, who'd recognized her voice. She hoped Phyllis wouldn't catch on.

Phyllis shook her head, annoyed. "That dog belongs to the owner's in-laws. Barks every time she hears someone come in."

"Is Anne here?" Art asked.

"No, she's gone for the day," she said. She eyed the etching.

"I wanted her to look this over. My client is interested in buying it but wants it authenticated," he said with a nod at Kate.

"I can do that for you."

"You sure?" Art asked. The woman frowned at his question.

"Yes, I can. Anne and I have worked together for years," she snapped.

"No offense meant, Miss…"

"Phyllis Van Houten," she said as she took the piece from his hands. "Follow me." Together they walked through the gallery to the workshop. Phyllis cleared a table, laid the etching flat, and began to study it with Art and Kate watching.

"Where'd you get this?" she asked.

"It was on consignment at a gallery. I came across it during an exhibition. The seller took it in trade for some custom jewelry and wants to unload it. My buyer has a good eye for a bargain. But it didn't seem quite right to me, so I have offered to check it out. The woman who owns the gallery agreed to let me bring it here for you to look at."

Phyllis leaned over the etching, lightly brushing one hand across several sections of the etching to feel the texture.

"It isn't right, as you say. There's one sure way to find out."

"Which is?" Art asked.

"Just a minute." Phyllis held up one hand. She retrieved a tool kit from a neighboring shelf. Then she turned the piece on its face, selected a thin-bladed scraper, and carefully began to pry at the backing. After several minutes of effort, she'd peeled it away. She pulled on thin latex gloves and lifted the etching and matting from the frame. Then she then turned them over face up. The matting came away easily. She leaned close and stared at the lower, left-hand corner.

"There." She pointed.

Art leaned in. "What am I looking at?"

"Nothing." Phyllis straightened up, brushing her hair back and smiling triumphantly.

"I don't understand."

"Each of Anne's pieces is numbered. She also adds a hallmark; it looks like two hands folded together. You'll find these at the lower, left-hand corner of every work. They're missing from this one. You were right; it's a fake."

"But I really like it," Kate exclaimed. Phyllis frowned disapprovingly. All during the exchange, Kate had been eyeing Phyllis. There was something familiar about the woman, maddeningly familiar, just below the threshold of perception. When Phyllis pushed her hair back, Kate noticed a faded scar running along Phyllis's hairline. It looked nasty and painful.

"Mr. Smart, Anne won't be happy to learn someone's faking her work. She'll want to be certain you don't go through with this transaction. If you do, that's fraud. Understand?" She glanced at Kate, her voice heavy with sarcasm. The condescending tone angered Kate, but she maintained her poise. It was apparent Phyllis thought she was a noodlehead. Good, that was the effect she'd hoped for.

"But I've already decided just where I want to hang it!" she retorted.

Art patted her arm. "We'll settle this later. Would you put this back together please?" he asked Phyllis.

"Okay. I'll be telling Anne about this."

"I understand." He took Kate aside while Phyllis reattached the frame. While she worked, she watched him gently scolding Kate, who meekly submitted to the lecture. Art left her standing aside and returned to the workbench. When Phyllis finished, she returned the piece to him.

"What will you do with this?"

"Return it to the owner. It's his property. I'll warn him about selling it as an Anne Patrick. Nothing else I can do. He'll have to get his money some other way."

"Does Anne know you?" Phyllis asked.

Art nodded. "We've met. I've admired her work for years." He handed her a business card. "Please have her call me so we can discuss this.. Thanks for your help."

"No problem," Phyllis answered. She shot a last contemptable look at Kate, who smiled innocently in return and followed Art out the door.

"Follow me around the corner," she snapped over her shoulder when they were out of hearing; she stomped to her car. When they had driven out of sight of the gallery, Kate parked and got out. Art did likewise and sighed, knowing what was coming.

"You really pissed me off back there!" Kate announced. "I—"

Art held up a hand. "In my defense, I was only staying in character. You did a great job acting like a self-absorbed, rich lady who's used to getting her way. I thought it all went well."

The compliment didn't make a dent in Kate's anger. "Don't interrupt. Lecturing me like I'm stupid or something. Don't *ever* do that again." She railed on for four or five minutes, stomping in circles and cursing at nothing. Art watched this display of pique with a bemused grin. When Kate had calmed down at last, she stopped and glared at him.

"John told me you tended toward the irritable side," Art said flatly.

"He said that about me?" Kate snarled.

"Now hold on. You're not going to, like, shoot him or anything, are you?" Art asked. "He said not to worry when your hair caught fire — just let the flames burn out. He told me he admires your spirit."

"Asshole."

"Him or me?"

"Yes."

"You played your part well. I'll return this to the gallery. And we need to let John know about Flavio Peralta." He gave out a hearty laugh. "You really looked silly, stomping around in circles and yelling."

Kate stared at him. Her glare began to soften, and the corners of her mouth slowly turned upwards. "You know what's funny? I was acting just like my nephew. I *hate* it when he does that." She began chuckling, which turned into a full-throated laugh. "Wow."

"Okay, that's settled. Meet at your office?" Art asked.

Kate nodded through her laughter. "Sure. Can't wait to tell John about this."

Driving to the task force office, Kate's thoughts returned to their encounter with Phyllis Van Houten. It was apparent the woman disliked her —

about that Kate could care less. But there was something more — a feeling, an attitude about the way she held herself. "Wonder if she was a cop or in the military?" Kate asked aloud. She shook her head. It might be important — or not. However, they *had* confirmed Peralta was in the game, and that was a development.

Her cell phone jingled.

"Hello?"

"Hi, Kate." It was David. "You finished at the gallery? Wanted to make sure before we come back."

"Yeah. Done."

"How'd it go?"

"Anne wasn't there, but her assistant took care of things. Phyllis, that's her name? What do you know about her?"

"Not a lot. Anne likes her. She keeps to herself most of the time. She's been with Anne for a while. Why?"

"Probably nothing. There was something familiar about her. She has a bit of an attitude. I wondered if she'd been a cop or in the service. Know what I mean?"

"I do. Beats me. I think Anne would have mentioned if Phyllis had been a police officer."

"Never mind. Anyway, we're done."

"Okay. Stay safe."

"I will. Give Tee and Taz hugs from me. By the way, Taz started barking while we were there. I think she recognized my voice."

"No doubt. She loves her Aunt Kate."

"Hope I can see her before you head home."

"Me too." He rang off.

"To work, Kate," she said out loud.

· · · · ·

NMSP Zone 1 Investigations office
"Dammit. Why's it doing this?" Phil Ortega cursed at his computer. Mike Charles looked up from his reading.

"Problem?"

"It keeps giving me an error message every time I enter my password. I'm tryin' to get into the warrants file and see if Vickery's warrant is online yet."

111

"Better call Orly in IT," Charles said, slightly amused as Ortega griped into the phone. Phil prided himself at being tech-savvy while Charles politely referred to himself as a "techno-peasant." It was justice that the master was having problems. Ortega banged down the phone in disgust.

"Well?"

"The standard answer. Orly says he has no idea why it would do that. He'll be here in a while."

"Ah, too bad," Charles said with feigned sympathy. He rattled the papers in front of him. "Take your mind off the computer and listen to this. This could be the lead we need to solve this case."

"Yeah?"

"Ten years ago Jim Vickery was indicted for first-degree murder along with another guy named Lewis Sanchez. They tortured and murdered a man named Dennis Ansel because Ansel stiffed 'em on a drug deal. They hunted him down, kidnapped him, took him out in the desert just south of Jemez, tied him up, and tortured him by burning him with cigarettes. They slit his throat and dumped him in an arroyo. Then they went to Ansel's apartment, took whatever money they could find, and set fire to the place. Like most crooks, they were stupid and bragged about what they'd done, so they got arrested a couple of days later. When he was brought in, Vickery offered to testify against Sanchez. Sanchez was a major meth dealer — suspected of a couple other killings — and the DA really wanted to put him away, so he went for it. Sanchez got life without parole. Vickery pled to involuntary manslaughter. Got eight years, did less than five."

"Really. You're right; he's our guy," Ortega cried.

"I think so. In his statement, Vickery admitted he was the one who tortured Ansel. Said he was scared of Sanchez and high on meth when he did it. The DA didn't like it, but making a deal was the only way he could put Sanchez away for good."

"Sometimes that's the way of it. Now we need to come up with something tying him to Marston. The torture points to him; it's the same M.O. Sure, he might have killed Mary out of revenge for what happened years ago. But we still can't put him at Marston's home."

"While you're fixing your little computer glitch, I'll call and see if they ran the prints they found at Mary's through AFIS. If one print matches Vickery's, we've got enough for a warrant."

"Then all we need to do is find him and see if he'll talk to us."

"Yep." Charles smiled. It seemed everything was falling into place.

. . . . .

Old Fort Marcy Park, Santa Fe

The bad news was Monje was late by nearly half an hour and that angered John Stephenson. The good news was Monje's tardiness gave Stephenson extra leverage with which to work. Informants periodically needed reminding who was in charge, and now was a good time. *What a miserable, little turd*, Stephenson thought when Monje finally appeared, shambling along with his strange gait. Stephenson stepped from his car.

"Hey," he called. Showing no sign of urgency, Monje ambled across the green, clearly indifferent to Stephenson's irritation. It was the nature of dealing with snitches.

"Sit down," Stephenson said, and Monje obliged. They walked to a nearby bench and sat in the pale sunlight.

"Hi," he said with a toothy grin.

"We agreed on ten o'clock."

"Sorry. I lost my watch."

"No more excuses," Stephenson said firmly. "You'll keep our appointments on time or your deal's off. Understand?"

Monje's smile evaporated. "Hey, wait a minute."

Stephenson shook his head. "That's the way this works. What do you have for me?"

Monje pouted in silence.

"Look, you don't like the way things are, I'll call DEA and tell 'em you're not living up to your contract. You know what happens then. Now what do you have?"

Monje gave Stephenson a sideways glance. "Come on, man, chill. I'm doin' good work for you."

"I'll decide whether it's good or not. So what's new?"

Monje shook his head. "Things are really quiet right now."

"Bullshit. The city's full of buyers here for the Market. You're moving your share of merchandise, I imagine."

"Oh man, things are really tight. I haven't sold—"

Stephenson held up one hand. "Save it. I know you're moving merchandise every day. How much of it is stolen, I wonder? You'd better watch your ass."

Monje feigned offense. "Officer Stephenson, the stuff I sell is legit. Come on."

Stephenson fully understood the situation with Monje. He was a snitch on loan from the DEA, and John had to allow him a certain amount of leeway. Snitches only knew about illegal activities if they were part of them themselves, and that was the risky bit. The trick was for the handler not to openly encourage the informant to violate the law, even when they suspected this was exactly what was going on. Using informants was a critical but seedy side of the job.

"Alright, there are a couple of buyers asking around the Market about santos. They're offering big money for a particular figure called the Weeping Friar of Chimayo. Heard anything about this?" Stephenson asked, all the while watching Monje's face for a reaction. There was none. *I'll give him credit, he's good*, Stephenson thought.

"Only what you just told me. I never heard of a santo that had a name. I'll find out more," Monje said. "Here's something for you. There's this lady selling pottery at the Market. Name's Maria Ferguson. I've heard she's a pot-picker. She lives out in Utah across the river from the Navajo Rez, a town called Bluff. She has some new stuff, but she also has a few pots that look Anasazi, real old. She's asking a lot of money for them."

"This her first time at the Market?"

"No, I saw her at the spring Market last year. But she wasn't selling Anasazi stuff then, only new ceramics."

"Okay. What else?"

"A lady claiming to be a dealer who says she has clients interested in santos. She's been here in Santa Fe a while. I don't know where she came from. Young, dark hair, kinda chunky, dresses nice. Has a funny name: Katerina something-or-other. She says she's interested in just about anything as long as it's antique. Talks like she's got a heavy bankroll." Now it was Monje's turn to watch for Stephenson's reaction. *Well I know who's doing countersurveillance*, John thought. He didn't take the bait.

"Okay, I'll check her out. Get her last name if you can. A business card or address would be good too."

"Right."

"What else?"

"There's a guy up in Taos: Don Levinson. He runs a little antique shop, takes stuff in on consignment, and doesn't ask where it come from. Also deals a little weed and ecstasy."

"Is he moving stolen pieces?"

Monje nodded. "Yeah. I know he sold some stuff that was ripped from that museum in Albuquerque last year. Talks like it was his biggest deal."

"Where'd it go to?"

"Don't know. You get him on the dope, he'll tell you."

"How about now? What's he selling?"

Monje shrugged. "Mostly junk. Only way he makes money is dealing E."

"I'll pass it along. How do you know him?"

"He used to buy E for me from another guy, then went into business for himself."

You probably ratted the source to the DEA yourself, Stephenson thought. "More?" he asked.

"Nothin, man. Like I said, things have been real quiet for me."

"Yeah, sure. Next Tuesday, ten-thirty at the Cross of the Martyrs. A place you can relate to, I think." Stephenson chuckled. He got up and walked away without looking back.

"Asshole," Monje muttered. At least his suspicions about Katrina had been put to rest. *And you're done, Levinson. That'll teach you to rip me off,* he thought happily. As he shuffled off, he took his wristwatch from a pocket and strapped it on.

In the car, Stephenson withdrew a pocket recorder and rewound it. Listening to Monje's description of Kate made him laugh. "Chunky. She won't like that." Taking out his phone, he called his contact at the DEA.

"Dan? John Stephenson. What do you know about a Don Levinson, lives in Taos, supposed to be an ecstasy dealer? Yeah? Look, I'm gonna come by and talk with you about him…"

• • • • •

115

Chinos' Coffee Shop, Cerrillos Road

Monje could tell Flavio Peralta was anxious. His shoulders were hunched, and one hand fidgeted with his cup while the other tapped a drumbeat on the tablecloth. Monje paid for his coffee and sat down opposite the jeweler. "So what's up?" he asked.

"The deal with the etching's off."

"How come?"

"Somebody woke the owner of the gallery. Whoever it was had it checked and found out it was a fake. She made me take it back." Peralta glared vacantly at nothing.

"Shit! Did she call the cops?" Monje asked.

"No, but she said if it showed up anywhere else, she would. You and your stupid ideas," he snapped. "We should've taken it to Dallas, like *I* suggested."

"Don't put this on me. *You* were the one said it'd be easy money."

"We're out three grand. I needed that money," Peralta whined.

You're such a dumbass. I'm the one who has to think for both of us, Monje thought. "That's the way it goes sometimes. Look, stash it for a while until we find an out-of-town buyer. You'll have to sit on it for now," he said quietly.

Peralta looked dismal. "That hurts. How 'bout a loan?"

"Me? Ha, I'm skinned. Maybe after the next ring." No way he'd loan money to Peralta.

"Ah shit," Peralta snapped. "When's that happening?"

"Depends on your guy. I can set it up for tomorrow night or the next. Want to see the merchandise first."

"Take my word for it, this one is really good. I think it'll bring fifty easy."

Monje thought for a moment. "Who's the artist?"

"Marjorie Villamos. My guy made a copy of one of her pieces from a photo I took at the Hacienda Martinez. It'll do."

Monje slowly rotated his cup, thoughtfully watching the coffee swirl. Now was the time for Peralta to step up and commit to something larger than swindling a few gullible collectors. "I've got a buyer who's looking for the Weeping Friar of Chimayo. You've heard of it. Think your guy could make one?"

Peralta blenched at the name. "Yeah, I've heard of it. I don't want anything to do with it."

"Why not? It don't really exist. Look, no one knows what it looks like. My buyer's from Spain. All he wants is a statue he can call by that name. He'll pay a lot for it. I figure three hundred thou."

"Uh-uh. My uncle told me stories about that santo. There's supposed to be a curse around it; they say if a sinful person has anything to do with it, they die. That's why no one's ever tried to fake it. My guy wouldn't think about it, not for any money we'd offer. And he's gettin' worried…too much exposure. I need to back off him for a while." Peralta was adamant.

"Ah you don't believe that bullshit. Besides, we wouldn't have anything to do with the *real* piece, if it even exists, so the curse wouldn't have any power, see? Look, you said your uncle probably knows more about santos than anyone in New Mexico. Talk to him about it," Monje said. Explaining things like this to Peralta was tedious but necessary. He needed the man's connections even if Peralta was dumb as mud.

"Uncle Roberto is all religious. He'd never fake a santo. He'd say it was a sin."

Monje leaned forward. "Have you ever considered maybe uncle knows where the real one is? If that's true, you realize how much money we could make? Find out what he knows. Quit bein' stupid about that curse." Monje reached across the table, rubbing his thumb and two fingers together. Peralta's eyes narrowed to slits. "Yeah, you're willing enough," Monje said. "You just figure out a way to convince uncle. Make it soon; my buyer wants an answer."

"You really think three hundred thousand?"

"For a fake. The buyer is a millionaire who's all hot to buy this thing and doesn't care what it costs."

Peralta pursed his lips. "If we find it, how we gonna convince him it's real?"

"Power of suggestion. He wants it, he sees it, and it looks right, he'll believe it's the real thing. And he'll pay anything to get it."

Peralta's face brightened. "Okay, I'm in. Look, I really need some money right now."

Monje shrugged. "I'll talk to my partner. Maybe I can interest her in the etching. I'll tell her we need five thousand out of it. Okay?"

"Sure, okay." Peralta was thinking about a way to approach his uncle. Then he had an idea. *Maybe the way to get to uncle is through* her. *Yeah.* The thought rejuvenated him.

"I have an idea. Anne Patrick is uncle's close friend. We get to her, we get to him."

"Good. How?"

"Don't know yet. You get the money; I'll work it out."

"'Kay." Monje drained his cup. "Call you later." He left. Peralta signed to the waitress for a refill. This was turning into a better day than he'd expected.

Eleven

Pilot Truck Stop, I-40 west of Albuquerque

Jim Vickery was sick. It had been at least nine hours since his last hit of meth; he was sick and getting sicker. The burning pinpricks the need for the drug produced had begun in his stomach; soon nausea and cramps would start in earnest. These sensations and his paranoia drove him toward only one objective: getting well. For that he needed money, *fast*. The girlfriend he'd acquired, May, was worse off than he was. She lay in the back seat of her car, comatose from fatigue, her dog huddled next to her. For a moment, Vickery considered how much he could make by selling the dog. Too much trouble. Instead he'd shoplift something from the truck stop store to sell in the parking lot.

The din of engines and voices swirled around him, exacerbating his paranoia. Batteries were always a quick way to cash; he would steal as many packs as he could. Once inside the store, things were quieter. He walked the aisles, trying to appear nonchalant while his withdrawal-driven anxiety increased. In reality he was sweating heavily, his steps were herky-jerky, and he continually ran his hands through his hair — the telltale actions of an addict on the edge. He found the rack of batteries and began stuffing them into his pockets.

"Hey!" someone exclaimed behind him. He whirled around and was confronted by a teenager wearing a red employee's shirt. "What're you doin'?" the boy asked.

"Sorry." Vickery mumbled and started to walk away.

"Wait a minute," the boy said in a shaky voice.

Vickery's eyes took on the faraway, thousand-yard stare of someone beginning to unravel. He snatched a black-handled knife from his back pocket, flicked it open with one hand, and levelled it at the boy. The youngster began backing away, eyes wide and fixed on the blade. "Hey, man, it's okay." He started raising his hands.

Vickery hesitated, trying to decide his next move while the sounds around him eddied through his brain. "Hands down. Move," he hissed. "Where's the back door?"

The boy dropped his hands but froze. Vickery stepped close. "Move," he said and poked the knife at the young man's stomach, goading him.

The boy stepped backwards and turned. "It's always locked."

"Move, you little f—k!" Vickery snarled. They started toward the back, ignoring the incongruous chatting and laughing of patrons oblivious to the drama unfolding in their midst. In what seemed an interminable time but actually took two minutes, they had reached a hallway leading to the storeroom. The boy pushed against the door.

"Like I said, it's locked."

"Unlock it," Vickery snapped.

"I don't have the key. Please don't kill me," the boy whimpered.

Vickery stepped in, thrust the knife against the boy's back, and turned him. "We're gonna walk outside. Now move!"

They hugged the rear wall, skirting shelves and displays while Vickery tried to see a door, any door. The area around the checkout would be the problem; maybe there was a side door they could slip through unnoticed.

Corrections Officer Ben Smith was tired after the overnight shift, but he'd promised his girlfriend a breakfast burrito, so he parked and hurried into the truck stop store. She had a thing about truck stop breakfast burritos. At the steam table, he made a selection and was heading toward checkout when he noticed a young man in an employee's uniform edging along the far wall, followed closely by a scruffy man in a soiled, camouflage shirt. Odd. He stared at the pair for a few seconds; the young man's eyes swept across him, and Smith saw the terror in his eyes. Suddenly he knew. He dropped the burrito and drew his Glock 40.

"Police! Freeze!" he shouted. Customers whirled to stare at him, saw the gun, panicked, and began scurrying away. Smith advanced on the pair, drawing a bead on the man in camouflage. "I said freeze!" he bellowed.

Vickery lifted the knife to the boy's throat. Sensing his chance, the young man twisted and raised one arm, flailing at the knife and cutting his palm in the process; blood sprayed everywhere. Vickery slashed at the boy's neck. As he did, the boy stomped down on one of Vickery's feet. Vickery stumbled backwards, then raised the knife. Smith saw his opening and fired a single shot, catching Vickery square in the chest; he dropped like a bag of sand. The boy fell to his knees, vomiting. Sour-smelling, powder smoke swirled in the air. Smith ran to Vickery, kicked the knife away, handcuffed him, and checked for vital signs. The eyes were fixed half-open in the death stare.

"Somebody call 911!" Smith shouted. He knelt next to the stricken boy and began examining his injuries.

· · · · ·

UNM Hospital #1, University of New Mexico, Albuquerque
It was nearly one in the afternoon when Charles and Ortega arrived at the emergency room of UNM Hospital. They weren't happy. The sketchy information the dispatcher'd relayed to them offered little hope they'd be able to question Vickery anytime soon, if at all. Checking at the admitting desk confirmed their fears. Vickery had been pronounced dead shortly after arriving at the ER.

"Shit, we really needed to talk to him," Ortega snapped. "Sorry," he said, apologizing to the clerk.

"It's okay. The officers from APD are over there. You want the skinny female." The woman pointed to a cluster of people in the hallway.

"Thanks." They approached the group. A short woman with close-cropped hair and pock-marked cheeks turned to them.

"Help you?" she asked tonelessly. They offered their IDs.

"Sergeant Charles, and this is Detective Ortega, NMSP. You're the investigating officer?" Charles asked.

"*Detective* Arless, APD. Wondered when you'd show up. You know the suspect's DOA?"

"We've been told, detective." Charles replied appreciatively, trying to soften the atmosphere a bit. "We wanted to look over his stuff. Can we do that? Might be helpful."

"Not until after the postmortem," she said. It seemed speaking with them was all a terrible inconvenience for her.

"Can you give us any details about what happened?" Ortega asked.

"Not much to it. An employee at the truck stop caught Vickery shoplifting, and he pulled a knife. An off-duty DOC officer walked in the store, saw what was happening, and shot him."

"Did Vickery say anything?"

"Not a word. Right through the pump. DRT."

"What?" Charles asked. He wondered whether she was always this contrary or making a special effort just for them. She rolled her eyes and exhaled an impatient sigh.

"DRT. Dead Right There," she said slowly, cynically emphasizing each word.

"Oh, sure."

A burly man wearing a corrections captain's uniform approached them. "Detective Arless, the PIO wants to talk to you." The woman strolled away.

"Sorry about that," he said. "Dan Wiley, Internal Affairs." He offered a hand to each of them. "Let's talk somewhere." They followed him to a far corner of the waiting area.

"She has a serious 'tude," Ortega offered.

"Yeah. The *good* news is, it's not personal — she's like that with everybody. You could say her people skills need some work. Okay, down to business. The notes on the warrant said you needed to talk to Vickery as soon as he was picked up. That won't happen. How else can I help?"

"He's a suspect in a homicide. Can we look through his stuff?"

"Well he had a car; it's been towed to APD impound. You'll have to go there to search it. APD has an inventory of what they found on him. There wasn't much. A customer at the truck stop pointed out a woman who was with him. We've got her in an office down the hall. She's a tweaker, so her story probably won't make much sense. Name's May Santiago. You're welcome to talk to her."

"Okay," Charles said to Ortega. Wiley led them to the security office, where an APD officer was posted at the door. They walked in to find May

Santiago curled up on the floor asleep. The room stank from the fetid body odor emanated by meth users. A white-and-tan puppy with huge brown eyes clung to her, trembling with fear.

"We figured letting her hang on to her dog might help," Wiley said. "Get her on our side, you know."

"Good idea," Charles said, kneeling beside May. He reached out and patted the puppy's head, who responded by licking his fingers. Charles poked the woman's shoulder. May moaned and stirred, then sat up. Her eyes were sunken, ringed black, and watery. She peered at him with a bleary eyed look of despair mixed with fear and sadness.

"May? I'm a police officer," Charles said. She nodded slightly and picked at a scab on one arm. "I need to talk to you. Okay?"

She kept picking at her skin.

"May? I need to know about you and Jim."

"Jim's dead," she mumbled. "Cops shot him."

"I know." Charles scooped up the puppy and handed it to May, who clutched it close to her chest. "Nice dog. What's his name?"

"Brit," she muttered. The dog nestled in her lap and instantly fell asleep. May had probably dragged the poor animal from one meth house to another in endless pursuit of the drug. Every time Charles had dealings with meth users there was a pervasive sense of fatigue affecting all who associated with them. He hadn't much sympathy for the addicts, but seeing their children and pets at the limits of exhaustion always stirred him.

"Brit's a nice dog. May, tell me about Jim."

"I'm hungry."

Charles glanced at Wiley, who held up a hand and hurried from the room.

"We're getting food for you. Can we talk about Jim?"

"'Kay." She picked at her arm again.

"How long were you with him?"

"About a month, I guess."

"Where'd you go?"

"Around." She looked vacantly at a corner of the room.

The questioning continued in this vein for ten minutes; she was evasive and indifferent, sometimes making no sense at all. Wiley reappeared with a Coke and two bags of Cheetos; May snatched them and began stuffing her mouth full, sharing the Coke with Brit. Tweakers always craved sugar. Between mouthfuls she related a fragmented tale of their wanderings in the past weeks, mentioning meaningless names and petty crimes, all woven around the ceaseless quest for meth. Charles struggled to keep the thread of her story, alternately asking questions and exuding considerable sympathy for the woman and asking her about meth. It worked. Tweakers were always afraid to talk to the police but would readily speak about the drug itself, vicariously fulfilling their cravings for it by talking about it. At last she'd reached the past week of their travels.

"So we went to my uncle's place in Socorro. Stayed there until last night. Then he got pissed 'cause he caught Jim ripping him off. So we split."

"What's your uncle's name?"

"Sam Quinones."

"Tell me about a week ago Monday. Were you at your uncle's?"

"Suppose so." She drained the Coke and hunkered down without another word. Within seconds she was breathing heavily. Charles stood. "Guess that's it," he said, looking at the others.

"Typical meth-head. They never know what's goin' on around them; they're only looking for dope," Wiley said.

"We can check out her story with the uncle," Ortega said. "See if they were there on Monday night. What about her?"

"We don't have anything to charge her with, so they'll kick her loose after she makes a statement. About Monday…that important to your investigation?" Wiley asked.

"Yeah, it is," Charles remarked.

"I'll make certain she puts some kind of a timeline in her statement."

"Thanks."

Ortega squinted in the glare of the afternoon sun as they walked out of the ER. "Well it's down to forensic, I guess. We can't eliminate him based on her statement."

"We'll find the uncle. If she's lying, Vickery's still in the frame. The lab is supposed to call me back before five and let me know about the fingerprint comparison. If none match Vickery…" Charles's voice trailed away.

"If none match, we're screwed," Ortega finished the thought.

"Screwed and not even a 'please' or 'thank you,'" Charles answered.

. . . . .

Santa Fe Place Mall, Cerrillos Road

Monje saw the silver Toyota 4Runner, strolled across the parking lot, and knocked on the window. The driver motioned him inside. In spite of his casual manner, his heart began pounding, and his throat tightened. It was always this way when he was around Veryle.

"What's so important you needed to talk to me about?" she snapped.

"A couple things. I've got an Anne Patrick photogravure, a really good one. The owner wants five thousand for it. It's worth double that, easy. Interested?"

Her green eyes bored into him as if searching for the roots of his soul. It unnerved him, and he had to look away. She despised any weakness; her reaction was like a fox seeing a rabbit.

"You must think I'm really stupid," she snarled.

Monje shrank further from her. "No, it's not like that. Easy money, that's all."

She laughed, a sinister popping-sound like hailstones drumming on the roof. "Money's easy to come by if you're smart. You and your pal Peralta aren't." Her hands began twitching as if she wanted to get them on him.

"How'd you know about Peralta?" he asked in a low voice. He couldn't keep his eyes off her hands. Her eyes remained fixed on him.

"He wanted eight thousand, now it's five. That's a lot to pay for a fake." How did she know these things? She had an unsettling knack for finding things out. Monje was playing a dangerous game, knew it, but the allure of money was too potent to resist.

"Yeah, but a good one." Sweat trickled between his shoulder blades.

"If it's so good, sell it yourself. What else do you want?"

Monje tightened every muscle he could trying to keep control. It was his only defense.

"I've got a line on a guy looking for a particular santo. It's called the Weeping Friar of Chimayo. People tell stories about it. It's one of those legends, but that's what makes it real valuable, see? There's this guy who wants it real bad. He might pay four hundred thousand, maybe more. Peralta's uncle is one of those woodcarvers who make santos. He could make one for us."

"You think the buyer won't know it's a fake? You're working this deal with Peralta? I told you what would happen if you cross me," she hissed.

"No, you don't understand. It's *our* deal, you and me. *I'm* the one with the contact. It's you and me, just like before. Peralta's not smart enough to do this on his own. Once it's done, we can cut him out real easy."

Veryle's smile was a thin slash across her face. Not a pleasant, relaxing smile. The sort of perverse smile you'd see just before someone slit your throat.

"You're getting careless, Monk. That's why *I* make the deals, not you. If you f—k up…" She left the threat hanging in the air.

Monje knew what that meant. "I'm bein' real careful. Look, I need some money for expenses. I'll trade the etching…it's worth the risk," Monje pleaded. It was best to plead and whimper with her. She liked it — at least he thought so.

Her hands stopped twitching.

"Keep it. You think Peralta's uncle will do this?"

"If we give him the right motivation."

"How?"

"Peralta says there's a way to get to him. He hasn't worked it out just yet."

"You think so? What's the uncle's name?"

"His first name is Roberto. He's some sort of hermit, lives out in the desert by himself. He knows a lot about this stuff. Like I said, Peralta's figuring out how to get to him. One problem though: They don't get along."

Veryle had been in the game long enough to know she couldn't do this entirely on her own. She needed these two, at least for the moment. If Monje had taken up with Peralta, it was safe to assume he was just like Monje — not two of God's most dependable creatures. They were risks she'd have to manage.

"That's his problem to solve. Tell me about your contact."

Monje's eyes shifted to and fro. He could only guess how Veryle would react if she knew it was Mirada. Would she kill him? Would she kill Mirada? Would she jump at the chance to screw Mirada one more time? But if he refused to say, she'd find out anyway. He had to chance it.

Veryle could tell there was some sort of inner debate going on, which raised her suspicions even higher. She knew Monje was a scheming, sneaky worm — the sort who'd slip a knife into you from behind but had no stomach for facing an opponent head-on.

"Well?"

Monje made up his mind and played his card.

"It's Luis Mirada."

He braced for an explosion of anger. Instead Veryle threw her head back and laughed.

"That's good! Very good."

"Really?" Monje stared at her. He'd never seen her laugh before. It was unnerving.

"Yes indeed. Tell me more." She kept laughing.

"His boss is some rich guy from Spain. He has this crazy idea about being a big man in politics, and getting his hands on this santo is supposed to make a difference. Mirada's agreed to get this thing for him, money no object."

In her mind, Veryle had already moved past how to work this and was considering the risks. It was a given Monje and Mirada would try to cross her. They'd assume she'd do the same to them. Peralta would probably do whatever they told him to. The sticking point was she needed Monje as the go-between with Mirada. In that she had no choice. However, maybe that could work to her advantage. She'd have another opportunity to finally settle Mirada as she'd settled his brother, making up for the one missed when he got away from the stupid Saudi police. It all fit together.

"All right, but we do this *my* way, understand?" She pulled several bills from a pocket and flipped them at him. "Here's two hundred for expenses. Now get out," she growled.

"But…"

The hands began twitching again. Seeing this Monje snatched up the money, grabbed at the door latch, and leapt from the car as she drove off. His chest heaved, and he felt like throwing up. Once he began to calm down, he realized the opportunity he had: If he found a way, he could cross Veryle, Mirada *and* Peralta and take the money for himself. His chest stopped throbbing. Sure it was risky, but all that money…

Veryle knew Monje would need careful watching from now on. His sloppy handling of the fake Anne Patrick was incredibly stupid; greed was getting the best of him. There was greed, and there was *managed* greed. Hers was under control. For now she'd let Peralta do the work for her in dealing with the uncle. If he failed, well…she knew how to find people. And how to motivate them once she did.

As for Mirada? Whoever said opportunity only knocks once was wrong.

Twelve

One Horse Dorp Gallery

"This still isn't quite right," Anne said aloud. She'd been working on several recent photos for hours, manipulating them using specialized software that allowed her to "smooth out" the natural imperfections and accentuate the characteristics she wanted to highlight. Normally the work was engrossing, but tonight it had become tedious. She checked her watch and sighed. "I need to step away from this for a while." She closed the program and shut off her computer.

Her usual cure for ennui was to venture out with her cameras. But twilight was fading into darkness, and she didn't feel up to driving anywhere. David, Tee, and Taz had gone to Taos and wouldn't be back until late. Phyllis had stayed over, working on the posters for an upcoming exhibition beginning three days from now. What to do? The storeroom needed attention. Cleaning it and sorting the chemicals kept there wasn't exactly liniment for the soul, but it would get her away from the computer screen. Preparing for the exhibition would take all Anne's attention in the next three days. Best to get this out of the way now.

"Phyllis? How's it going?" she called. Phyllis appeared, hair disheveled and jeans ink-stained, but she was smiling.

"Good. You'll like them. Want to see?" she asked eagerly.

"Not right now. I need a break. I'm gonna clean up in the storeroom."

"Oh okay." Her voice dropped in disappointment.

"Sorry. We'll look them over together tomorrow. At the moment, I need to clean out my brain. When you're finished, take off; you must be exhausted."

Phyllis shook her head. "I'm fine. Creating gets me stirred up. You know how it is." She grinned.

Anne returned the grin. "Yeah, I do. But right now I need some mindless task to clear my head. I promise we'll look over the posters tomorrow. Okay?"

"Okay. I'll let you know when I leave." She walked back to the workshop.

The storeroom was actually a separate building just behind the main gallery. From the shadows across the road, Monje and Peralta watched Anne walk to the door, unlock it, and step inside.

"She's by herself. Come on," Monje whispered. They snuck out of the shadows.

As Anne stepped inside and switched on the light, she frowned; it was worse than she'd thought. "Glad I'm doing this now." She donned rubber gloves and picked up a bottle of ammonium thiosulfate, stretching to put it on an upper shelf — a photographic fixer and highly toxic, it was the worst of the chemicals she kept there.

The light went out.

"Shit!" she snapped. Then the door closed behind her. She turned and cracked an elbow against the workbench. "Ow!" The bottle crashed to the floor. Almost immediately the room filled with sour, choking, ammonia fumes. Anne's eyes began watering; she scrabbled for the light switch, found it, and flicked it on and off several times. Nothing happened.

"Ugh, ugh. Damn!" The fumes choked her. Amidst her rising confusion, she suddenly felt, or sensed, that someone was in the room with her. Reaching out, her hands brushed something soft like fabric. There was a slight rustle as it recoiled. Terror engulfed her.

"Who's there?" she cried between coughs. "Ugh! Who's there?"

Silence. She stepped carefully backwards, her shoes crunching on broken glass, trying to recall anything in the room she could use as a weapon. Then the wall was hard against her spine; she was trapped at the back of the room.

"Who's there?" she cried again. She put one hand over her mouth and concentrated on slowing her breathing. The miasma of ammonia was getting stronger, wrapping itself around her. Fear clutched at her, pulling her toward the threshold of panic, but she fought it down.

A second later a hand was on her shoulder and spun her around; something sharp pushed against the middle of her back. Someone leaned close to her.

"Do what I tell you or you get hurt," a voice breathed. The pressure against her back increased. She could feel the harsh scrape of whiskers against her ear. A man.

"What? Why are you (ugh, ugh) doing this?" Anne asked, trying to sound firm while her body shook. Her coughing grew worse.

"You're gonna help me, understand?" Coughing interrupted. The voice wheezed; the knife pushed harder against her spine. "You need to...ugh, ugh, UGH!" The knife wavered. "I want (ugh, ugh)...I want...UGH!" the man said. Suddenly he was gone, and the door slammed shut.

Then she heard voices outside — at first just murmurs, intermixed with harsh coughing, just below her hearing. One voice said what sounded like "knife," and a second voice, a man's voice, more loudly said, "What did..." The first voice spoke again, but she couldn't make out the reply. There seemed to be whispers interrupted with coughs. The second voice said, "Next time..." but dwindled away. There was a gentle thump and the snick of the lock being turned. Bile rose in her throat, driven by fear and toxic fumes; she kept fighting the urge to cough but failed.

"Ugh! UGH!" The fit took hold, and she couldn't stop. "UGH!" Bending over only made it worse. She tried holding her breath, pushing her hands against her mouth with such force she tasted blood. "UGH!"

"HELP!" she gasped as the choking closed in. "HELP! UGH!"

A shout came faintly from outside. "Shit! Someone's coming!" a man's voice exclaimed. There were a series of thumps, cries, and unintelligible sounds all mixed up. Then they stopped. Anne stepped in the direction of the door. She heard the lock turn, and light suddenly flooded the room. She recoiled. What was happening?

"Anne! Oh God. What happened?" It was Phyllis. She rushed forward, grabbed Anne, and pulled her out the door. Coughing engulfed Anne, and she fell to her knees, spitting, gasping, and choking. She sucked in deep buckets of the night air as Phyllis knelt beside her, holding her.

"Breathe slow, deep breaths. You're okay now," she said. Anne sagged against her, tears streaming from her eyes.

After a few minutes, her breathing slowed. She took a last deep breath, relishing the sweetest air she'd ever tasted, and wiped a hand across her face. She looked up at Phyllis.

"I'm okay," was all she could manage.

"What happened?"

Anne inhaled several more times.

"I…the lights went out, and I dropped a bottle. I tried the switch, but it wouldn't work. Then I felt someone in the room with me."

Phyllis shook her head. "I thought I heard someone running away, but there's no one here." She helped Anne to her feet. "Take it easy." She reached inside and flicked the light on and off. "Light's working now."

Anne stared at her; tears began running down her cheeks. "What?" She flicked the switch. "But it wouldn't work. I tried it!" she barked. "There was someone, a man inside with me. He pushed a knife or something like a knife against my back. He said I had to do what he wanted or he'd hurt me. Then he started choking and ran out. Then I heard people outside the door talking. I couldn't make out most of it, just 'knife' and 'next time.' Then the door was locked, and there were noises. And then you opened the door."

Phyllis shook her head. "When I got here, there wasn't anyone around. I was coming to tell you I was leaving, and I heard you calling, 'Help,' and I pulled the door. It was locked, so I knew something was wrong." She hesitated. "I thought someone might have been running away, but I didn't see anyone."

Anne stared at her, then squinted at the door, the light, and the shattered bottle on the floor. She turned her stare back to Phyllis.

Phyllis eyed her closely. Then she stepped inside the storeroom, covered her mouth, and leaned over the broken bottle. "Ammonium thiosulfate! You could have died. You weren't wearing the dust mask?" Anne shook her head. Then Phyllis pointed. "Look, there's broken glass outside the door. It must have been on the shoes of whoever attacked you. Look, sit down. I'd better call the paramedics."

"No, I'm okay!" Anne cried. "I…just…don't…understand." She stared at the broken glass, coughing a few times, less violently than before.

Phyllis turned off the light and closed the door. "I'll get some kitty litter tomorrow to clean this up. I'd better stay with you for a while just to make sure you're all right. You want me to call the police?"

Anne sank against the wall of the building. She felt sick to her stomach, and a headache was forming behind her right eye.

"I don't know. You think I should?" She rubbed her temples trying to forestall the pain.

Phyllis nodded. "This is serious. If I hadn't shown up...who knows?"

"But what do I tell them? Someone came at me in the dark, threatened me with what felt like a knife, but I don't know what he wanted? Then he locked me in and ran off? It sounds completely idiotic."

Phyllis pursed her lips. "I think you should report this. This wasn't a random attack; someone was after *you*. The police might be able to find out why."

"But I don't have any idea why. Unless I can tell them something, they wouldn't know where to begin. I'd be wasting their time." The ground was cool but beginning to feel hard against her slender frame. She pushed herself to her feet. "No, I'm not going to call the police."

"Well...let's go in and talk some more. I'll make you some tea." Phyllis took Anne by the arm and led her to the gallery.

Two blocks away Monje caught up with Peralta, who was at his truck trying to make the remote work with shaking hands.

"Hey! Ugh! Ugh! Wait!"

Peralta got in and fumbled with the keys. Monje yanked open the passenger door and leapt in. "You f—cking coward! You're not gonna leave me here," he snarled, punching Peralta in the face with such force his head struck the driver's window.

"Ow!" Peralta swung at Monje, who waved his knife.

"I'll cut you! Get us outta here," he ordered, thrusting the knife close to Peralta's ribs. Peralta shrank from him and turned the ignition, and they roared away into the dark.

"You said she was by herself! Who the hell was that woman?" Peralta shouted.

"Drive, stupid!" was Monje's reply.

•　•　•　•　•

The orange herb tea went down nicely and would have been even better spiked with a jigger of Bailey's Irish Cream. Anne thought about it and remembered she was out. She sipped again with less enthusiasm.

"How's your throat?" Phyllis asked. She wished for a bit of orange schnapps in hers. They were sitting in the gallery office; Gershwin's "Lullaby for Strings" purred on the radio.

"Better." Anne swallowed and rubbed her throat. The pain was a bit scratchy but livable. "I was trying to remember what the man said to me. He started to say something and then coughed. The ammonia got too much for him, and that's when he ran away."

"You couldn't tell what he tried to say?"

"He said he wanted me to help him, or he'd hurt me...then he coughed. But what did he want? It's not like I had money or a purse." Anne raised her eyebrows. "Could it be information? Maybe that's it. But what information?" She stared quizzically at Phyllis, who shrugged. "What information?" A thought began nagging her: Did someone know she'd offered to work with John Stephenson? How would they know?

Phyllis was insistent. "Who knows what he wanted? That's why I think you should call the cops. You know, he might come back again. You shouldn't take this lightly. I mean, what saved you was dropping that ammonia."

"*You* saved me, Phyllis. But I'm not calling the police. Talking it over with you now, it's *really* embarrassing. Look, I'm all right. You go on home; you look really tired."

Phyllis smiled. "Not until I'm certain you're okay." She drained her cup and held it up. "More?"

"No, this will do me just fine. I know you're not happy with me, but I'm not gonna call the police," she said over the rim of her cup.

Phyllis sighed. "Don't take this wrongly. You're an amazing woman. You've been very kind to me, and I really appreciate that. I've learned so much from you. But...once your mind is made up, well, you're the most stubborn woman I ever met."

Anne threw back her head and gave out her throaty, room-filling laugh. Phyllis began to giggle, which evolved into full-throttle laughter. It was a singular moment between them.

· · · · ·

NMSP Zone 1 Headquarters

Captain Charles "Chico" Villalva walked out of the press conference wearing the look of a man who'd just had his annual exam from the proctologist: edgy with a slight tingling sensation in his lower regions and happy it was over. Mike Charles was waiting in the adjoining hallway.

"How'd it go, Cap?"

"This winter I'm sending you and Ortega to PIO training so you can handle these things yourself."

"Aw, you did just fine. I listened in. Phil and I couldn't do better," Charles said with a sly grin. Like most officers, he hated dealing with the press, although in this case, they might be useful. As far as he was concerned, press conferences were for command staff. He also believed good detectives shouldn't rely on the press to generate leads. But they had no place to go; May Santiago's story had checked out. She and Vickery had been at her uncle's during the time Mary had been killed.

"Keep repeating the phrase 'duties as otherwise assigned.' Hope this generates some leads," Villalva said.

"So do I."

Villalva checked his watch. "Well I've got some memos on the stove. Let me know if you hear anything." He chuckled and walked out. Charles returned to the investigations section. Ortega was frowning as he perused a report.

"What's up?" Charles asked as he sat down at his desk.

"Report from the lab on those prints they lifted at Marston's. No matches for Vickery. Most were Marston's. Two are unidentified. They were lifted from the desk next to the cash drawer, so they could be from a customer."

"Did they run them through AFIS?"

"No, the system was down. They'll run 'em when it's back up. How was the press conference?"

"All the locals were there. KBRQ said they'll run it as the third lead tonight. Wait and see. Maybe we'll get lucky with those unidentified prints."

"Hope so. I really don't want this case to go cold."

Both men were realists and knew not every case could be solved. However, this was one of those cases that called for maximum effort. Mary Marston was a decent person who deserved a better fate than lying dead in a ditch, discarded like so much trash. Citizens might think detectives' egos drove them to solve every case. Truth was they saw themselves as the only advocate for the victim. Nothing was more satisfying than when they spoke with the victim's voice, confronting the perpetrator with evidence of their crime. Likewise nothing was more frustrating than when a case went unsolved.

"Any ideas?" Ortega asked.

"Yeah. We go back to the beginning. Go through everything, see if there's anything we missed."

Ortega opened his cell phone. "Better call Isa and tell her I'll be late tonight."

Charles did the same. "Hi, babe. Look, it's gonna be another late night…" he began.

· · · · ·

Casa Elegante, Agua Fria Street

When he entered the room, Luis Mirada could see Estefan La Vaca was enjoying a special moment. He was smiling broadly, his eyes had a lustrous sheen in them, and he was completely relaxed, sitting back with his legs crossed. He cradled the phone in one hand and signaled to Luis to set down the mug of coffee on the table next to him. He did so and sat opposite his boss, who murmured into the phone with an excited schoolboy's gaiety. After another minute, he kissed the phone and snapped it shut.

"Ah thank you, my friend," he said, picked up the mug, and sipped appreciatively.

"You look particularly happy this afternoon. Maria Elena?" Luis asked.

La Vaca was all smiles as he sipped. "Yes. I need scarcely remind you not to mention her to *anyone here*."

If Luis took exception to the warning, his face betrayed nothing. "Understood. I want you to know I am making progress. But we may need to extend our stay a few days."

La Vaca considered this. "How long?"

"Four or five days more. I have told my contacts we want a result very soon."

"These contacts — can they be trusted?"

Luis snorted. "Of course not. But they are the sort of people I have handled before. They won't be a problem."

"You are close to acquiring the Weeping Friar? Wonderful!" Estefan was more excited by this prospect than his conversation with his fiancée in Spain. This tendency to the ephemeral made him easy to handle in spite of his self-described shrewdness. The only thing Luis appreciated more than this trait was Estefan's money.

Luis nodded. "Yes. The santo may be in the care of an old man, a believer. But as we both know, even the most passionate of believers has a price."

"That is excellent. Staying a few days won't be a problem. You're arranging to take the santo to Spain without any trouble?"

"There won't be any trouble. The Spanish consul here is being very co-operative."

"Good. Now where shall we have dinner tonight?" Estefan drained his coffee.

Thirteen

One Horse Dorp gallery

Tee wandered about the gallery, enjoying the afternoon warmth; the gallery was quiet, and she took the time to study her sister's work. Anne was outside playing with Taz; David was on the patio, watching the two of them while he enjoyed a late cup of coffee. Tee relished this uninterrupted opportunity; she'd never truly appreciated Anne's talents, not really. Truth be told, she'd harbored serious misgivings about Anne's Santa Fe venture, and now she felt a twinge of guilt. Anne was successful; her pieces were quite good, and several were exceptional.

From the back garden Tee could hear Taz barking excitedly as Anne chased her about. In the way of dogs, the two had quickly become buddies, and Tee wondered why Anne had never gotten a dog herself; she'd always loved animals. But now she had a very busy life, on top of which she was engaged… and La Vaca didn't strike Tee as the dog type.

Anne's phone jingled; she'd left it next to the cash register. Without thinking Tee answered.

"Hello?"

"You got my message?" a voice whispered.

"Who's calling?" Tee asked.

"Don't act stupid. Do what I want or you'll get hurt. Understand?" the caller hissed.

"Who is this?" Tee barked. The call abruptly ended. She looked at the screen; the number had been blocked. Holding the phone, she hurried into the garden. "Anne."

Anne picked up Taz and smothered her with kisses. "I just love you, Anastasia!" Taz excitedly licked Anne's face.

"Anne, come here," Tee said. The tone of her voice caused David to look over.

"Something wrong?" he asked.

Tee held up the phone. "Someone called for you."

"Oh not now. That's what voicemail is for," Anne replied. She put Taz down and resumed chasing her.

"No. Stop that," Tee snapped. Anne stopped, turned, and stared at her sister.

"You sound just like Mom," Anne teased.

"I'm serious!"

"I see that," Anne said, annoyed. The interplay between them intrigued David; he'd never seen them square off like this.

"Anne, whoever called threatened you."

"You're joking. That's not funny."

"I'm not joking. They said you'd better do what they want or you'd get hurt. What's going on?"

Anne quickly turned away to stare at the garden. Puzzled, Taz began jumping side-to-side, inviting her to play. Anne looked down at the little dog, snatched her up, and clung to her. She turned back to Tee, her eyes dark with worry.

"What's going on?" Tee asked, irritated that she'd become annoyed at Anne. Something was terribly, terribly wrong.

Anne sat down; Taz began licking her face.

"Anne?" Tee pulled a chair close and sat opposite her sister.

"There was a problem the other night, the night you went to Taos."

"What happened?"

Anne told them the story of her encounter in the storeroom. Tee's hands clutched the arms of the chair; she found herself holding her breath. David's face tightened with anger. When Anne had finished, Tee leapt to her sister and clutched her.

"Oh, Anne. Thank God Phyllis heard you and you weren't hurt. Did you call the police?"

Anne shook her head. "No. I didn't want to waste their time. It all seemed so…unimportant."

"That's crazy!" David exclaimed.

Tee kissed Anne's cheek. "You could have been hurt. I know you always think things will work out and you can take care of yourself. You're as stubborn as Mom."

Anne managed a meager smile. "So are you. Please don't be angry with me."

Tee stood. "Well I am. It'll pass. But I'm adamant — call the police."

Anne sat quietly. Contrary to what she'd told John Stephenson, she'd never discussed their conversation with Tee and David, putting it off long enough until it had slipped into a disused corner of her mind. In light of the incident in the storeroom and the threatening call, this could be the only explanation for the threats. Her self-assurance was badly shaken.

"Why would someone threaten you? Anne?" David had shifted from brother-in-law to cop. "What went on between you and John Stephenson? This has something to do with that, doesn't it? Are you in some sort of trouble?"

She nodded. "I offered to work with him."

"Why'd you do that?" Tee asked.

"He needs information, and I offered to help."

David shook his head. "You should have talked this over with us."

"I know. I wanted to. I kept putting it off." She looked from Tee to David and back to Tee. "I should have; I made a mistake."

David took a deep breath. "I should be mad at you. But one thing my old sergeant, Eddy, taught me: Getting mad doesn't make things any better."

"What now?" Tee glanced at David. If someone knew Anne was giving information to the police, there was no telling what they might do. "I think you should call Stephenson and tell him no. It's too dangerous."

As Anne listened to them, she became angry. "No, the more I think this over, the more I'm resolved to work with him." She stood up. "No one is going to make me afraid." She handed Taz to Tee. "You remember when Margaret Scofield kept picking on me when we were at Bowles Middle School? I finally had enough and punched her. That's the way I feel right now, dammit."

Tee chuckled at the memory. "Mom and Dad were shocked when the school sent you home. I think Mom was secretly pleased. Of course Dad had to make a show of being angry. Dads are supposed to be angry when their daughters get in trouble, right?" She gave David an amused grin.

"The Fleming sisters. You two are a pain in the—" David began.

Tee put a hand over his mouth. "Don't say something you'll regret later, dear heart."

David screwed his face into a frown. "All right. But we can't just go on like everything's okay. I'm gonna talk with Stephenson. He needs to know. Agreed?"

Tee and Anne both nodded.

"One thing more: We keep tabs on one another."

"That works," Anne said. She reached down and scratched Taz's ears. Tee patted David's arm and mouthed, "I love you." He leaned down and kissed the top of her head. But he had the feeling this was only the beginning of trouble. And that worried him a lot.

· · · · ·

Santa Fe Flea Market, Montezuma Avenue, Santa Fe
Surveillance was tough under the best circumstances — doing it alone compounded the difficulties by a factor of ten. Finding the subject at any given time was problematic until patterns of behavior were identified.

Where to begin? The flea market. Anyone looking to buy or sell anything could usually find it here, provided one didn't ask or expect too much. Merchandise showing signs of wear was considered "antique," items "new in the box" had probably been shoplifted the previous day, and many offerings were little more than junk. When buying or selling, one needed to remember this: Price had no relationship to value. One was based on economics, the other on emotion.

He'd spotted the woman first. There was something notable about the way she held herself: always balanced, poised, as if she was prepared for trouble. Most shoppers browsed casually; she focused only on stalls displaying artwork, primarily acrylics and santos, and never spoke to the vendors. That was left to her companion, a slouched, shambling fellow indifferent in manner and appearance. He did all the talking and, occasionally, the buying.

Surveilling anyone was always a study in human behavior. The more one learned about the target, the more fascinating (and unpredictable) they became. Subtle inquiries discovered the man was asking around the stalls in a casual way about santos — in particular about The Weeping Friar. The hours of tedium had paid off.

Every Saturday they showed up at the market mid-morning, strolled the market for an hour or so, and disappeared. Once he'd managed to follow them to their car: a silver 4Runner. The woman always drove.

This Saturday was different. When he spotted her, she was alone. With practiced care, he followed her through the throngs of buyers. She stopped at one particular stall where she'd stopped before. This time the vendor, a thin-faced Latino, waved her behind a quilt that hung at the back. He knew the man: Juan Ramos, well-known for his crooked dealings. Because of them, he'd been banned from the Indian Market and resorted to selling at the flea market. Quickly he walked to the stall and began examining the works displayed. Within seconds Ramos pulled back the quilt; the woman's profile was partly visible behind him.

"I'll be right there, señor," he said.

"Just looking." He picked up a piece, casually turned it over once or twice, and moved away. Ramos watched him leave, then turned to the woman. She was examining a small, carved figure of St. Anne.

"You have the money?"

She handed over a folded wad of bills. "We agreed on fifteen hundred." Ramos thrust them into a pocket. He proceeded to wrap the figure in heavy paper and handed it to her.

"Now there's the other matter; what's your answer?" she asked.

Frowning, Ramos shook his head.

"No way. I won't do it."

"Afraid?" she snapped.

"Damn right! It's not smart, messing with something like that."

Her entire body tensed. "Don't tell me what's smart. You're a coward," she hissed. Picking up the parcel, she flipped aside the quilt and disappeared into the crowd. After she'd left, Ramos crossed himself.

When she emerged, her shadower was waiting. He followed as she walked toward the parking lot. Picking his way through the slow-moving crowds, he reached his truck just in time. She drove out of the lot, headed toward Paseo de Peralta. He followed as best he could, keeping her in sight while trying to conceal himself among the heavy traffic. The Plaza District made things dicey. The narrow, one-lane streets made concealment nearly impossible. He'd be spotted. Sure enough, the car ahead of him turned suddenly, and he found himself right behind her. If a game of hide-and-seek commenced, he'd know she'd seen him.

But she turned north in an ordinary way, drove past La Posada Hotel, and then pulled into a driveway on the left. He continued along the street, eyes on the rearview mirror to see if she emerged. Then he pulled to the curb and stopped. How long should he wait? If she'd spotted him and ducked into the first available driveway, she could only remain for a few minutes. The SFPD continually prowled the Plaza neighborhoods — parking was always a problem, and complaints were constant. He took a chance and quickly got out, walking back the way he'd come. At the driveway, he slowed; a house was hidden behind the trees, but he could make out the shape of the parked 4Runner, now empty. The layout of the property precluded any possibility of close surveillance. He noted the address; tomorrow evening he'd walk past and get a good look at the place. Just then a parking warden's car passed him. He trotted back to his truck, arrived just ahead of her, jumped in, and pulled into traffic, heading north toward the Taos Pueblo. He needed to tell Uncle Antonio what he'd learned.

Thus he missed seeing her leave the house sans parcel but carrying a thick envelope. When she reached the 4Runner, she slid into the seat; keeping one careful eye on the house, she tripped a switch hidden beneath the ashtray, causing the radio console to rotate out and downwards. The envelope was tucked inside, and then she pushed the volume button, and the console returned to its proper position. Wheeling into traffic, she drove away. Transaction completed.

· · · · ·

Southwest Trafficking Task Force office
Kate Cordova sat across the desk from John Stephenson, who was alternately nibbling on a cranberry-orange muffin and leafing through the endless forms the feds required from him. When her cell phone rang, she immediately checked the number before picking it up. It was a habit she'd cultivated after joining the unit. One careless mistake with the phone, and her cover would be blown.

It was Monje. Kate held up a hand, calling for quiet.

"This is Katrina."

"It's Monje. The ring tonight is cancelled."

"Oh too bad. Is it rescheduled? I have a buyer who's only here a couple of days."

"I'll let you know." He rang off.

Kate looked across the desk at John. "Monje cancelled tonight's ring. I think something's up."

"Why?"

Kate wore a handsome, silver-and-turquoise ring on her left pinky. She fiddled with it while she thought.

"He's a greedy sonuvabitch. Never misses a chance to make a buck."

"Think you're blown?" Stephenson asked. Since David's warning, he'd worried Kate would be found out and had done some discreet surveillance on her himself. But there'd been no sign of anyone tailing her.

"Don't think so. When I talked to him yesterday, everything was fine. Cancelling the ring tells me he's got something else on. I'm gonna call Peralta and feel him out."

"Do it." Stephenson resumed working over the paperwork. Kate walked to an adjoining office and closed the door in order to make the call without interruption.

A short while later she emerged and sat down.

"Find out anything?"

"Left a voicemail." There was a copy of the *Santa Fe New Mexican* on the desk; Kate picked it up and idly turned the pages. One article caught her interest: a follow-up about the shooting on Highway 582.

"Wow, that's interesting."

Stephenson looked up. "Is this work-related?" he asked with a smirk.

"Sort of. It's about the OIS (officer involved shooting) the other night near Okayh Owinge."

Stephenson frowned. "Maybe I should have said *work related to the task force*. Stretching it a bit, aren't we?"

Kate giggled. "I guess. No, the article has profiles of the officers involved. One of the tribal officers, Rick Hayes, has a degree in journalism with a minor in Native American studies. Now he's a cop. Sounds like an interesting man.

He's good-looking too. Wonder if he's single." She held up the paper, pointing to a photo of Hayes.

Stephenson inspected the photo; a wry smile spread across his face. "Ever tried one of those online dating services? You know, single female with Rambo-like personality seeking male who enjoys shooting, being handcuffed, and casual interrogation?" he teased. Kate's personal life was littered with the wreckage of several social mishaps. She had a tendency to treat boyfriends like suspects and was always surprised when they took umbrage with such behavior.

"That's not fair. He seems like someone I'd like to get to know," she snapped. Stephenson dissolved into choking laughter. Kate sat and fumed until he stopped.

"Finished?" she growled.

Still chuckling he wiped his face. "I really got you this time."

Kate threw the paper on the desk. "Glad you enjoyed yourself."

"Ah come on, I was teasing. Look, you're really interested, why don't you call the tribal police and talk to him?"

"If I do, you'll be that last to know," she snapped.

Stephenson was about to return to his paperwork when he glanced down at the newspaper. "Look at this. When you've finished drooling over Officer Hayes, check out the lead article." He pointed. "Spanish Donor Builds Legacy with Museum Donation," it read. Accompanying the piece was a photo of Estefan La Vaca, Luis Mirada, and Anne Patrick. Stephenson skimmed through the article and then began reading aloud. "Senor La Vaca is not only a generous patron of the arts in New Mexico but an *enthusiastic collector.* He is especially fond of works with religious themes." He shook his head. "Wow. In the past three years, he's donated over two million dollars to the museum." He put the paper down. "If it doesn't interfere with your social schedule, check with ICE (Immigration and Customs Enforcement) on this guy La Vaca. I'll bet he's the bankroll behind Mirada. See if he's applied for any permits to take artwork out of the country," he said

"Right."

"And let me know what you hear from Peralta."

Still miffed Kate walked to her desk and dropped into the chair. Before she signed on her computer, she discreetly fished the phone book from a drawer, found the number for the Okayh Owinge Tribal Police, wrote it on a pad, and tucked it into her purse. Stephenson's teasing notwithstanding, he'd given her an idea.

While Kate got busy, Stephenson sat at his desk staring at the papers arrayed before him. Ever since his meeting with Anne Patrick, he'd harbored the vague hope the two of them might "get together." The news piece stomped that idea flat — La Vaca was wealthy and influential. How could John think Anne Patrick would throw him over for a shopworn police officer who lived one paycheck to the next? Shaking his head to clear his thoughts, Stephenson forced himself to concentrate on the uninspiring task before him. But the pain of a crushed dream lingered.

· · · · ·

One Horse Dorp gallery

This morning was a good time for David to talk to Phyllis; Tee and Anne had left for a girls-only breakfast. Taz was happily ensconced in the guesthouse, crunching on a Nylabone. The gallery wasn't open yet, but he'd seen Phyllis walk inside. He went looking for her.

It wasn't that David didn't believe Anne's story about her encounter in the storeroom; rather, experience had taught him important details emerged when different witnesses were interviewed. He wanted to know what Phyllis knew that might differ from what Anne had told him. As he walked past the gallery office, a noise from within attracted his attention. He pushed the half-open door and was surprised to see Phyllis inside. She was bending over the desk, looking at something. At the sound of the door opening, she whirled round.

"What do you want?" she barked angrily, her eyes cold, almost menacing. David stopped in his tracks. Upon seeing him, Phyllis's demeanor instantly transformed itself to the meek, shy woman he was accustomed to.

"I'm so sorry. You scared me!"

"Sorry I startled you. I want to talk to you about the other night," David said. "What are you doing?"

"Anne asked me to call a man for her this morning. I thought his number was in my phone, but it's not, so I was checking Anne's." Phyllis stepped away from the desk. "Why do you want to talk about what happened?" She smiled, but her tone was suspicious.

"See if there's anything you remember, any detail Anne might have missed. She told us you heard someone running away. Could there have been more than one person?"

Phyllis shook her head. "It sounded like only one. Everything was happening all at once, I couldn't say for sure."

"The lights went out, but when you tried them, they worked. Maybe someone switched off the power at the box. Is it close by?"

"Yes, it's around the corner from the door. I didn't think to check it."

David nodded. "No worry. It must not be padlocked."

"No, we need to correct that."

"We're just grateful you were there and rescued Anne."

Phyllis blushed. "Well..."

"You tried to convince Anne to call the police, but she refused. Any idea why?"

"She kept saying she was embarrassed because she didn't have much to tell them. I kept telling her to call anyway and let them figure it out. She's very stubborn and wouldn't do it. I still think she should've called them."

"I agree. Did you notice any suspicious people hanging around earlier in the day?"

"No, but I'm usually in the workshop, so I probably wouldn't notice... sorry. Are you gonna call the police?"

"Not much point. Any evidence there was is gone now. I just wanted to satisfy my curiosity. Thanks again for helping Anne. If you hadn't been there... " David smiled. "Well thanks."

"She's my friend. I'm just glad she's okay," she said and hurried past David toward the workshop, leaving David to sort through several thoughts. Phyllis couldn't offer any new information and that disappointed him; she might be quiet, but she was also bright and observant, and he'd hoped she had something new for him. That brought him to Kate's reaction to the woman; it seemed out of place. Phyllis didn't strike him at all like someone coming from a regimented background such as military service or law enforcement. She was shy and awkward with people, not the sort of assertive personality typical of those professions. Her outburst with him could be readily dismissed as the reaction of a frightened woman. Even so David trusted Kate's judgement. There was a way to find out about Phyllis's background, though not something Tee or Anne would approve. He opened the desk drawers and began leafing through Anne's business files. In a few minutes, he'd located the one he wanted and opened it.

"Strange," he said softly. The file contained only a single sheet of paper. No payroll record, no resume, no letters of reference — only a cover sheet. He hovered over it, thinking. Anne was maddeningly anal about details, everything having its proper place. The contents *could* have been misplaced…he shook his head. No way. A thorough search of the desk didn't turn up the missing documents. He carefully returned the files to the desk and closed the drawers. Something was going on, but he wasn't sure what. How to proceed? He glanced around the office, looking at the photos, thinking what to do next.

Telling Anne and Tee would be awkward. Kate's assessment of Phyllis was no more than a vague hunch, hardly justification for rummaging through Anne's files. Both would feel he'd violated her privacy. An idea formed. Before saying anything, there were two other avenues he could pursue. If he came up empty? "No harm, no foul," he murmured. He hurried out and headed to the guesthouse.

· · · · ·

1840 Metate Street, #11, Santa Fe
Mike Charles was in a bad mood. Phil Ortega kept quiet; there was little point trying to lift his spirits with casual conversation. So he concentrated on following the twisting warren of streets near the Santa Fe Railyard. At last he found the address: an unprepossessing, two-story, blond brick apartment block built in early 1950s style.

"Here it is," he announced. Charles grunted in reply and climbed out of the car.

Their rehash of the case file had taken all night and much of the next day and produced no new insights but revealed one glaring omission, which they were in the process of correcting. They'd neglected to follow up and find Phyllis Van Houten. Ortega had argued (unsuccessfully) that it was an oversight and nothing more. Charles wasn't buying that; he took his supervisor's responsibilities seriously and insisted the blame was his alone. Hence his brooding silence. They'd obtained her address from DMV, along with a photo.

Apartment 11 was on the backside of the building. When Charles's knocking produced no reply, he tucked a card in the door, and they began checking adjacent apartments. Number 12 was vacant. After a few minutes knocking, the door to apartment 10 opened slightly; a bleary eyed young man with tousled hair and several days' beard peered through the crack. Charles thrust his ID in the man's face.

"State police. You know the woman who lives in apartment 11?"

The man stared at him briefly, obviously roused from sleep even though it was after 2 P.M.

"Sorry, I work nights." He rubbed his eyes. "Nah. Seen her once or twice."

Ortega produced the DMV photo. "That her?"

He studied it for a minute. "Yeah. I talked with her a couple times, just said hi like you do, you know?"

"Sure," Charles replied. "She live by herself?"

"I think so. Never seen anybody with her. She in trouble or somethin'?"

"Just need to talk to her." Ortega handed him a business card. "If you see her, call us, okay?"

The man accepted the card without enthusiasm. "Sure."

"There an on-site manager here?" Charles asked.

"Apartment 1."

Charles turned away. "Thanks," Ortega said.

The manager was young, obese, and sucking on a malodorous cigarette when she opened the door. Charles squinted and stepped back from the bluish cloud of smoke; he had an aversion to cigarettes after watching his father chain-smoke his way into an early death at forty-three.

"Help you?" she asked, exhaling a huge cloud.

Ortega offered his ID. "We're looking for Phyllis Van Houten."

"Apartment 11."

"She's not home. Is there anything you can tell us about her?"

"Sure, come in," she said, smiling at the two of them. She liked police officers.

"No, thanks anyway," Charles said.

"Your name is...?" Ortega asked.

"Amy Luna."

"Nice to meet you, Amy. I'm Investigator Ortega; this is Sergeant

Charles." He gave Charles a sideways glance, hoping he was loosening up a bit in spite of the smoke. Charles nodded at Ms. Luna.

"Is Phyllis in trouble?" Amy asked.

"We're doing some background work, and she may know something about a case. We just need some information," Ortega offered. "Does she work anywhere?"

"Yeah, at some art gallery. Sorry, I don't remember the name. It's an unusual name. Would you like me to check her tenant application?"

"That would help," Charles said.

"Why don't you come in? I keep all the records in here."

The woman was so eager to help, Ortega couldn't refuse.

"Sure, thanks." Charles glared at him, which Ortega ignored. They stepped inside. The apartment was ripe with the stale aroma of smoke; a squeaking ceiling fan didn't help much. Charles sucked in his breath, his discomfort painfully clear. Amy saw this and switched on a table fan.

"I'm sorry. Smoke bothers a lot of people," she said, apologizing.

Ortega smiled at her thoughtfulness; he didn't like cigarette smoke either. "Thanks."

Amy searched two file cabinets, located the file she wanted, and opened it. "She's lived here about three years. Always pays on time. I haven't had any problems with her. She used to work for the Catholic diocese. Then she got this job at a gallery. Here it is — called One Horse Dorp," she read and chuckled. "Like I said, it's got an unusual name." She handed the file to Charles.

"She's a good tenant?" Ortega asked.

"Yes. She's not around much. Works a lot of hours."

Charles looked over the application. "Can you make a copy of this?" he asked in a pinched voice.

Amy scowled. "We're not supposed to give out information about tenants. But..." she hesitated. "Sure."

"Thanks a lot," Ortega said. Amy took the application and placed it on the copy screen of a printer next to the cabinets and hit the copy button.

"It's kinda slow," she said.

"No problem," Ortega replied.

"While we're waiting, I have a question for you," Amy said.

151

"Sure," Charles said. Of course you do. Never met an apartment manager who didn't want advice from the police.

"There's a man lives in apartment six. I can smell marijuana coming from inside when I walk by. What should I do?"

Ortega chuckled. Marijuana had become ubiquitous; the police paid little attention unless someone was flaunting its use or they discovered large quantities.

"Call Santa Fe PD," he answered.

"The last time I smelled it, I did. The dispatcher said they were too busy and gave me the number for the drug detectives. I left a message, but they never called back," she said in a disappointed voice.

"Yeah, that happens. Have you talked to him about it?" Ortega asked.

"I did once."

"My advice is warn him again."

"Okay. Probably won't do any good. There's another thing."

Charles tried to hide his impatience. "Yes?"

"A few weeks ago, Phyllis showed up with an SUV. She asked if she could keep it here for about a week. Said a friend of hers was moving, and she offered to store it for him. I said okay."

"What's the problem?" Charles snipped. In spite of the fan, the smoke was getting to him.

"Each tenant is allowed one parking place. I have two new tenants moving in real soon and need the parking. I mentioned it to her, and she said she'd move the car somewhere else. That was two weeks ago. It's still here."

"Tell her she's got to move it soon," Ortega said. "You said she was a good tenant. She'll understand."

Amy frowned. "I left a note on her door. The next day I found it in the parking lot, all torn up. Somebody must have took it off her door. Some people! I haven't seen her, but the car's still here. It's covered and out of the way, but I really do need the space."

"Well next time she's home, talk to her about it. There won't be an argument."

"Oh okay. Thanks." The copier was finished; she retrieved the copy and handed it to Charles. "Did you want to ask me anything more?" she offered eagerly.

"No, thank you. We appreciate your help," Ortega replied. They left.

In the car, Charles sniffed his shirt. "I'll need to take all this to the cleaners now. Ugh!"

"We should go to that gallery where Phyllis works," Ortega said.

"Yeah." Charles scanned the papers they'd collected. "It's not far."

. . . . .

One Horse Dorp gallery

"Where're we gonna park?" Ortega asked as he looked around. The gallery parking was overflowing with people and vehicles. A banner over the porch announced "Fourth Annual Fall in New Mexico exhibition by Anne Patrick. Friday, Saturday, Sunday and Monday." The porch steps were as crowded as the entrance to The Pit before a UNM home game.

"On the street somewhere." Charles shrugged. After driving the environs for several minutes, Ortega was able to squeeze their Impala into a space between a Kia sedan and a King Ranch pickup. They walked back to the gallery, threaded their way inside, and looked for Phyllis. After several minutes of fruitless search, an attractive woman dressed in a flowing, yellow blouse and blue slacks approached them.

"Welcome to our exhibition. I'm Anne Patrick." She offered them a hand each in turn. They showed her their identification.

"How can I help you?" Anne asked in a puzzled voice.

"You have an employee: Phyllis Van Houten. We'd like to talk with her," Charles said.

"She's not here right now but should be back soon. What's this about?"

Ortega could see this worried her. "We're doing some background on a case, and she may be able to help us."

"Is she involved?" Anne asked. The question took him off guard.

"An acquaintance of hers was murdered. We're putting together a profile of the victim," Charles interrupted.

"That's awful! She's just a really nice person. I can't imagine her mixed up in something so terrible. Would you like to wait? Like I said, she should be back in a little while."

"Sure."

"Please look around. Help yourself to refreshments."

"Thanks," Ortega said. With a smile, she walked away, trying to put aside this disturbing news and concentrate on her patrons.

They idled around the gallery for thirty minutes or so, examining the works without enthusiasm. Customers kept piling in, and it became difficult to move about. Finally Charles checked his watch.

"Wanna stay?" Ortega asked.

"No. Look at this place. She won't have time to talk to us. Let's find Ms. Patrick and leave her our cards." Charles cast his gaze around the room. "There she is." They made their way through the crowd to Anne; she was expounding on a particular photo to a short, balding man who was eagerly asking her questions.

"Ms. Patrick? Sorry to interrupt. We have to go. Would you give these to Phyllis and ask her to call us?" Ortega handed the cards to Anne.

"She should be back any time now."

"Thanks, but we can't wait any longer. Please ask her to call us." Charles waved a hand at the crowd. "Looks like your exhibition is going well."

Anne smiled and nodded. "Yes. Please come back when you have time," she said. They returned her smile and left.

Walking back to their car, Charles mused out loud. "Hoped we'd be able to interview her before the weekend. That ain't gonna happen."

"Nope," Ortega answered. The Friday traffic was ferocious, and it took them half an hour to reach Cerrillos Road. All they could do was inch along and fret.

Fourteen

The Plaza

Anne hurried along the sidewalk. Estefan's lunch invitation had come at an inconvenient time, what with her exhibition in progress. But the pull of seeing him was too strong, so she'd done a quick repair job on her hair and driven to the Plaza. As always parking was a headache. She'd found a spot some blocks away, all the time regretting the decision to drive instead of walk. Too late for that now.

She hurried along and was passing the Basilica of St. Francis when a high-pitched voice called to her. "Anne! Hey, Anne!" A man zigzagged his way across the street to her — Simon Lansbury, a freelance writer and casual friend.

Anne waved. "Hi, Simon. I'm in a hurry — can't stop."

"Wait. I've got something important to show you."

Anne frowned, stopped, and checked her watch. Simon was thirtyish and nice-looking in a scraggly way, with close-cropped, brown hair. His shirt was untucked, and his jeans showed white wear lines along the pockets. Appearance notwithstanding, he was a talented writer whose work routinely appeared in several regional publications. He'd written pieces about her a number of times before she won the Osgood Prize, and she appreciated his work. He liked to dig, and what he wrote was fair-minded. Right now he thrust a wrinkled sheaf of papers at her.

"You need to see this."

"Can this wait? I'm meeting my fiancé for lunch."

"Well this is about him. I've been carrying these around for two days, hoping I'd run into you."

Anne took the papers and began reading. After a minute or so, she turned her eyes to him. "How'd you find this?"

"I saw that piece about you and Mr. La Vaca in the *New Mexican* and was curious about him, so I did a keyword search. These came up. I called a buddy who works for an English-language newspaper there. He verified the stories, says La Vaca is in the news a lot. He's very connected to Spanish power politics."

Anne resumed reading, carefully turning each page; she began to frown, and as she read, her eyes took on a deep, dark, near-black lustre. She nervously licked her lips; the papers began shaking.

Simon watched all this. "I'm sorry to bring this to you, but you needed to know."

Anne reached over and patted him on one arm as she continued reading. When she'd finished, she folded the papers, nodding. "Thank you. I really appreciate this. May I keep these?"

"Sure. And don't worry. I'm not going to write a story about this. But we should get together soon, okay?"

"Yes, we will. I need to go. You're a decent man, Simon."

With determined steps, she made for her destination, a new "boutique café" near La Fonda called Puerco Feliz. Simon watched her leave, knowing there was a story here but fighting the urge to write it. He hated people who broke a trust; someone always ended up getting hurt, and what he'd showed Anne had hurt her, he could tell. Sometimes friendship was more important than a story.

Approaching the restaurant, Anne saw Mirada and La Vaca seated together at an outdoor table, engaged in animated conversation. As she walked up, La Vaca was jabbing a finger at Mirada — his face red, and his voice loud, almost a shout.

"No more delays! You get that santo. Understand?"

Mirada angrily pushed his chair back and stood, nearly tripping over Anne in the process. He glared at her and left without a word. At the sight of her, La Vaca's demeanor changed; he became the solicitous, caring suitor. He stood and reached for her hands.

"My dear Anne. I'm sorry. Luis and I were having a small disagreement."

Anne remained standing; she pushed the papers into his hands. Later she would remember, and relish, the look of surprise and dismay on his face. "You're quite a media figure in Spain, Estefan. Tell me about your friend — or should I call her your fiancée: Maria Elena Questanones."

La Vaca looked down at the papers; the flesh tightened across his cheeks, and anger flickered in his eyes. Then he stared at her, trying to hide the anger and failing. He did manage to soften the tone of his voice; it became soothing, syrupy, so that he almost cooed. Revulsion mixed with outrage began rising in Anne's chest.

"Mi cariña, it's all nonsense. You know how the press can be; they print lies about people like me who are wealthy and successful. Maria Questanones is the daughter of a friend; I know her family. Nothing more. These stories are planted by people with a grudge against me. I have no real interest in politics. Please, this should not come between us and our future." He dropped the papers on the table and reached for her; she pulled her hands back.

"It sounds like you have a *very* interesting future planned for yourself. It apparently doesn't include me, but according to this, it *does* include Ms. Questanones. Contrary to what you're saying, it appears you have a rather strong interest in politics — and in becoming prime minister...now there's news. The story mentions your pursuit of an...what did the paper call it? Oh, an artifact from the Spanish conquest of New Mexico. Just now you were ordering Mirada to get a santo, a particular santo. Which santo would that be, Estefan? And why are you looking for it?" She squared herself, facing off with him.

He shook his head. "As always the facts are all wrong. It is a small thing that Luis has located, something I hope to donate to the museum."

"Oh, again the facts are all wrong. Isn't that always the way of it? Funny thing is, here are several editions of this newspaper printed months apart. There's no response from you in any of them. They keep printing lies about you, and you never bothered to correct them? Why is that, Estefan?" Anne ridiculed him. This produced the result she'd intended.

La Vaca didn't try to hide his anger. "How I deal with the press is my concern, not yours!"

Anne switched from the outraged fiancée to the obliging lover; her eyes turned soft and silky and her voice winsome. "Perhaps I'm being unfair; I'm sorry. Tell me, what santos is Luis finding for you? Perhaps I can help. If you're donating it to the museum, I'd like to be included."

La Vaca sensed he'd turned the tables on her; she was coming around. Nothing was lost. He skirted the table and stepped close to her. "I'm sorry we've quarreled. Don't concern yourself over this antique; Luis will take care of it. Let me make things right between us. Please?" He stepped closer still. For a brief second, Anne felt the last vestiges of love surging through her. She gazed at him with longing in her eyes...and shoved him away. He staggered back and crashed heavily against the table, tipping over cups and plates. Hearing the noise nearby, diners looked over; one man stood.

"You all right, ma'am?" he called. Anne ignored him.

"You contemptable, lying, cheating bottom-feeder! You think you can dazzle me with your money and your phony manners and your oily voice and I'll just melt in your arms? Stay away from me, stay away from the museum and stay out of Santa Fe! If I ever see you here again, I'll make sure your real story is printed in all the newspapers...you know, the newspapers that never print the facts." She snatched the papers off the table and started walking away. Hesitating, she turned toward the man who'd spoken to her. "Yes, thank you, I'm all right *now*." She smiled at him and disappeared. La Vaca could feel the eyes on him; he brushed himself and scurried away.

· · · · ·

1425 Baca Street #15, Santa Fe

The knock on the door produced a reciprocal knocking between Monje's ears. He pushed himself onto one elbow, squinting in pain. There'd been too much tequila the night before; being awakened from blissful unconsciousness was agony. The knocking got louder; his head seemed to vibrate. "Who's there?" he burbled, pushing his tongue against his teeth. Now the knocking became pounding, which rattled the entire trailer home.

"Who's there?" he yelped. Pushing himself up, he stumbled to his feet, scrabbled on the nightstand for his knife, and unlocked the door. Sunlight pierced his eyes; he jerked, trying to shade them, dropping the knife in the process.

"Wake the f—k up!" Luis Mirada barked. Before he could respond, Mirada pushed past him as he made a feeble attempt at blocking the door. Mirada picked up the knife. "You look like shit." He chuckled. Monje blinked several times, realized he was naked, and stumbled across the room to pull on jeans.

"Man, what do you want?" he muttered. His head was throbbing.

Mirada tossed the knife on the table. "I need that santo. Soon! You get it yet? Talk to me."

Monje sank onto the bed, holding one hand against his temple.

"You said your pal's uncle might have it…well?"

Monje tried to swallow and couldn't, tried to spit and couldn't. "He's not sure."

"You also told me you might know someone to fake it."

Monje started to shake his head, which made the room spin. He bent over. "Didn't work out," he said in a small voice.

"My boss will only be here a few more days, and he wants the Friar. Instead of working, you get drunk. There's too much money involved for you to screw this up." Mirada slapped Monje across the back of his head, producing the result he wanted: Monje rolled onto the floor, moaning.

"Leave me alone. I'll get it," he whispered.

"For your sake, you'd better."

Mirada shoved him with one foot. Monje lay motionless; dry heaves started. He managed to stand and stumbled to the bathroom. Mirada screwed up his face in disgust at the nasty retching sound. It stopped, and Monje reappeared, clinging to the door frame, his chest spattered with vomit.

"Can't we do this later?" he asked, weakly licking his lips.

"No, now!" Mirada barked.

With eyes closed, Monje felt his way to the bed and flopped. He opened one eye and peered at Mirada. "Can't we just buy one? That'd be quicker — probably cheaper too."

Mirada snorted. "No shortcuts on this one. My boss knows his stuff. He's read all about the Friar. He won't go for just anything you might find." Mirada leaned close to Monje, wrinkling his nose at the stench. "You get me that santo or else. Understand?" he growled.

Monje rolled away from him. Mirada grabbed him by the hair and pulled him close. "What do you think Veryle would do to you if she knew you were crossing her?" Monje forced himself onto an elbow, eyes wide with fear. "I see you understand. Good. Get to work."

Mirada spat and walked out. Monje sank back on the bed and closed his eyes, hoping the room would stop spinning.

· · · · ·

Southwest Trafficking Task Force office
Kate was pounding away at the keyboard when her cell jingled. She checked the screen, recognized David's number, and answered. "Hey Sarge, what's up?"

"Hi, Kate. How's everything?"

"Good. Just finishing a report."

"Is John there?"

"He's at the federal courthouse meeting with the assistant AG. He'll be back in an hour or so."

"I need to talk to both of you. I also need you to do me a favor."

"Anything."

"Remember the woman who works for my sister-in-law? Phyllis Van Houten?"

"Yeah, the one I thought I knew from somewhere."

"Right. I'm doing some checking on her. There's been some strange things going on."

"Like what?"

"I'll tell you when I see you. Is there anybody you know who could run a check on her through DOD (Department of Defense)? Maybe you're right that she was in the military."

"Yeah, I know some people in the Guard who can help."

"Good. I don't have a DOB for her, but she's probably in her mid-forties. That's all I have right now. I'll clear this with John so you don't get in trouble."

"He won't mind."

"Professional courtesy, kiddo. Look, I'm driving to Albuquerque. I'll be back by this afternoon. Anything going on your end?"

"Nothing."

"Okay, see you in a while." He rang off.

Kate flipped through her cell phone, found the number she wanted, and hit the send button.

"Hi, Jerry. It's Kate Cordova. I'm fine, thanks. Look, I need a favor."

. . . . .

One Horse Dorp gallery

Anne spontaneously looked at the number when her phone jingled. Blocked. She hesitated; ever since Tee's warning about the threatening call, she'd taken to screening them more closely. This time curiosity got the best of her, and she answered.

"This is Anne."

"I want some information." The voice was muted, but she was certain it was male.

"Sure, why not. Maybe I can meet you somewhere," she chirped, determined to find out more.

"No chance. You have a friend: Roberto Arturo."

"He's not a friend, just someone I know."

"You're going to help me find him."

"Why do you want him?"

"He has something I want."

"Really? What's that?"

"None of your business. Get me his number. I'll call tomorrow. Remember, what happened in the storeroom can happen again. Understand?"

"Sure. I'll be waiting for your call," she said casually, almost cynically, baiting him.

The call ended. Anne stared at the phone. Should she tell Tee and David? Should she tell Roberto? To her surprise, she wasn't scared but angry. She *really* wanted to find out what this was about. Tee and David might offer to help — more likely they'd tell her not to encourage this mumbling clown and leave it to the police. This was something she could handle herself.

. . . . .

Diocese of Santa Fe Catholic Center offices

Walking inside the center was a step back in time for David. The atmosphere reminded him of his brief flirtation with the priesthood as a teenager. How many times had he visited the Maryknoll fathers, talking with them and praying with them until he'd finally rejected the "calling"? A large statue of the Blessed Virgin, Our Lady of Peace dominated the foyer. As the husband of a non-Catholic, he was considered estranged even while he held to his beliefs. It was difficult to feel at ease.

The receptionist casually greeted him. "May I help you?"

"Yes. I'm here to talk with a priest. I only know him as Father Bob. Is he here today?"

"I'll see if he's in his office. Your name?"

"David Harrowsen. I'm the brother-in-law of a friend of his: Anne Patrick."

She dialed a number. "Father Bob, there's a man here to see you. He doesn't have an appointment but says he's related to Anne Patrick." She listened briefly. "I'll send him up." She pointed to the elevator. "Third floor. His office is on the left."

"Thank you."

David found the office without difficulty. The door was open. Inside a tall, nice-looking man was peeling off an orange cyclist's jersey stenciled "Santa Fe Cycling"; he extended a hand.

"Father Dunleavy. Call me Father Bob."

They shook hands. "David Harrowsen. Anne Patrick's brother-in-law."

"Nice to meet you. Sit down. Would you like water or coffee?" Father Bob wadded up the jersey, tossed it on a shelf behind him, and sat down at the desk. David couldn't help but smile; he wasn't accustomed to seeing a priest in a sweat-stained T-shirt.

"No thanks."

Dunleavy stretched and yawned. "Um, sorry, David. I like to get in a bike ride before work. Today was a tough one. Getting ready for a fifty-mile charity ride this weekend, and it's wearing me out. How is Anne? I haven't heard from her in a while."

"She's fine."

Dunleavy studied him thoughtfully. "You're a police officer, right? Sure, Anne mentioned you one time when we were talking about her family. I'm proud to have several officers as friends."

"Nice of you to remember."

"Tell me about yourself," he said, extracting a handful of mixed nuts and dried fruit from a plastic bag on the desk. He offered it to David, who shook his head.

David was usually cautious talking about himself with strangers, a necessary safeguard. But for the next few minutes, he recounted his life and background. Father Bob chewed and listened, occasionally interjecting a question. He was an easy man to talk with.

"Almost became a priest, eh? Sounds like you've found your true calling. As for me, I thought about becoming a hunting guide, but winters in the UP are brutal. Then I thought about joining the military. I tried studying finance in college but couldn't handle the math." He chuckled. "I gave up on the military after talking with a recruiter — wasn't my thing. Can't say I had a calling to the priesthood — more of a whisper." He laughed. David laughed with him.

"Enough of this. What can I do for you?"

"This is a complicated situation, so bear with me." David told Father Bob about the recent events at Anne's gallery and Kate's intuitive reaction to Phyllis, culminating with this morning's encounter with her.

"Strange stuff! I see why you're concerned. I'm glad Anne has you on the scene, so to speak."

"Well sometimes she's too trusting of people. From a cop's perspective, that can be dangerous. I hate feeling suspicious, but she's my wife's sister, and I love her, I don't want anything to happen to her."

Dunleavy nodded in agreement. "This will sound strange coming from a priest, but I agree people can't always be trusted. Now let me tell you about Phyllis. She was cousin to a woman I knew. They grew up together. I didn't really get to know Phyllis until she was grown up. She had a sister but never talked about her. She never mentioned being in the service; she doesn't strike me as someone who would be drawn to it, you know? Anyway, she worked for me as youth group coordinator. When she applied for the job at Anne's gallery, I gave her a reference. She's a really nice person, great with kids."

"She has a sister?"

"Yes, but she told me they weren't in touch with one another. They were night and day apparently. I think the sister's name was Vera...no, Vicky. The only time Phyllis talked about her, it seemed to upset her. Something bad must've happened between them." A look of sudden realization crossed his face. "Oh shit!' he exclaimed, then muttered, "Dear Father, forgive me." David twitched at the profanity.

"My apologies, David. I've just remembered something, and I feel really stupid about it."

"No problems, Father. I'll bet you like to fish."

"Yes. But—"

David interrupted. "The assistant pastor at our church was quite a fisherman, and I used to go with him sometimes. That's where I first learned to swear."

Father Bob blinked and scowled. "I *am* a fisherman, but that's no excuse for my language."

"Mind if I ask what triggered your memory?"

Father Bob twisted his lips. "Some time ago, a friend of mine, a state police officer, came to see me. He's investigating a murder, and I once knew the victim. He needed some background information. One of the things he asked was if she had any friends with the initial P. I didn't make the connection until just now. Phyllis was her cousin...I'll bet she's P. I need to call him right away and let him know. Do you mind?"

David checked his watch. "Actually I need to get going. Thanks for talking with me."

They stood and shook hands. Turning to leave, David glanced at several photographs standing on a shelf next to the door. "Is that Phyllis?" he asked, pointing.

"Yes. That's her with the youth group. I sure miss her. Haven't found a decent coordinator since she left."

David picked up the photograph and stared at it.

"When was this taken?"

"Must've been three years ago. Why?"

David kept staring at the picture. "She looks different."

"Really? Well people change. I haven't seen her in a long time."

"It's probably nothing. She just looks different from the way she looks now." He returned the photo to its place. "Thanks again."

"My best to Anne."

After David left, Father Bob called Mike Charles's office, feeling more than a little foolish. The phone rolled over to voicemail.

"Hi, Mike. Father Bob here. Someone was here asking questions about Phyllis Van Houten, and I just remembered something about her and Mary

Marston. When you talked with me about Mary, you asked if she had any relatives or friends with the initial P. Phyllis Van Houten was Mary's cousin. I'm almost certain she's the P you asked me about. Guess my gray cells aren't firing on all cylinders after all. I'm really sorry. Hope this helps." He rang off. The foolish feeling lingered.

Fifteen

"I told you not to call me during the day," Veryle snarled into the phone.

"Mirada's getting impatient. The mark is leaving in a few days, and he wants the santo." Monje's voice was shaking with panic.

"Thought you had a line on Peralta's uncle," she said in a simpering, mocking tone. She should have known this would happen.

"I'm working on it. I'll know tomorrow."

"For your sake, you'd better!" She snapped the phone closed, shaking her head. Once this business was finished, she was finished with Monje; he'd become a liability. Liabilities had to be eliminated.

"I'll find him myself," she said aloud and smiled.

$$\bullet \quad \bullet \quad \bullet \quad \bullet \quad \bullet$$

David had almost reached the Southwest Task Force office when his phone rang. He flipped it open as he slowed, bringing a blaring horn and upraised middle finger from the driver behind him. He waved the man on and pulled to the shoulder.

"Hello?"

"It's Kate. Can't meet now. DEA needs us to help out with a search warrant. Maybe tomorrow?"

"Sure. Stay safe, okay?"

"We will." Click.

Maybe this was better. He'd return to the gallery and talk with Phyllis. All the way back from Albuquerque, he'd been picturing the photo in Father Bob's office, comparing it with his mental image of the woman. Something didn't seem right. He should've asked Father Bob to borrow it — too late for that. Kate had connections — maybe they'd turn up something.

The gallery was busy, though less so than the previous three days, so David was able to park without much problem. First he headed to the guesthouse, hoping Tee was there; she wasn't, and neither was Taz. So he returned to the gallery. Anne gave him a nod and continued talking to a short, round woman. Phyllis was at the counter finishing a sale.

"Thank you. We hope you enjoy the piece," she said gaily and handed a wrapped parcel to the customer. At David's approach, she smiled.

"The exhibition's going well," he said.

"Yes, this is the best one yet."

David nodded. "I know you're busy, but think you could spare me a minute?"

"Why?"

"I met an old friend of yours today. Father Bob. He said to say hello."

"Who? Oh sure, Father Bob. I haven't seen him in a long time. How is he?"

"Fine. Said he'd stop in someday soon."

"That was nice of him." She began sorting receipts, then looked up. "Was there something else?"

"He mentioned your sister, Vicky." Hearing the name, Phyllis's face suddenly froze. After a few seconds, she blinked.

"Haven't thought about her in a long time," she murmured. "Why'd her name come up?" She stared at David.

"Just talking, you know. No special reason."

Phyllis's eyes narrowed to slits, as if the recollection was painful. "Bad memories. She did some terrible things when we were kids."

"Sorry to bring her up. I won't keep you."

She resumed sorting the paperwork, but David could see she was aggravated. He made his way through the crowd to the door. Outside he spotted

Tee and Taz walking up the driveway. Immediately Taz hit the end of the leash, barking excitedly. "Taz! How's my girl?" David spread his arms, and Taz leapt into them and smothered his face with happy kisses. He grinned at Tee and stuck out a hand.

"Sure, Taz gets kisses, and I get a handshake. Sleeping in the car tonight?" she asked.

David set Taz on the ground, took Tee in his arms, bent her over, and planted a lavish kiss on her.

"Whoa, let me breathe," she gasped. She wrapped her arms 'round his neck, then gave him a lingering kiss. "That's more like it," she breathed. "Busy tonight?"

"Whadda you have in mind?"

"Thought I'd ply you with liquor and take advantage of you."

"Okay by me. Come along," David said and led them to the guesthouse.

· · · · ·

All the customers had finally left. Anne stood on the porch watching the last car disappear. Phyllis was at the counter, balancing the cash drawer.

"Why don't you leave that to me? You're very tired. Go home. I'll see you Tuesday. No, come back Wednesday. You deserve the extra day off."

"You sure? There's a lot to do," Phyllis asked. Her eyes were sunken with fatigue.

"I'm sure. Thanks. We did well. Oh don't forget to call those officers. You have their cards?"

"I won't forget. G'night," Phyllis said with a touch of irritation.

She reached under the counter, retrieved a backpack, picked up her cell phone, and quickly left. Well it'd been a long four days, which would explain her brusque manner. Anne dismissed it. She glanced at the register, considered whether to finish balancing it, and decided not to. She locked it, turned off the lights, and headed for the guesthouse. All afternoon she'd been edgy, the emotional hangover of her confrontation with La Vaca weighing on her. She needed to tell Tee and David all about what had taken place — not for their affirmation but because she needed some loving-kindness. At her knock, Taz began barking and scratching at the door. After a few minutes, David opened the door, barefooted, wearing jeans and no shirt, and rubbing his hair with a towel.

"Hi, Anne. What's up? Just taking a shower," he said, sounding a bit annoyed. There'd been little time for him and Tee on this trip. Well perhaps later. Taz was jumping and whining to be picked up. Anne obliged.

"I'm sorry. I need to talk with you and Tee. I'll come back."

"No worries. Come in. We'll be out in a minute." He disappeared into the rear. Anne sat on the sofa and stroked Taz, who playfully began gnawing on her hand the way bichons are inclined. Shortly David reappeared fully dressed; Tee followed wearing a bathrobe and sandals, her hair wet and straggly across her forehead. Anne immediately felt embarrassed at disturbing them. They sat down opposite her.

"What's going on?" Tee asked.

Anne's jaw set. She put Taz next to her on the sofa.

"I found out Estefan was cheating on me. Of course he denied it — well sort of. Come to think of it, he never *actually* did deny it. Regardless I told him off but good. I'm glad I did but am feeling rather embarrassed about all this."

"I'm so sorry. Oh, Anne!" Tee exclaimed. Anne reached out, and Tee took her hand. Tee looked over at David with tears in her eyes. He clenched his teeth; his instincts about La Vaca had been justified, but he hated being right.

"Don't be embarrassed, dear heart. We've all been there," David said, trying to sound reassuring.

Anne let go of Tee, who then sat down next to her. Anne leaned and kissed her cheek.

"Right now I wish I'd hit him. Oh he really took me in. Those put-on manners and that voice. I'm sorry now I didn't punch him out."

Tee wiped her face and sighed. David leaned forward.

"How'd you find out he was running around on you?"

Anne's eyes darkened with anger. "A friend of mine, a reporter, told me. He showed me some articles from an English-language newspaper in Spain. Estefan is engaged to the daughter of an important government minister — has been for quite a while. He's also been mentioned as a candidate to become prime minister. The stories have been around for months."

"Asshole," Tee muttered.

Anne nodded. "Yep. Also there was mention of him acquiring a relic from the Spanish colonial period here in New Mexico and taking it back to Spain with him. When I asked him about it, he told me the papers got it all wrong — it was something Luis Mirada had located, and he was donating it to the museum. By that time, I'd had enough of his lies. I let him have it right in front of God and all the customers."

David chuckled. "Good job. Best you didn't slug him; you'd be in a cell by now if you had."

Tee laughed. "What would Mom think about that?"

Anne looked away. "I can't laugh about this, and it's too soon to cry. Once I'm over being mad, I will." She squeezed Tee's shoulder. "Mom always used to say, 'You can't hold in your anger. If you keep it to yourself, you'll never be able to cry.'"

David walked over, squatted, and hugged both of them. They remained this way for some time while Taz circled their feet, sensing something was wrong. Anne reached down and scratched her ears; she stood on her hind legs, begging to be picked up. David did so, and they huddled together again. Finally Taz began squirming to be let down; they separated. Tee shivered.

"You're getting chilled. Please get dressed," Anne said.

"I'm fine. What's this relic La Vaca is looking for?" she asked.

"I was thinking about that. When I got to the restaurant, he was arguing with Mirada. He said something about 'that santo.' He didn't elaborate, but he ordered Mirada to get it right away. It has to be the relic mentioned in the newspaper. The way he talked about it to Mirada, I got the impression it was a particular piece."

David bit his lips. "Maybe John Stephenson can help. You never called him to tell him you'd decided not to work with him, did you?"

"No, I kept going back and forth. Getting ready for the exhibition crowded it out of my mind."

"That's okay. I'm gonna see him tomorrow anyway. He'll probably ask. Want me to tell him?"

"No, it should come from me."

"Why're you seeing John?" Tee asked. She'd wondered if Anne had spoken with him and explained her decision but avoided bring up the subject, reluctant to crowd Anne about it.

171

David looked at both of them. Now was the time.

"I took it upon myself to check out Phyllis." Surprise registered on both their faces. Tee opened her mouth to say something, and David held up a hand. "Let me explain. It started with something Kate said to me. She happened to meet Phyllis and got the feeling she'd met her before."

"How did Kate meet Phyllis?" Anne asked.

It was David's turn to look surprised. "I thought you knew. Phyllis didn't tell you?"

Anne shook her head.

"Isn't that interesting?" David said in a half-whisper. He turned to Tee. "Remember the day Kate called and asked us to disappear for an hour or so 'cause she was coming here on business? Anne, Kate came here with a man who works with the task force. They were checking on an engraving that was supposed to be one of yours. They wanted you to authenticate it because they thought it was a fake. You weren't here; Phyllis offered to help. She verified they were correct; it was a fake. She told them she'd let you know about it."

Anne held up a hand. "She never did. I'm sure she meant to. I'll ask her about it." Tee shook her head. Anne always thought the best of people and could be maddeningly loyal to a fault. "Go on," Anne said.

"Anyway, Kate told me there was something familiar about Phyllis. She had the impression Phyllis had been in the service or might have been a cop. I trust her intuition, so I started a little investigation of my own. A few days ago I went to talk with Phyllis while the two of you were out. It was the morning you two went to breakfast. I surprised her going through your cell phone; you'd left it behind."

"I made her do that. I thought she needed the break," Tee said.

"Why was she looking in my phone?" Anne asked.

"You ever tell her it was okay to do that?" David asked.

Anne shrugged. "I don't think so. She wouldn't have any reason to. What did she tell you?"

"She said you were supposed to call someone that morning, and she thought she had the number, but it wasn't in her phone. So she was looking in yours."

Anne raised her eyebrows. "I don't remember telling her to call anyone for me…wait a minute," she mused. "When was this?"

"Tuesday."

"There was a vendor who'd called about the exhibition. I called him back on Monday, the day *before*. I'm sure I didn't ask Phyllis to call him. Maybe she got her days mixed up."

"It didn't sound plausible to me, but I let it go. We talked a few minutes about the incident in the storeroom, and then she left. I decided to go through the files in your office, looking for her employment record. Sorry about that. I found her file, but there wasn't anything in it."

"What?" Anne exclaimed.

"Nothing. No letter of reference, no W-4, just a cover sheet. Then I remembered your friend at the diocese here, Father Bob. You mentioned he'd recommended her to you. Today I went to see him."

Anne was annoyed with David but also alarmed by what he was telling her. "I'm sorry, Anne. I wasn't expecting anything like this to happen. I guess I wasn't expecting anything at all. I figured if everything checked out, I'd never say anything about it."

"It's all right," she snapped.

Tee's expression was a mixture of surprise, annoyance, and curiosity. "What did Father Bob have to say?"

"He's a nice man. Told me all about Phyllis, how he got to know her. Said she never mentioned serving in the military. While we were talking, he suddenly remembered something about her. Some time ago the state police came and talked with him about a homicide. He'd known the victim, and they were gathering background on her. While we were talking, he made a connection between Phyllis and the woman who was murdered — Phyllis was her cousin. He also told me Phyllis had a sister, whom she never talks about."

"She never told me about a sister," Anne said.

"There's a lot Phyllis doesn't tell you, it seems," said Tee.

"When I got back today, I talked to her again and mentioned her sister; it upset her a lot. She didn't want to talk about her at all. I was hoping to see Kate today because I asked her to check out Phyllis's military connection. She had to cancel — something came up. I'll see her and John tomorrow."

Tee looked over at Anne. "If Phyllis was in the service, why didn't she tell you? If she left it off her job application on purpose, she lied. That's serious. Then there's her not telling you about the fake engraving and going through your phone. And what happened in the storeroom. Something serious is going on, and I'll bet Phyllis is mixed up in it."

"Anne, what do you think?" David asked.

Anne sat back. "I'm not sure what to think right now. It's been a busy week, and today's been crazy. What you're telling me about Phyllis has me worried. Oh, something I neglected to tell *you*. There were two detectives from the state police here Friday wanting to talk with Phyllis. They're investigating a homicide and told me Phyllis knew the victim. You've just handed me an awful lot to digest. I don't know what to say."

Tee patted her arm. "Take it easy. One thing at a time." She looked at David. "What now?"

"Check her out with the military folks. Try to find out what happened to her personnel file. Oh I just remembered one other thing. When I was leaving Father Bob's office, I saw a photograph of Phyllis from when she worked with the diocese youth group. She looked different from the way she does now."

Anne scowled. "Are you sure? You're not just being overly suspicious?"

David chuckled. "Touché. Maybe I *am* being overly suspicious, but I really don't think so. The photo was taken three years ago. But people change over time."

Tee scooted closer to Anne, putting an arm around her. "We'll sort this all out. First things first: I'm really sorry for you, sis."

David nodded his agreement. "So am I forgiven?" He leaned over, put his hands on Anne's shoulders, and looked her squarely in the eyes. She smiled.

"Of course. You're just looking out for me."

"We're kinda fond of you, you know?"

Tee stood. "We are. And forget feeling embarrassed about La Vaca. Be glad you found out now and not after you married him!"

"I don't think he would have married me. He was just using me; it was just a ploy. There's something important about that santo. Whatever it is, we need to find out and stop him," Anne said.

"Leave that for later. None of us have eaten, and it's getting late. Think I'll get dressed." Tee said, standing.

"Oh why? That's a very fetching ensemble, especially at this time of night," David replied, reaching for the belt holding her robe closed.

"You're insatiable," Tee exclaimed. "Go outside and cool off." She retreated to the bedroom. David looked at Anne.

"You're probably not hungry right now."

Anne stood. "A few minutes ago I would have agreed with you. Now I'm famished. Thirsty too."

"Want to order in? Something simple, share a few glasses of wine, figure all this out?"

David asked.

"Wine? No, I think a cocktail. Under the circumstances, something strong sounds good. Maybe a cosmopolitan or a sidecar."

"Whatever you want; you deserve it. Taz, what do you think?" David asked. Taz's legs bounced off the floor as she gave out a terrific yelp. She whirled around the room, yipping and squeaking.

"That's settled," David said. "Where's *The Bartender's Bible*?"

· · · · ·

The Plaza

He chose a spot near a coffee kiosk, bought a cup, and hung out. The coffee was just turning cold when his target appeared, slinking into view. Whoever this guy was, he also had a knack for being nondescript, invisible. The female partner wasn't with him.

The man wandered past the vendors, stopping only where other shoppers stopped. Was he a pickpocket too? Maybe. He would lean in close to people as if he was listening; that was very curious.

After a turn around the square, he stopped, bought a coffee, walked to the war memorial, and sat in the sun, casually sipping and watching the crowd. Shoppers were beginning to pour in; it was time to move. Why not approach the man directly? Cradling his now-cold coffee, he walked to the memorial and sat down a few feet away.

"This market is amazing, don't you think?" he said.

The man glanced at him and nodded.

"My first time here since I was a kid. My uncle made jewelry and brought me along when he came here. It hasn't changed much. Boy, I sure miss him."

The man ignored him.

"How about you? First time?"

The man shook his head and kept watching the people.

"Oh you know your way around then?"

The man took notice at this. "Yeah."

"Maybe you could help me out. I've been told it's real easy to be cheated."

"Happens." The man eyed him over the edge of his cup, studying his clothes, sizing him up.

"I'm looking for something special. My aunt, she's real religious, you know? She has this little shrine, like an altar, in memory of my uncle. I want to get her a statue or a painting of a saint. I didn't see anything I liked here this morning."

"Hang around. The best vendors will be here soon. How much you want to spend?"

He produced a money clip; several hundred dollar bills were easily visibly. "Depends."

The man slid over. "Sure, I'll help you." He stuck out a hand. "Call me Monk."

"That your real name?"

"Nah, my working name."

"Don't know if I want to do business with someone called Monk." The money clip was barely visible tucked into a pocket; Monk's eyes flicked to it and then looked up.

"Ellis."

"Got a last name?"

Monk hesitated. "Why you wanna know my last name?""

"Just being careful."

"Rubaldo."

"That's better. Richard Begay."

"Navajo?"

"Navajo-Irish. I live in Window Rock."

"Okay, you want a santo or a retablo. Whatever you want, Monk can get." A smarmy grin accompanied the comment.

Now was the time. Begay stood and squared himself in front of Rubaldo.

"I've been waiting for a chance to talk to you. I know quite a bit about you. You've been asking questions around, about a special santo called The Weeping Friar. What's your interest?"

Monje started to stand. Begay stuck out a hand.

"You need to hear what I have to say," he said in an even, commanding tone. Rubaldo stayed put.

"You a cop?" Now there was anxiety in his eyes.

"I work for some important people who want to know why you're asking about the Friar. It's to your advantage to talk to me."

"Really? What advantage is that?"

Begay leaned forward and stared directly at him. "Take a guess. If you keep this up, I might just go to the cops and tell 'em what I know about you and your female friend."

"You don't know nothin'." Monk stood. "I'm outta here."

"Also do you know there's a curse around the Friar?"

"I don't believe that bullshit."

"You should. Especially since I can make that curse come true." Begay balanced on the balls of his feet, waiting for Rubaldo's next move.

"What's that mean?"

Begay stepped closer, lowering his voice to a near-whisper. "Just this: There are some people who are very upset about this. They don't like what you're doing. If I tell them I warned you and you ignored it, they might take matters into their hands. It's better for you to stop looking for the Friar. Understand?"

Monje's face reddened. "F—k off!" He stomped away.

Begay shrugged. "Didn't think it would work." At least he'd found out the man's name. Rubaldo's reaction was more fearful than angry. Whether he'd heed the warning or not...

Sixteen

410 Zia Road

Before Flavio Peralta answered the knock at his door, he tucked the .32 auto into his back pocket — success as a silversmith had made him wealthy but also cautious. People with less-than-honorable intentions might assume he had bags of silver lying around to be picked up.

"Yes?" he asked, peering through the peephole. A UPS driver stood on the step.

"UPS, Mister Peralta." He received deliveries nearly every day, so he unlocked the door without hesitation.

"Two for you today." He accepted the parcels, put them inside the door, and scribbled his signature on the electronic pad.

"Thanks." He turned to close the door when something hard pricked the back of his neck.

"Move." He was pushed inside and at the same time relieved of the gun.

"Please don't kill me!" Peralta begged. "I don't have much—"

"Move." He was steered to his workshop at the rear of the house and, with sinister efficiency, guided to a chair.

"Sit."

"Please, take anything you want. Aaaaa!!" One hand yanked his head backwards while the gun was thrust against his groin.

"Now. I want information," the driver snarled. "Or else…" Flavio heard the snick of the safety being let off.

"No. Pl…please!"

Low, harsh laughter. A woman's voice.

"Don't want to lose your jewels?"

"What do you want?" he gasped.

"There is an artifact I want, and your uncle has it. It's called the Weeping Friar. You're going to help me get it from him."

"I don't know if he has it. Really it's true."

"Let's refresh your memory."

The gun barked; the bullet tore through the inside of Flavio's left knee, spraying blood and bone across the floor. He screeched in agony.

"Lesson one in telling the truth. More to come." He writhed in the chair until the pistol moved to the knuckles of his right hand. In spite of the pain, he froze, terrified. "What good is a silversmith with no fingers? Lie and you lose them one at a time. Let's try it again. Where is your uncle?" His head was wrenched back. "Don't you pass out on me! You uncle has it, doesn't he?"

"Yes."

"That's *much* better. How do I find him?" She mocked him.

"Lives in the desert," Flavio gasped. Tears mixed with sweat coated his face.

"*Very* good. You learn quickly for a sweating pig. Address?"

"No…address. In the hills. Chimayo," he mumbled as shock began taking over.

"Sorry, not good enough." A fist cracked down on Flavio's right collarbone, snapping it and knocking him to the floor; the chair toppled on top of him. One hand grabbed his right arm and twisted it upwards so that the fractured bones grated against one another. A further twist and one shattered end poked through his skin. He passed out.

The world was tinged with red when he regained consciousness. Searing, unimaginable pain surged through his body. He was sitting upright in the chair again.

"You don't learn quickly after all. Uncle's address?"

"Not marked," Flavio whispered.

"Dear, dear." His head was yanked back again, something was shoved into his nose, and water squirted into it, choking him.

"Playing dumb isn't helping you, Flavio."

More water; he choked and coughed, fighting to breathe. On the verge of suffocating, his head was pushed forward. Blood, water, and vomit spewed across the floor.

"What a pig you are. It's a disagreeable sight. What would your customers think, those fat, yuppie women with perfect hair and too much jewelry. What would they think if they saw you now? Would they still buy?" His head was yanked back again. "Address!"

"Take…you…there."

"Not likely." More water, more vomiting, and then he was shoved to the floor.

"Who knows how to get there? Who knows the way?"

Flavio choked and vomited again. He reached for his shattered knee…a foot stomped on his arm. He shrieked. "Tell me! Who knows how to get to Uncle's house?"

"Patrick," he gasped. "Anne Patrick. Friend…uncle."

"Very good." A vicious kick to the groin. He lay on one side, chest heaving. "Death concentrates the mind most wonderfully." There was a cruel, throaty laugh and then footsteps receding into silence, leaving him sprawled unconscious in a bloody, motionless heap.

Outside she peeled off the UPS smock, thrust it into the backpack brought for the purpose, and walked quickly to the next street, where her car was parked. Once inside she flipped open her phone and auto-dialed. Monje answered almost immediately.

"Hi."

"You pick up the car?"

"Yeah. Just waiting for you to call."

"Any problems?"

"No."

"Meet me where Highway 466 joins Rodeo Road. I'll be there in half an hour."

"Did you talk to Peralta?"

"Don't worry yourself about him. Half an hour." She snapped the phone shut and smiled. All the loose ends were being gathered up.

. . . . .

Southwest Trafficking Task Force office

Art Smart walked in carrying a box of Dunkin' Donuts. The sight of it produced a glare from John Stephenson and a grin from Kate Cordova.

"Greetings, fellow art sleuths. How's everything?" he announced loudly. Opening the box, he offered it to Kate, who snatched an M&M-covered donut and took a healthy bite. Stephenson recoiled as if he'd been shown a live rattlesnake.

"No? Your loss," Art said. He sat and selected a jelly roll.

"Your gain," Stephenson answered. "You know how much fat—?" he began.

Art cut him off. "Spare me the health-nut lecture. Cops and donuts go together like barbecue and French Fries." He took a bite and chewed happily.

"That's a tired, old joke," John said, turning his disapproval on Kate. "You *do* know better."

Kate stared at him defiantly and thrust the remainder of the donut into her mouth. John closed his eyes in disgust.

"What's up?" Kate asked as she reached for another.

"What was it Monje said about you? Oh yeah, that sort of chunky woman," John said and snickered. Kate mouthed "asshole" at him, getting a snarky grin in return. But she put back the chocolate donut she'd selected.

"No bickering. We're all friends here," Art said with a smile. He truly enjoyed Kate and John's company. "I got a lead on the bronze that was stolen from the Indian Pueblo Cultural Center last year."

"Really? How?" Kate asked.

Art wiped a bit of sugar frosting from his lip. "A tipster." He smiled.

John sighed. God, next he'll be calling himself a gumshoe. They'd created a monster. "Well what did you find out?" he asked.

"That mystery woman, Mrs. Scott. She moved the dingus out of the country. The good news is I know who has it," Art said, relishing the moment.

"Dingus?" Kate turned and asked John.

"Ever see *The Maltese Falcon?* A dingus is something stolen, in this case the stolen bronze," John sighed.

"Oh." She looked at Art. "So you know who has it. What's the bad news?"

"A billionaire Russian banker has it in his private collection. No way to get at it," he answered.

John held up a finger. "I have a friend who works for the State Department. I'll give her a call. Maybe there's something she can do. Give me all the particulars."

Art deposited the box on John's desk and pulled a notebook from a pocket, flipped through several pages, and then pushed it across the desk so John could copy his notes.

Kate ran her tongue over her teeth. "That reminds me. I need to call David." She flipped open her phone and dialed. "David? I heard back from my friends in the Guard. They couldn't help. But there's someone in Santa Fe who can: my sergeant from the 220th. He's in the state police here. Sure. See you then."

"What's going on?" John asked.

Kate shrugged. "Helping David check out someone." She could see the skepticism in his face as she rubbed her hands together. "He's on the way. Be here anytime."

"You're not going outside the box on this, are you?" John chirped.

"Come on, John. Would I do that?" Kate have him her wide-eyed, innocent look.

"Frequently," he answered. "Art, how reliable is this 'tipster'?"

Art crossed one huge leg over the other. "On a scale of one to ten, probably a six." One foot began dancing up and down. John glanced at it. The dancing stopped. "Okay, maybe four." John nodded. "He's the one who stole the bronze, but it'll be hard to prove." Art tucked the last morsel of roll into his mouth.

"Really? How do you know him?"

"We used to run around together. He took one path, I took another. A few days ago, he rang me. He's broke and needs money."

"Why'd he give up Mrs. Scott? You didn't promise him anything?" John asked. Art was a good man and very helpful, but John was worried he might overstep his bounds.

"I asked him why the rat? She paid him part of the money for the bronze. He kept after her, and she started threatening him. He's scared of her, so he gave her up. I gave him a few bucks for the info."

"Fair enough." He turned the notebook around and pointed at it. "What's this about a car? Silver 4Runner and part of a license number. That hers?"

"Yeah. I asked him if he'd try and get the rest of the number, but he said no. Like I said, he's scared of her."

John closed the notebook and handed it back. "Good work. Got anything else?"

"Just the rest of these." Art pointed to the box. "There's one with your name on it. Hear it calling to you?"

John chuckled. "Thanks anyway. I can hear your arteries hardening from here."

Art hoisted himself out of the chair. "Well I'm off. I'll leave these." He slipped on a pair of cheap sunglasses. "Like my cheaters?"

John sighed. "'Bye, Art." After he'd gone, John turned to Kate. "You think maybe he's getting into this a little too much?"

Kate grinned. "Nah, Art's the goods."

John held up both hands. "All right, I give. Enough with the Sam Spade references."

Five minutes later David walked into this hotbed of silliness. "Good morning, you two."

"Hey Sarge, we've got donuts," Kate teased. She held out the open box. David had a long-standing aversion to deep-fried anything, particularly donuts. He grimaced in disgust.

"You promised you'd lay off those," he snapped. "John, you're letting her fall into bad habits."

"Only so much I can do," John answered. "Kate said you're checking out someone. What's up?"

David sat down and pushed the donut box away. "Ugh, I hate the smell of those." He leaned forward. "This has to do with Anne Patrick."

"She never called me back. She up to something?"

"No. It's the woman who works for her, Phyllis Van Houten. I've been doing a little investigation into her background, and there's some things about her that don't make sense. The day Kate and Art Smart came to the gallery, Kate thought she recognized her. I asked Kate to see if she had any military background."

"Not easy to do," John said, twisting his lips. David turned to Kate.

"Who's this friend of yours with the state police?"

Kate eyed the donuts but resisted. "He was my sergeant in the 220th. Mike Charles. Good guy. I thought we could go and see him so I could introduce you. If that's okay?" She looked at John. He picked up a pen and flipped it around between two fingers.

"You don't need to worry. I'll keep the task force out of this," David said.

John stared at the pen. "All right. David, you're sticking your nose into something *again*. You sure about this?"

David nodded. "I'm sure. This is mostly conjecture on my part. I doubt anything'll come of it."

John stared at Kate. "Okay, but I don't want you spending much time on this. You haven't finished your report from last week. You call Monje today?"

Kate leapt from her chair. "Yesterday and today — three voicemails. I'll call him again. And I'll finish the report this afternoon. *Promise*. Let's go," she said to David.

"Thanks, John. I owe you."

"You do. I'll remind you later. Get going," John said. As they left, he dropped the donuts into the wastebasket. Kate watched with a tinge of regret and walked out.

• • • • •

County Road 67J, southeast of Santa Fe

There was a reason Monje hadn't returned Kate Cordova's phone calls: He was dead.

Veryle's instructions to him were straightforward. He followed her into the desolate sand hills southeast of Santa Fe until she turned onto a rutted track. In less than a half mile, it ended at a trash-strewn flat surrounded by several small berms. Broken beer bottles littered the sand; the picked-over carcass of a coyote was drying in the heat. It was the ideal spot to dispose of the SUV. Veryle parked ahead of him, opened the rear hatch of the 4Runner, and removed two gas cans. Monje got out. She hefted one can and handed it to him. "Here."

He obligingly poured gasoline onto the seats and in the rear compartment, then tipped the can on its side beneath the chassis. He turned to reach for the other can…Veryle stood in a bladed stance, aiming a .40-caliber Glock at his head.

"What? Wait. Please!" Monje shrieked.

"Give me your phone," she growled.

"Please, what's wrong?" he pleaded.

"It's very simple. I'm sending a message. The phone, you simple bastard," she ordered. He pulled the phone from its holster on his belt and stepped toward her.

"No, no. Put it on the ground. Now get in." She waved the handgun at the open driver's door.

Monje put the phone down, shaking uncontrollably. "Oh God! No, please just shoot me! Goddamit, PLEASE!"

Veryle's eyes had a hard, bright, excited sheen. "Get in!"

Slowly Monje shuffled toward the SUV. He spun and started to run. The pistol barked, the round catching him in the lower back; he tumbled to the ground.

"Agghhh!" He thrashed on the sand, tried to stand, and couldn't; his legs wouldn't move. A hand grasped the back of his shirt. He was dragged to the car and roughly pushed inside like so much refuse. The stink of gasoline was overpowering.

"PLEASE, OH GOD!" Gas was poured over his head and legs. Choking he tried to push himself out the open door; she slammed it against his legs. There was a sudden whoosh, and flames rose into the sky.

"AGGHHH!" he screamed. His last conscious sight was Veryle holding up his phone to record his demise and leering at him, her smile cruel and taunting. Then his hair ignited, and he could see no more. Flames engulfed the car as black smoke rose into the sky. After a few minutes, the screaming stopped. She took one last satisfied look and drove away.

Seventeen

"Think he'll remember you?" David asked as they walked into the building.

Kate laughed. "Sure he will. I was the biggest pain-in-the-ass in our unit."

The guard at the security desk examined their identification, gave them an indifferent frown, and waved them through. They followed the signs to the investigations area. Mike Charles was impatiently rummaging through a drawer when they walked into the cubicle.

"Sergeant Charles," Kate announced. He turned, and his face went from an exasperated frown to a broad grin.

"Kate Cordova. What the hell are you doing here?" She rushed him and gave him a big hug. "Look at you all dressed up!"

"It's so good to see you," she said and released him. "Sarge, this is David Harrowsen. He's my partner at CBI."

David shook his hand. "Nice to meet you."

"Sit down," Charles said, waving at two chairs. "This is a surprise. What's new? What are you doing in Santa Fe?" he asked.

Kate nodded to David.

"This isn't really official business, Sergeant. Kate's on a detached assignment here in New Mexico. I'm here on vacation. I'm checking into something, and she suggested I talk with you to see if you can help me." He flipped open his notebook.

Charles wagged his head side to side thoughtfully. "Call me Mike. If I can help, I'll be glad to."

David outlined the recent events at the gallery. At the mention of Phyllis, Mike took immediate interest.

"Phyllis Van Houten? She's involved in a homicide case I'm working."

"My sister-in-law told me you came to the gallery looking for Phyllis. How involved in this case is she?"

"She has a connection to my victim. I've been trying to meet up with her for an interview, but she hasn't called me back."

"I'll make sure to tell my sister-in-law; she can remind Phyllis to call you. Anyway, Kate happened to be at the gallery recently and thought she recognized Phyllis as someone she might have known from the army. Make a long story short, Kate found out you work for the state police and you have the contacts to check her out with the DOD. That's why we're here."

"Sure. Give me a minute." Charles opened the Marston case notebook and flipped through the pages. Finding the one he wanted, he handed it to Kate. "This Phyllis?"

Kate studied the grainy DMV photo for a moment. "I think so." She lingered over the photo. "Wait! There's no scar. Look." She pointed at the picture. "Her hair's pulled back; if there was a scar, it would show. The woman at the gallery has a nasty scar just below her hairline. She wore her hair down in bangs across her forehead." She pushed the notebook back to Charles. "I'm not sure she's the same woman."

"When was this taken?" he murmured. "License renewal date…three years ago. Well it's possible something happened since this was taken, an accident maybe?" He looked up at the two of them. "There's someone who might be able to help. He's a priest at the Santa Fe diocese and—"

"Father Bob Dunleavy. I've met him," David interrupted.

Now Mike looked surprised. "Really? How—?"

David held up one hand. "It's all part of this. He knows my sister-in-law; he gave Phyllis a reference for her job at the gallery. So I went to see him. There was a photo of Phyllis with a youth group in his office. She didn't have a scar in that photo."

"All that tells us is she didn't have a scar when the pictures were taken and she does now. Shouldn't make too much of it just yet," he said, glancing at Kate, who frowned at him in return.

"You *can* run a check on her with the DOD, right?" she asked.

Mike nodded. "Do it right now. There's coffee if you want to wait." He turned to the desk, searched his Rolodex, and found the number he wanted. David sought out the coffee while Kate stayed in the cubicle. When he returned they sat quietly while Mike spoke for several minutes and then hung up.

"They'll call back in five or ten minutes." He grinned at Kate. "You're here on assignment? Can you talk about it?"

"I can tell you I'm working for the feds but nothing else. What about you? How's things?"

Mike grinned. "I'm married and have a little boy, nine weeks old." He retrieved a framed photo from the desk and handed it to her. "Jack and Kirsten, best things in my life."

"Ah, he's sweet. Takes after his mom, fortunately for him," she teased.

Mike laughed. "You're right. How about you?" At this David turned away to hide his smile. Kate saw the look; her eyes narrowed.

"Haven't found the right man yet. I'm pretty picky."

The interplay between David and Kate amused Mike; he remembered Kate's social "issues" from their time together in the Guard.

"I'm sure you haven't." He chuckled. "I—" the phone interrupted him.

"Sergeant Charles. Hi, Melanie." He listened for a moment. "You sure? Okay, thanks." He hung up. "No record of her. Sorry, Kate. Guess you were wrong."

She shook her head. "I'm certain I know her from somewhere."

David sipped, wrinkled his nose, and set down the cup. "Pretty bad."

Mike laughed. "My partner likes it strong. I shoulda warned you."

"Can you tell us about Phyllis Van Houten's connection with this case you're working?" David asked.

Mike sat back and sighed. "She and the victim were cousins. We were putting together background on her, and Phyllis's name came up. Father Dunleavy was the one who put us onto her. Strangely he knew both of them years ago. She's not a suspect. But until we talk to her, we're kinda stuck. All our leads have dried up."

"I wonder why she hasn't called you. My sister-in-law tells me she's very reliable."

Mike shrugged. "I'll keep after her until she comes in. You know how it is. People have unreasonable fears about being interviewed by the cops. I always thought that was kinda strange; it's not like we use torture or anything."

"That's it!" Kate shrieked, almost falling out of her chair. "I remember," she added with a huge grin. David and Mike both gave her the "Well?" look.

"Sarge, remember Captain Vicky McNee? She worked in intelligence, was in charge of interrogating Iraqi POWs."

Mike's mouth dropped open and his entire body tensed up. "Wow. That's a name I thought I'd never forget."

"Or me. We heard lots of rumors she used torture to get information. The POWs called her 'Shitan zu el oudon khatraa,' devil with the green eyes. I met her a couple of times, got this real bad feeling about her. She had these creepy, green eyes — dark, almost black. And she had a scar running across her forehead right at the hairline. She tried to hide it with makeup, but if you looked close, you could see it. I'm telling you that's the woman at the gallery."

"Let's see what we can find out," Mike said and picked up the phone. "Hi, Melanie. I've got another name for you. Vicky McNee. She was a captain in intelligence during the first Gulf War. Age about mid-forties. I really appreciate anything you can find on her." He hung up and turned back to Kate. "I remember we turned that information over to CID and never heard anything back from them. Things were so crazy right then, we just let it go."

"Kate told me you were assigned to intelligence. You and McNee never crossed paths?" David asked.

Mike shook his head. "Nope. I switched to that assignment after we came home. I was the intelligence liaison for the Guard with DEA and Customs, assisting with drug investigations, part of the HIDTA (High Intensity Drug Trafficking Area) initiative in Colorado. Thing is, regular army don't interact a lot with the Guard, at least not when they aren't deployed, so there wasn't much chance I would have run across her." He reached for a half-consumed Pepsi that stood on the desk and drained it. "Kate, if you're right, you've sure turned my case on its ear."

"She has a knack for it," David said and dodged a punch from Kate. "I could tell you some stories."

"I didn't know you spoke Arabic," Mike said to Kate, then glanced at David. "When she joined the Guard, she could barely speak English."

"Thank you, sir, may I have another," Kate groused.

"Your day in the barrel, kiddo." David laughed. He closed his notebook. "We'll stick around until DOD calls back if that's okay."

"Sure. Kate and I can tell you a few stories about our time in the Guard, how great it was." He laughed loudly. "Not."

For the next half hour, the two amused David with their experiences as MPs during the Gulf War. Mike told the best tales, with much drama and flair. Kate's sounded like sanitation reports.

"So like I said, Colonel Tidy-Bowl was always busting us about keeping everything neat and clean, always bitching about the sand and the dirt and the smells. He was one of these officers who looked the part: uniform pressed, boots shined, just in case some big brass showed up. Had all the right credentials too, punched the right tickets. Thing was, he couldn't decide whether to drink his coffee or sip it unless he "consulted higher authority." But man, he looked good! Anyway, one day he's creeping around like he always did, and he has to take a crap. He's way on the other side of the compound, too far from the officers' latrine, so he heads for enlisted latrine instead. Something we didn't know until that day, he was a secret smoker — seems his boss didn't like smoking, so the colonel hides it. He walks right past the sign saying the latrine's closed for cleaning, has a seat, and lights up. Now look, the army has this nasty stuff they'd pour down the holes to disintegrate the waste. Typical military, this stuff is toxic and highly flammable. Maintenance always closed the latrine for several hours to let the stuff work. Well our colonel's sittin' there, probably dreaming about his next promotion, finishes his smoke, and drops it in the hole. Ka-whoomp! There's this big explosion, whole place goes up in flames. He comes stumblin' out covered with shit with his pants around his ankles and his boots on fire. Burns down the latrine, and he gets second-degree burns on his ass! It was great." Mike doubled over laughing, Kate dissolved into giggles, and tears were running down David's face. Sadly the phone rang, ending the interlude.

"Sergeant…ugh, ugh…Sergeant Charles. Hi, Melanie. No, I'm okay," he said, choking down his laughter. "What've you got for me?" As he listened, his eyes got wide, and his face turned dark. He began scribbling hastily. "Can you email me all this? It involves a homicide I'm working. Are there finger-prints in the file? Good, can you send them too? Thanks, sweetie, I owe you. Okay, I owe you twice. Take care." He hung up, finished his notes, and turned to them.

"Captain Vicky McNee deserted right before the cease-fire. She'd been under investigation for some time for smuggling: drugs, booze, stolen prop-erty, whatever. She was about to be arrested when somebody put her wise, and she disappeared. She's also wanted by the Iraqi government as part of an on-going investigation into war crimes. She's accused of torturing and murdering several Iraqi soldiers and a couple of civilians too. They want her real bad. There's not been a trace of her since the war."

"Jesus," David muttered. Kate's eyes glittered with satisfaction but "Wow," was all she could muster.

Mike nodded. "Wow indeed. Kate, you get a major attaboy for this one — *if* it turns out you're right." She glared at him but saw the softness in his eyes. "Not to worry. I'm certain you are. There's probably a photo of her in the file they're sending, so we can confirm the woman you saw is McNee. In any event, we need to...wait a minute. I wonder..." He flipped through the case-file notebook for a couple of minutes. "Worth a try," he mumbled. He reached for the phone.

"John, it's Mike Charles. How are ya? Good. Remember those prints you lifted from that little shop on Water Street? Did you run the unknowns through AFIS? Oh sure. Look, I'm gonna email you some prints in a while. Would you compare them to the unknowns? Great."

At this moment, Phil Ortega walked in. Mike hung up and made the in-troductions. "How was court?" he asked as Ortega sat down.

"Bound over for trial. Looks like the DA is gonna offer her a deal. She pleads to one count of aggravated assault, they drop the robbery charge, and she gets at least ten years."

"Good. We came up with some information, which may not have anything to do with Marston, but then again it might. The DOD is emailing it to me."

"DOD?" Ortega mouthed at him.

Mike nodded. "It seems Phyllis Van Houten is an alias; we think she's really an army deserter wanted for a bunch of stuff by us and the Iraq government."

"That's wild."

"Yep. I'm waiting for her prints. I asked John Erickson over at SFPD to compare them to the unknowns lifted from Marston's shop. Just an idea."

Ortega smiled at Kate and David. "Mike tell you how crazy this case has been?"

"Not really," Kate replied.

"Well it wouldn't surprise me if this deserter turns out to be involved. Do we know where she is right now?"

"Soon as I get the email, let's head over to her apartment and try to snatch her. You two want to tag along? Unofficially of course," Mike asked.

"Sure. I'd better phone my boss and let him know," Kate said.

"Good idea keeping your boss informed," David reproached her. She gave him a nasty glare. "If you don't mind, I'll call my sister-in-law and see if Phyllis, I mean Vicky, is at the gallery. I won't tell her why I want to know."

"Okay," Mike replied.

David called three times, but Anne's phone immediately went to voicemail after each. This both worried and annoyed him at the same time. So he called Tee.

"Hi, dear. Is Anne around? I called her but keep getting her voicemail. Really? How long ago? Did she say where she was meeting her? Oh. Look, if Anne comes back, have her call me right away. Tell her to stay away from Phyllis. In fact both of you keep away from her; I think she's dangerous. I'll tell you later. Love you."

Worry lines were deep in his cheeks when he turned to the three of them. "Phyllis called Anne earlier and told her she was in some sort of trouble and she needed Anne's help. Anne told my wife and left an hour ago to meet her somewhere. We need to find her right now. You have an address for Phyllis?"

"Sure do. Want backup from SFPD?"

"Let's see if she's home first. Come on," Mike barked. They rushed out.

· · · · ·

Casa Elegante, Agua Fria Street
Luis Mirada snapped his phone shut. "Still no answer."

Estefan scowled. "Sit down and have your lunch. After we'll go find this Monje together. It's not that I don't trust you, Luis. Perhaps I can motivate him in a different way. Time is short."

Mirada sat and began indifferently picking at his food. True, Monje was sneaky and unreliable, except where money was concerned. It wasn't like him not to return Luis's calls. Once this was over, he'd make Monje squirm for putting him in a bad light with Estefan. He avoided Estefan's stare; disapproval was etched across his face.

"I'm not happy with the way you've handled this, Luis," La Vaca said through a mouthful of roll. "But once the Friar is in my possession, things will be better. Don't worry yourself," he added in his most patronizing tone. In truth he'd had enough of Luis's bungling; the man would have to go.

As Mirada sipped his water, the phone jingled. He looked at the screen and smiled. "At last!" he said. He flipped it open…after a few seconds, his face turned white, and his hand began to shake. La Vaca was stunned by Mirada's reaction; he'd never seen him act like this. Mirada's eyes were fixed on the screen even as he tried to look away. After another moment, the screen went dark. He laid the phone on the table. His lips were greenish purple.

"Luis? What's happened? Luis?"

Mirada stood, wavering on his feet. "I…I…She's coming for me," he said vacantly. With unsteady footsteps, he started toward the door.

"Luis! What's happened?" La Vaca threw down his napkin and snatched up the phone. On the screen were the words, "You're next." A video appeared — a video of a screaming man engulfed in flames. Revolted La Vaca held the phone away from him. "Luis?"

Mirada turned to him. "No. Keep it away from me!" He reached the door and opened it. Two men stood on the veranda. He stepped back.

"Who are you?" Mirada asked, his voice shaking.

"Luis Mirada, isn't it? Recognize you from your picture. I'm Special Agent Samuels, and this is Special Agent Yokada from U.S. Customs." He nodded to the logo stitched on their shirts. "We have reason to believe you have information about illegal trafficking in stolen artworks and artifacts. We'd like you to accompany us to our offices." He looked over at Estefan. "Señor La Vaca? You too."

La Vaca stood, puffing himself up and thrusting his shoulders forward. "We have diplomatic protection under international law. I demand to speak to the Spanish consul immediately."

"Don't worry, we've taken care of that already," Agent Yokada said. "You need to know the consul is under investigation by your government concerning these matters. I understand he's being very cooperative. Now take a step back." He stared directly into La Vaca's eyes. A few seconds passed; both Mirada and La Vaca stepped backwards.

"Thank you," Agent Samuels said as they entered the room. "By the way Mr. La Vaca, both of you hold tourist visas, not diplomatic. It's a felony to misrepresent your status. Turn around and put your hands behind your backs. You're under arrest."

"He's the one you want," La Vaca shouted immediately, pointing at Mirada. "This was all his doing. See what you've done, you moron!" he shrieked at Mirada, who turned and lunged at La Vaca, who in turn aimed a karate kick at Mirada.

"You fool! This was *his* idea, not mine. You and your delusions of grandeur. Hijo de puta," Mirada shouted and punched La Vaca square in the stomach.

La Vaca fell to his knees but managed to head butt Mirada in the groin. They tumbled to the floor, kicking and spitting. The agents had a busy couple of minutes separating and handcuffing the pair. Finally they were secured.

"Okay, boys, no more of this nonsense. One other thing: We have a search warrant for this place, as well as for your phones and computers — just in case you think we don't have any evidence," Samuels announced. "Let's go."

"Wanna bet which one snitches the other one out?" a smiling agent Yokada asked after they'd tucked the sullen twosome inside their cars.

"My money's on La Vaca." Samuels grinned at him. "Rich guys always have a way of putting the blame on someone else."

Eighteen

1840 Metate Street, Santa Fe

He'd give this another ten minutes; it was getting late, and he'd have to get to work soon. In the beginning, he'd been happy to take this on for his uncle. But his "investigation" had run its course and become tiresome; there wasn't anything else to be plucked from this bird. He'd learned of several people snooping around asking about the Friar. Only this woman was apparently still interested; the rest had drifted away after being rebuffed by most vendors, who'd been discreetly warned off. She seemed to be involved in other questionable deals; he'd report this to the folks who needed to know. Rubaldo hadn't surfaced recently, so perhaps their interest in the Friar was waning. It struck him (not for the first time) what a pointless waste of time it was for people to chase such a myth...Uncle Antonio had satisfied him on that point.

Bored he unwrapped a stick of gum and tucked it inside his cheek. That's when things started happening.

A tan Honda Accord raced into the parking lot and stopped next to the woman's silver 4Runner. "Who's this?" he muttered, raising his binoculars. Almost immediately his target appeared and hurried over to the Honda. The driver leapt out and hugged her. There was an animated conversation between the two. Suddenly the driver stepped back. He could see her face; she looked bewildered and frightened. The other's face had turned dark, angry. She waved the driver into the car through the passenger side and slid in next to her, all the while keeping one hand close to her waist as if holding something; his instincts told him it was a gun. Within seconds they drove away. He had no choice but to follow; whatever was going on inside the Honda, it wasn't good.

Late afternoon traffic was accumulating on St. Francis Drive, but he was accustomed to the crush. His problem was simultaneously trying to keep the Honda in sight, avoiding a crash, and dialing his phone while deciding what he would say to emergency dispatch so they'd believe him.

· · · · ·

Mike Charles horsed their Tahoe through traffic like he was still riding his NMSP motorcycle. Phil, David, and Kate sat helpless as he neatly worked through the traffic while keeping up a running commentary. Ortega was relieved they'd been assigned the Tahoe; it afforded more protection than their Impala in the event of a crash, which he assumed was imminent.

"Our case would be dead filed if it wasn't for the info you gave us. I keep thinking there's a connection between Vicky McNee and our homicide. Just don't know what," Mike said.

Ortega squirmed as they brushed past a concrete truck with a few millimeters clearance.

"Maybe…maybe forensic will turn up something," he gulped.

"Hope so." Charles accelerated and switched lanes. David glanced over at Kate, who gripped the door handle tightly. "He drives like you do, Sarge," she murmured through clenched teeth. He was too uncomfortable to respond.

"Kate, remember that CID lieutenant — short guy, bald? We gave him all that information on McNee?" Charles kept up his running banter.

"Don't remember his name. Sorry," she replied. Her hands were sweating. "I—"

The emergency alert tone warbled on the radio.

"All units stand by. All units in north Zone 1, possible kidnapping just occurred, 1800 block Metate Street. Suspect vehicle is a tan Honda Accord occupied twice, New Mexico plates. Female driver, female passenger who's possibly armed. Heading northbound on St. Francis Drive. SFPD responding to the scene."

"Shit!" Charles barked. "You don't suppose—"

"Yeah, I do," David snapped. Ortega leaned forward, listening to the radio chatter.

"All units, suspect vehicle is now heading northbound onto 84/285. RP is off-duty tribal officer. We've lost cell contact."

"Head to the scene?" Ortega asked, glancing back at David and Kate.

"No, SFPD will handle that. Try to catch up to 'em," Charles snapped as he accelerated.

· · · · ·

When Anne arrived, she was surprised that Phyllis greeted her outside and even more surprised to see her smiling; from what she'd said on the phone, Anne expected the weepy, downcast face. Nevertheless she jumped from the car and embraced her.

"Now tell me all about this trouble," she said firmly.

Phyllis pushed herself away. "There's trouble — just a slight problem — and you're going to help me solve it." It was a command.

"I don't understand." It was then Anne saw the gun Phyllis held close to her waist. "What's going on?"

"Get in the car. You drive." Quickly she ushered Anne to the passenger side. Phyllis motioned her to slide behind the wheel and got in

"Why?"

"Shut up. North to Pojoaque," Phyllis said, cutting her off. "Don't do anything stupid. Drive."

Anne did as ordered. *Think, think,* she told herself and concentrated on slowing her breathing to calm herself. They drove in silence for a few minutes. Anne chanced a bit of conversation.

"Phyllis, why are you doing this to me? I thought—"

"My name's not Phyllis…it's Veryle. Phyllis is dead." She smirked. "I don't care what you think."

Anne followed the highway north. She realized she'd need to keep talking; it was her only chance for survival.

"What's in Pojoaque?"

"I'll tell you when we get there. Enough questions."

. . . . .

The radio chirped again.

"Re-established contact with the RP. Suspect vehicle still northbound approaching Pojoaque exit. Victim is an unknown female, five-feet-eight, light brown hair."

"Phil, tell dispatch we think the victim's name is Anne Patrick, and the suspect is possibly Phyllis Van Houten," Charles said.

"Dispatch, 121. Victim is possibly Anne Patrick, suspect possibly Phyllis Van Houten."

"121, copy. Switch to data channel for further."

"Can't right now. We're on 285 trying to catch up to the suspect. What's the RP driving?" he asked while Charles deftly negotiated the traffic. "Come on, come on!" he barked.

"121, RP is in a blue Ford Ranger."

"121, copy."

All of them scanned the traffic ahead, but the Ranger was nowhere in sight. A semitractor directly ahead of them stopped at a light adjacent to the Cities of Gold casino; Charles slammed on the brakes. "Shit!" He checked behind him, backed and drove onto the shoulder, squeezed past the truck, and barreled through the intersection.

"Want lights and siren?" Ortega asked.

Charles shook his head. "Don't want the suspect to hear us — too risky. We'll manage."

Ortega gulped and nodded. He wasn't so sure.

"See if there's an air unit available."

"One twenty-one, any air support up?"

"Negative, it's shift change. Won't be in the air for at least forty-five minutes."

"Dammit!" he snapped.

. . . . .

They'd passed Pojoaque and the highway leading to Los Alamos. Just then his cell chirped; signal lost again. "Shit!" Up ahead the Honda switched lanes left to right and back again. He stayed put in the right lane, found himself blocked by a slow-moving truck sagging under an overhanging load of vegetables, and jumped on the brakes. "Come on!" There was the slightest opening ahead, and he wormed through it — ignoring the angry honking from another motorist — and passed the truck. The Honda was nowhere in sight. Where to?

"Keep going," he snapped. Maybe they were headed to Espanola. With one hand, he dialed but still no signal. Cresting a hill, he caught a fleeting glimpse as the Honda turned east on Highway 503. Rolling through the stoplight, he nearly clipped a panhandler standing at the corner, swerved, and accelerated. On this road, the traffic was thinner, which would make it easier to keep visual on the Honda but increased the odds he'd be spotted. He raced through a series of twisting curves, past Nambe…but still no Honda. Farther on the terrain opened up a bit; just west of the turn to Chimayo, he spotted them continuing east on 503. He hung back now and dialed. A connection!

"Dispatch, it's 303 again. We're eastbound on Highway 503 passing the turn to Chimayo."

"10-4. We have possible ID on suspect and victim from SP, 121. Stay on the line as long as you can. We'll simulcast."

"Okay."

· · · · ·

Charles slowed as they approached the intersection with the Los Alamos highway, giving Ortega a worried glance.

"Dispatch, any update?" Ortega asked.

"Still no contact. We're calling the RP every two minutes. Must be in a dead spot. Wait…stand by."

"Okay, keep us advised. Whadda you think?" he asked Charles, who shook his head.

"David? Kate?" Charles asked. David shrugged.

"Okay, let's try westbound." He made the sweeping turn onto Highway 502. The road ahead was empty. After a couple of minutes, he pulled to the shoulder. "No good. Let's wait for an update."

"What if there isn't one?" Kate asked, knowing the answer. David pulled his cell phone and began scrolling.

"Here, give this number to dispatch and have them ping it. It's Anne's cell." He read the numbers to Ortega, who relayed them.

"Hope Van Houten didn't make her turn it off," he said. David nodded wordlessly in reply.

"121, Dispatch."

"121."

"We have contact with the RP. Suspects heading east on 503."

"Copy," Ortega replied. Charles whipped the car in a U-turn.

"121, we're pinging that number. They're eastbound from Nambe. Tribal police have a unit en route, also Santa Fe County."

"Copy. What's the RP's call sign? Can we go car-to-car?

"Call sign is 303, but he doesn't have a radio."

"Damn! Hey, 303 is Rick Hayes. He's good; he'll stick with 'em," Ortega said. At the name, Kate's eyes glowed.

"Dispatch, we're eastbound passing the Nambe community center."

"10-4." Ortega checked their GPS.

"It's no good, keeps bouncing back and forth between Nambe and Chimayo."

"Yeah, coverage sucks out here," Charles said. They continued eastbound.

· · · · ·

The Honda was just about to cross the dry Rio Frijoles when it veered right onto an unmarked track. Hayes slowed; should he keep following? Once on these single-lane tracks, discreet surveillance would be impossible. Should he accelerate and try to intercept? He scrabbled in the gear bag next to him for his gun, swerved in the gravel, and thumped to a stop in deep sand on the shoulder.

"Dammit!" He jammed the truck in reverse, rocked it several times, and finally extricated himself. It was clear he was falling behind; the dust from their passage was settling. Adding to his fear was the lowering light of approaching dusk. Tracks weaved across the road; at every crossing he slowed, looking for fresh tire marks. His cell jingled.

"303, it's Dispatch."

"We're on an unmarked road heading southeast from 503, just west of Cundiyo. The turn's west of the river crossing."

"Copy. We're pinging the victim's cell. All we know is the phone is hitting a tower in your area."

"I've lost visual. I gotta put the phone down to drive."

"10-4."

· · · · ·

"Stop right there," Veryle ordered.

Anne's fright had dissipated; now she was hurt and, even more so, angry. With instinct born of experience, Veryle looked behind them but saw no one suspicious.

"What now?" Anne asked.

"We're going to Roberto Arturo's. He has something I want."

Anne shook her head. Veryle slugged her, knocking her head against the window.

"Get going." She prodded Anne in the ribs with the gun. Anne pulled onto the road and continued east.

"How far?" Veryle asked.

Anne wiped a bit of blood from her nose. "A few miles. What is it you're after?"

"You take me to Roberto, and you'll find out. Now shut up."

Anne drove silently for a moment.

"I can't believe you're doing this. After everything I did for you!" Anne looked sideways at Veryle, who avoided her gaze. Anne took notice. *You can't look at me, you're not comfortable doing this,* she thought.

"Be quiet!" Veryle snapped.

"We were friends. How can you do this to me?"

This time Veryle made eye contact. "Friends? You and your goody, sham respectability? I hate you, people like you. I used to know someone like you. She was gonna help me too. Said she'd pray for me. She was *so* pious, always praying for somebody. She said the same thing to me: How can you do this? " Her voice was stinging with sarcasm. "Never got her anything but dead. Just keep driving."

Approaching Cundiyo, Anne turned south. The road was washboarded, and she watched carefully for any deep ruts. If the spot was just right...

203

"Slow down. How far now?"

"Couple of miles."

Up ahead Anne saw a deep rut where the monsoon rains had cut across the track. Quickly she gunned the engine, and they bottomed out in it. The jolt bounced both of them against the roof of the car; she slammed on the brakes and grabbed for the door handle. Before she could open the door, there was a blow across the side of her head; colored pinpricks of light swirled before her eyes for a few seconds. She blinked, and her vision cleared; the barrel of Veryle's gun was pushed beneath her chin.

"Any more tricks and I'll decorate the car with your brains." The gun was shaking; Veryle's voice was low and deadly earnest. Anne froze, waiting for the explosion. Veryle lowered the gun. "Get going."

They headed south. Up ahead was the turn to Roberto's. Instinctively Anne slowed ever so slightly, then picked up speed. Too late — Veryle had noticed.

"You missed your turn. Back up."

Anne braked, backed up, and turned right. She'd begun to realize Veryle would let her live just long enough to get what she wanted from Roberto; the threats weren't empty, just delayed. There was still time. What she had to do was think the way Veryle would think. That wouldn't be easy.

• • • • •

Hayes squinted against the sun in his eyes. The track was getting rougher. He was bouncing around like a baseball on concrete and nearly dropped his cell phone. He had to slow down.

"Dispatch, 303. We're still heading south. I've lost visual again."

"10-4. I have three units heading for your location."

"Okay. I'll…wait, stand by." The light was getting muddy…there! Tail-lights glowed red against the sand just below the bright skyline, about a hundred yards ahead. He sped up…the lights were gone.

"Dammit!" He slowed again and studied the tire tracks in the sand. They stopped, backed up, and turned southeast at a side road marked with a fence-post draped with a tire carcass. He stopped. What to do now? Wait! He scrabbled in the gear bag again, jumped from the truck, ran to the post, and stuck his Tribal Police cap on it.

"Okay, we've turned southeast now. I've marked the—" The phone chirped. Lost signal.

"Shit!" His tires sprayed sand as he accelerated into the gloom.

. . . . .

Charles saw the turn just in time. The Tahoe bucked and swayed as they turned and began bouncing along the iron-hard clay.

"Dispatch, 121, we're heading south from Cundiyo." Ortega's voice vibrated, making him sound like Elmer Fudd, incongruous given the circumstances.

"121, 10-4. 303 has lost visual. Stand by...suspects turned southeast... we've lost contact with 303."

"Dammit all!" Charles barked.

"Start watching for his taillights," David said. "Try to catch up to him." Charles accelerated; they began swerving side-to-side on the sand.

"No good. Can't go any faster," he said and slowed.

They bounced along in rising frustration, staring into the lowering sun. David kept picturing Anne's face; no, now was not the time for sentimentality. "You need to know I'm not carrying," he announced.

"That's okay. There's a shotgun in the back," Ortega replied. "We're good."

"121, Dispatch."

"Go ahead," Ortega replied.

"SFPD just made entry into the suspect's apartment. It's clear. They found a holster and ammunition but no weapon."

"10-4."

The road and the light got worse. There was no sign of Hayes.

. . . . .

Up ahead Anne could see Roberto's home and slowed.

"This it?" Veryle asked. There was an undertone of excitement in her voice.

"Yes." Anne stopped the car. "Course he might not be home."

"If he's not, we have plenty of time. Out. This way." Veryle backed out the door, covering Anne with the gun and motioning her to slide out. Keeping her distance between them, Veryle directed Anne to the door. It opened. There stood Roberto.

"Miss Anne! I'm so happy to see you." He stepped out and stopped when he saw the gun; his eyes grew wide.

"We have business with you. Inside," Veryle ordered. Roberto backed inside the door. Once inside Veryle positioned herself with her back to the door, holding the gun at low ready. "Sit down." Both dutifully sat at the table.

"What's this about?" Roberto asked. "There's no need for a gun."

"It's simple, old man. You have a santo, a very special one called the Weeping Friar of Chimayo. I'm here to take it from you. And don't waste my time telling me you don't have it. I know you do."

Roberto looked at Anne, his cheeks contorted in pain and disbelief.

"I didn't know what she wanted, really I didn't. I didn't know you had the Friar. I'm sorry." He nodded.

"Aren't you two so nice to each other. Isn't this touching?" Veryle's voice mocked them. "Enough! Get that santo."

Roberto frowned at her. "Why do you want this? It can't have any meaning to you. Taking it will bring you death."

Veryle chuckled, a chilling, snapping noise like sand blowing against the windows. "Oh you mean the curse of the Friar? Curses only work if you believe in them. I don't, so I'm immune. Don't try to scare me with some religious fable. This isn't about fairy tales; it's about *money*. A lot of money."

"Is that so? Then I'm sorry for you," Roberto said.

His expression of sympathy enraged Veryle. "Save your sympathy for each other." She stepped close to Anne, aiming the gun at the back of Anne's head. "I'll kill her if you don't get it. Now!"

Roberto looked directly into Veryle's eyes. He was unflinching; she didn't see fear, and this surprised her. Instead there was a calm resolve. She inched closer to Anne.

"If you kill her, you'll have to kill me too. And you will never have the Friar," he said. They faced off for perhaps thirty seconds. Veryle lowered the gun.

"No problem. There are things I can do that will change your mind. You can watch while she begs me to kill her." Her smile was a thin slit on a canvas of mockery. With her free hand, she pulled a butterfly knife from a pocket and flicked it open. She laid the blade against Anne's right earlobe, pricking it slightly. Anne winced as blood slowly trickled from the wound. Roberto grimaced; his lips moved but made no sound, as if he were praying.

"Prayers won't help you," she said. She poised the knife over Anne, waiting, almost eager. "Want me to continue?"

"No, no...please stop. Come. Follow me to my workshop."

"So much for devotion between friends. All right. Try anything and I'll peel her like an apple," Veryle snapped. She prodded Anne with the knife, guiding her along, following Roberto toward the rear of the house.

· · · · ·

"Dispatch, 121. Any contact with 303?" Ortega asked.

"Negative."

"Keep your eyes open. It'd be easy to miss him in this light," Charles said and slowed even more, until they were crawling along. David's hands twitched; the strain was becoming unbearable. Kate found herself leaning forward, hovering at the edge of the seat. Ortega's head was on a swivel.

"There's a side road up ahead." He pointed. Charles stopped the car. "I don't see any tracks...keep going." They continued on.

"There's another...no, just a pullout. Shit, it's like a maze," Ortega snapped. The radio was ominously quiet. "Dispatch, 121. Any update?"

"Negative, no update."

"There's another," Ortega said. They slowed. "No good. Keep going."

"Wait!" Kate pointed. "Look! See, on the post? It's a police cap. Turn here. He marked it with his cap."

"Well spotted, Kate." Charles made the turn. "Advise Dispatch."

"Dispatch, 121."

"121."

"Now we're southeast on a side road. The turn is marked by a police cap on a post. Who're the responding units?"

"BIA 414 and County 27. Switch to Tac 3 for car-to-car."

Ortega switched channels. "121 to BIA 414 and County 27, watch for a side road marked by a police cap on a post. Turn southeast there. We don't have visual on 303. No emergency lights. We'll advise."

"County 27, 10-4. Be advised my tactical units will stage on 503 west of Cundiyo."

"BIA 414, copy."

"121, copy." They crept along in the twilight.

· · · · ·

The road got rougher and narrower; Hayes sensed it was coming to an end. He glimpsed a house up ahead; the road transformed itself into a wide lot in front. And there was the Honda; it looked empty. He rolled to a stop next to a large juniper for concealment. The quiet settled around him as the light continued fading. Sit and wait? That wouldn't do. He checked his cell phone… still no signal.

"It's on you then," he murmured. Collecting his pistol and flashlight, he silently stepped from the truck and moved forward to his left, keeping to the shadows offered by the scrub.

· · · · ·

Roberto pulled aside a curtain and disappeared through a doorway.

"Wait," Veryle ordered. "Turn on the light."

A match flared in the darkness; Roberto put it to the wick of a lantern. As the flame took hold, he thrust it close to her face.

"Watch it. Back up."

Keeping the lantern between his face and Veryle's, Roberto retreated into the room. Inside was a workbench — chisels, planes, and knives were scattered amongst wood shavings. In one corner were stacked, gnarled, cottonwood limbs and roots. The other corner was cloaked in darkness. In the flicker of the lantern, Veryle glimpsed a face — no, several faces. Discarded santos huddled there, peering at them as if they were actors performing before a macabre audience of the dead. The idea unnerved her, and she shuddered, then angrily clamped down on her fear. *Concentrate!*

"Where is it?"

Roberto had seen the glimmer of fear in her eyes. "They're watching. They know what you're doing. You feel it, don't you?"

"Stop gibbering, old fool. Where is it? I told you what I'll do to your friend." With a flip of her wrist, she turned the blade toward Anne's cheek. "All right."

"To touch the Friar with an unclean heart means death."

"What're you afraid of? I thought you people weren't scared of dying? Just get it. No more stalling." The blade pushed against Anne's flesh. "Shall I begin?"

Roberto set the lantern on the workbench. He reached underneath and withdrew a large bundle wrapped in rags. Reverently he placed the bundle on the bench.

"Let me see it."

As Roberto began to unfold the cloths, his hands began to shake. He shuddered, and his legs began to buckle. "Ahhh!" he moaned. He slumped against the bench.

Veryle had expected something like this. So had Anne.

"Stop acting or I'll slice off her ear. Stop it." The tone of her voice changed from exasperation to anger to fury.

Roberto's eyes rolled back in his head. As he sagged to the floor, his hand pulled the bundle toward the edge of the bench; it teetered and began to fall.

"Shit!" Quick as a thought, Veryle kicked Anne's legs out from under her. "On the floor." She threw the knife away and leapt at him. Anne dropped and rolled. Veryle thrust the gun at Roberto's face while making a grab for the bundle.

"Time for you to die," she barked.

Anne's idea to grab the knife was impossible now — no telling where it was. She scrabbled in the corner behind her, felt something hard with her hand, and struggled to her feet.

CRACK! The room exploded with noise, smoke, and fire. Roberto dropped like a stone.

"ROBERTO! OH GOD!" Anne shrieked. Veryle spun round, aiming the gun at Anne...

As Hayes got close to the house, he heard voices. A quick peek through a side window...the room was empty. He sidestepped his way around the outside.

At the rear corner, the voices were louder, coming from somewhere just inside. He daren't risk a light. Focusing on the sounds, he stepped cautiously through the sage and low scrub, grimacing at every crackle of boots on dry leaves. Closer now he squinted in the dark, looking for cover…

CRACK! A gunshot ripped through the silence. Someone was shouting a name. Then came a shuddering wail. Everything went quiet.

Keeping his eyes trained just above the fluorescent night sights of his Glock, Hayes scuttled around the building, kicked open the front door, cut the corner, and headed for the rear. A curtain swayed in a doorway; he ripped it away and stepped into the room. On his right, a tearful woman cradled a man sprawled on the floor. Blood was running down his pale face; he looked dead. In the center of the room lay another woman. A large, metal spear had pierced her right eye and jutted through the back of her head. Her left eye was fixed and staring, almost in seeming surprise. A pistol lay at her feet.

Putting his gun aside, he knelt down next to the other woman.

"Ma'am, I'm a police officer. Let me look at him."

At that moment, the man opened his eyes. She wiped away the blood.

"Dear God, I thought you were dead!" she cried and pulled him tight against her. Then she noticed Hayes.

"May I?" he asked. "It's all right. You're safe now."

"Go ahead." She clutched Roberto to her as Hayes examined his head. The light caught Veryle's face; Anne shuddered and looked away.

Hayes stood. "He's gonna be all right; it's a flesh wound. I need to get my medical bag. Be right back." He disappeared.

Anne wiped the blood from Roberto's face. "Roberto, Roberto," she whispered.

· · · · ·

The cavalry began arriving in response to Hayes's call. By this time, he'd moved the two of them into the main room, away from the staring horror. Roberto was sitting up and taking a bit of water. "I think you're all right, but we'll get you checked out at a hospital just to be sure. You could have a concussion."

"I don't need that. I'll be just fine." Roberto dismissed the idea.

"He needs to be seen. Convince him, will you? I'll be back in a minute," Hayes said to Anne before he left the room.

"Thank you, officer," Anne called after him. She gave Roberto's shoulder a squeeze. "You must have a thick skull."

He nodded. "My father would agree with you."

"You need to see a doctor," she added. There was a frown, then a sigh of resignation.

As Hayes stepped out the door, Mike Charles appeared out of the dark. "Hey, Rick Hayes! How'd you get mixed up in this?"

"Can't take time to tell you much. My uncle asked me to look into some shady art deals. I checked around and found out this woman was asking a lot of questions, so I started watching her. Tell you more later."

"Glad you were on the spot. Everyone okay?"

"The man is wounded, very slight. The woman, er…Mrs. Patrick? She's okay, not much shaken up, which is amazing. The suspect is DOA. Stabbed through the eye with a spear."

"You got her? Good work."

"Not me. Mrs. Patrick stuck her through the eye with a spear."

"A spear?"

"Crazy, huh? Not sure—"

Just then David rushed past them into the house. "Anne! Anne!" He found her sitting on the floor next to a small, wizened man with a bandaged head. Kneeling he embraced her. "Thank God you're okay." They held each other for a time. She looked back toward the workshop door. "I killed her. She was going to kill Roberto and then me. It was horrible."

"Thank God you're all right," he said again and gently pulled her head to his shoulder. "Don't worry. It'll all get sorted."

Then Kate was at his side. Radios were blaring and officers were hurrying about. Two medics arrived and gently placed Roberto on a gurney. Anne smiled at him as they hefted him past. He reached out and grasped her hand.

"Wait. Do you want the—?" Anne asked

"It's not necessary. Bless you, dear Anne." His face was peaceful, and that was all she needed. She fixed her eyes on him until he was out of sight.

"What's that about?" David asked.

"Something between the two of us."

"All right," he said, obviously puzzled. "Let's get you away from all this." He led her toward the waiting Tahoe.

"Won't the police want to talk to me?"

"There'll be time for that later. Right now you need to chill." He turned to Kate.

"Find out where they're taking Anne's friend. Then get in touch with Tee, tell her where we're going and to meet us there."

"Okay."

"Oh, better call Stephenson and fill him in."

Kate frowned. "Do I—?"

"Just do it, okay?" David barked. But he smiled when he spoke..

"Yes, sir!"

. . . . .

Nineteen

Roberto Arturo's home, two days later

Roberto stopped at his front door, opened his arms wide, and stood in silence. Anne held back a few paces; when they'd arrived, he'd asked her for a "moment with God." After a moment, he lowered his arms and turned to her.

"Thank you for bringing me home." He opened the door and showed her inside.

A quick check and Roberto determined everything was as it should be. Any signs of the violence of two nights before had been removed. He retrieved two chipped mugs from his sideboard and put them on the table.

"You will share coffee?"

"Yes, thank you." Anne sat and surveyed the room while Roberto busied himself with the coffeepot. His home felt different to her now, as if the events had left a permanent stain on its soul. She wondered if she'd ever feel at peace here again.

"Roberto, does anything about your home feel different now?"

He sat opposite her. "I know in my head it could. I suppose that's inevitable. I prayed that God will bring peace to my home, that in my heart I will always celebrate your courage in saving my life." He reached across and took her hand. "Thank you." Anne's eyes sparkled.

"You're welcome. I'm glad we visited Flavio. I could tell it meant a lot to him."

"I am too. I think he expected a lecture from me about how his sinfulness brought him to this. I hope his recovery continues to go well. I think I will ask him to stay with me when he leaves the hospital. He still has a lot to learn about our relationship."

For a few minutes, they sat in the quiet, listening to the finches calling one another in the junipers outside. Steam began to swirl from the spout of the coffeepot; Roberto fetched it and poured with a shaking hand, adding two spoons of sugar to his cup. Anne watched him as she sipped hers, letting the bittersweet nuttiness roll across her tongue.

"Your hands shake."

"Yes," he answered as he sat. "The doctors said that might go on for a time. Don't worry. I'll be able to work." He drank deeply and sat back, contented.

"Roberto, about the Friar. At the hospital, you said we'd talk about it later. Well?"

The lines in his face curved upwards as he smiled. "Why do you want to know? Is it the artist in you? Or something else?"

She stared down at her cup. "When they took you to the ambulance, I asked if you wanted to have the Friar with you. When you said it wasn't necessary, I was surprised. But later I realized it wasn't in the bundle at all."

He grinned at her over his coffee. "You're right. The bundle is an old, wooden marking gauge my father gave me. It's a treasure I keep in his memory. I keep it wrapped to protect it. I grabbed it without thinking."

"And the Friar? Do you have it? Does it really exist?"

He rubbed the Band-Aid on his temple but said nothing. When their eyes, met she understood.

"All right, I won't ask again."

"Thank you."

· · · · ·

One Horse Dorp gallery

Tee and David lolled on the porch, waiting for Anne's return. The afternoon had been a soft one, the clouds edged with tints of rose and lavender bringing the promise of a clear evening. Taz lay on the deck and chomped on a red dragon chew toy, having given up presenting it to David so he could toss it for her. Tee's phone chimed; she checked the screen.

"Text from the restaurant confirming our reservation. I hope this place lives up to Mike Charles's recommendation."

"Me too. Kate says he knows his way around Santa Fe."

"Does he know anything about haute cuisine in Santa Fe? He looks like a steak-and-potatoes man."

David shrugged. "We'll find out. Nice guy, good cop. Anne said he was very kind to her when he interviewed her. The comment Phyllis...er, Veryle made to her amounts to a confession to murdering Mary Marston. They found Mary's fingerprints at Van Houten's apartment. Charles believes Marston went there to visit the *real* Phyllis, not knowing that McNee had assumed her sister's identity. McNee attacked her and knocked her unconscious, tortured her, drove her out near Okay Owinge, drove over her, and dumped her body."

"Hideous! Why was she tortured?"

"Charles has a theory about that. McNee had a reputation for it; she threatened to torture Anne. He thinks she tortured Mary Marston out of sheer cruelty. She hated her, seemed to hate anyone who was kind and decent, anyone who reminded her of her past life. We'll never know for certain, but it sounds plausible.

"They don't know what happened to the real Phyllis Van Houten?"

"No, but it's highly likely McNee murdered her too."

"That's so terrifying. All over this santo? Isn't it rather extreme?"

"The santo was only a small part of it. According to John Stephenson, McNee was deeply involved in smuggling of all sorts: drugs, artwork, human trafficking. When the Santa Fe police searched her apartment, they seized her computer. The feds have a forensic expert going through it. Kate told me there's very detailed information about smuggling networks, contacts, where she stashed her money, all kinds of stuff, going back to the end of the Gulf War. They'll be following up on it for months."

"And Veryle...sorry, I can't call her any other name than Phyllis. She finagled the job here at the gallery, which gave her a respectable image *and* access to lots of information about the art community here."

"I think you've nailed it. You're a pretty fair detective yourself, Mrs. Harrowsen...for a theater person," David said and blew her a kiss.

"Thanks, dear heart. But I'm worried about Anne, about how she'll handle all this. And what are the chances she'll be charged with murder?"

"Don't worry about Anne. She's a tough lady, just like her sister." He smiled. "The DA will want her to testify for the grand jury, but I'm sure they'll find it a case of self-defense."

"Even though she stabbed Phyllis with that spear? It's so brutal! Will that matter to the grand jury?"

David shook his head. "It's not the method, it's the motive."

"And why a spear?"

David lounged against the railing, drinking in the sweetness of the early evening air. "Anne talked about that when we were driving to the hospital that night. It seems Roberto kept his discarded works in the workshop — you know, pieces he wasn't satisfied with. Even though he wasn't satisfied with them, he has a special place in his heart for them. As Anne once said, they're an extension of himself, his faith. Instead of chopping them up for firewood or throwing them away, he burns them. Sort of a purifying ritual, that's how she described it. One of them was a carving of St. Michael the Archangel, the great defender. He was holding a spear. When McNee knocked Anne down, she was trying to find anything she could use to hit her to stop her from killing Roberto. She felt something hard and grabbed it, not knowing what it was. McNee turned to shoot her, and Anne lunged at her with it. That's all there was to it."

"Wow. St. Michael...he *was* the great defender in this circumstance. Makes you think, doesn't it? I mean...well, it makes you think."

"Mmmm. My mom used to say—"

A car turned in at the entrance. "Hey, it's Kate," Tee said eagerly. "Who's that with her?"

"Dunno."

The car parked. Kate and a tall, thin man emerged from the front. A woman stepped out of the back, followed by a huge man who squeezed himself out with some difficulty. He sported a knee-length overcoat, baggy trousers cuffed at the bottom, a rumpled shirt buttoned at the collar, and a wide-brimmed hat tipped over one eye, accentuated by an overwhelming puce-colored tie. They were all dressed to the nines. Kate had even had her hair done.

"That's the officer you met at the hospital, the one who spotted Anne being kidnapped. His name's Rick Hayes. Kate's kinda taken with him," David said.

"Think we're underdressed for dinner. Who're the others?" Tee asked as the couples approached.

"The guy in the suit is Art Smart, a dealer Kate works with sometimes. I don't know the woman."

"Hey, Sarge. Hi, Tee. Taz, come see your Aunt Kate." Kate opened her arms and Taz leapt up, smothering her with licks. Tee smiled at her companion.

"Nice to see you again, Officer Hayes. Thank you for my sister's life." She stepped up to him and gave him a huge hug. Hayes's eyes widened.

"If you're gonna be around this bunch, better get used to it," David said and offered his hand.

Hayes took it with a touch of embarrassment. "Glad I was there."

"So are we. Hi, Art. Nice getup."

Smart stretched himself in a full preen. "I call it Bogart-casual. You like it?"

"On you it looks good." Tee laughed. "Bogey would be proud." Smart beamed.

David wrinkled his lips in mock disgust. "Art, this is my wife, Tee Harrowsen. She was in theater; you two will get along fine," he said sarcastically.

Smart ignored the jab. "I remember you well. It's a privilege," he said with a bow. Tee blushed. "This is my good friend, Jaime Estes."

"Nice to meet you. We're just waiting for my sister, Anne, and we'll be off. I'm sure the restaurant can squeeze in two more," Tee said as she opened her phone. "Hungry?"

Kate twisted her lips. "Ah, change of plan. There's a film festival in Taos, lots of old movies, and they're sponsoring a film-noir night. There's a dance to old, really old music. We're heading there instead. Sorry." She checked her watch. "We'd better scoot." She gave Taz one last squeeze and put her down, hurriedly kissed Tee, and hugged David. "Bye." She took Hayes by the hand and led him to the car. Art and his date scurried after them.

"Good luck," Tee called.

Hayes looked back at Tee and rolled his eyes. But he was smiling. Gravel skittered across the drive as they raced away.

"Whew. I'd forgotten how high octane she can be. Think Officer Hayes will be all right?"

"A lamb amongst wolves. Who can say?" David chuckled. "Bogey would be proud? He was maybe five-six. Smart's at least a foot taller."

"Artistic license, dear." Tee gave him a grin of pure superiority.

"Think I've had enough of artists for a while." He checked his watch. "Speaking of which, hope Anne shows soon."

Five minutes later Anne's Honda pulled up. "John Stephenson's with her?" David gave Tee quizzical look.

"Great. I'm glad she asked him along," she said without a hint of surprise.

"I'm in the dark as usual," David groused. "What's going on?"

"Later." Tee put a finger to her lips.

They stepped from the car. Stephenson retrieved a black-and-white puppy from the back seat, tucked the dog under one arm, took Anne by the other, and led her to the porch.

"Hi, John. Nice to see you. Hope you're hungry," David said, eyeing the dog.

Stephenson approached Tee and gave her a peck on the cheek. "Hello, Tee."

The dog squirmed to be put down. Taz squared off, retrieved her toy, and stood poised, waiting for developments.

"We've a favor to ask," Anne announced. Tee looked at her, then at John, then at the puppy, who stretched and licked her face. She returned her gaze to Anne.

"It's only until we get back," Anne said. "John and I are going to a little, out-of-the-way place he knows for a nice, quiet dinner. Just the two of us. Okay?" she asked. Her eyes begged Tee's approval. Tee frowned, and then her face relaxed.

"Sure." She scratched the puppy's ears. "What's his name?"

"Her," John said. "She's called Smidge. My daughter showed up with her yesterday. She's a Havanese. She and her fiancé rescued her. They can't have pets at their condo, so they pretty much blackmailed me into taking her. Not sure what *I'm* gonna do with her. There's a lot going on in my life right now." He gave Anne's arm a squeeze and put Smidge down.

Slowly Smidge walked over to Taz, who backed up a step. Carefully Smidge sniffed the toy, then took hold of one end and gave it a tug. Within seconds the two were engaged in a raucous tug-of-war that quickly transformed into a game of chase along the porch and then inside the door. Their happy barking faded as they disappeared into the gallery.

"They seem to have hit it off," John said, casting a broad grin at David, who frowned in return.

Anne gave Tee's arm a squeeze. "Remember some time ago you told me you were thinking of a companion for Taz? I...er, we thought..."

"No. Anne. No," Tee said firmly. She looked at John, who turned his sappy grin on her. "No."

"Gee, look at the time. We've got to go," Anne said and gave Tee a hug.

"We'll discuss this further," Tee replied. She looked at John, who took Anne's hand without a word. They hurried to the car and drove off.

Tee turned to David. "Hi, sailor, new in town? Guess it's just the two of us. Want a drink? Or are you hungry?" she asked without enthusiasm.

David stared inside the open door, listening to the happy dogs scampering across the tile. His hands dangled at his sides, shoulders slumped, defeated.

"Thirsty. Gin and tonic, please. A large one."

"I'll make it two," Tee said.

And Last

The hills east of Nambe

The land rises and falls here, sculpted by years of wind and rain. In the folds of sand lie nooks and caves, hidden from human eyes. One cave lies far from roads, tracks, and trails, away from even the most diligent of explorers. It is cramped and craggy; a man could scarcely squeeze inside; the ceiling is low. It holds a secret, a secret best kept hidden until…well, until the time is right for it to be revealed.

In this dusty cavern stands a carved figure of a saint, a figure with a thin, kindly face, dressed as a monk. On one cheek a tear has traced its way downward, wept over lives lost to violence, greed, and anger — for above all else, this saint is a man of peace. His garments are simple, his arms outstretched, his hands open. A tiny bird rests on one, content and without fear.

Occasionally a man visits, a small man stooped now with age, his face careworn by years but whose eyes have the bright sheen of hope and happiness. He kneels before the figure, lights a crude candle, and prays in silence, head bowed. After a time, he rises. With reverent care, he brushes away the accumulated dust. Then with a final genuflection, he extinguishes the candle and departs, leaving behind only footprints.

Outside the wind whistles, birds call, and clouds drape their shadows over the land as the seasons pass. When winter comes, a fox enters the cave. She has done so before. The face of the figure does not frighten her, for she knows in this place, she is safe. She lays herself down and sleeps, nestled at the feet of the Weeping Friar of Chimayo.

CPSIA information can be obtained
at www.ICGtesting.com
Printed in the USA
FSHW021110210219
55830FS

9 781480 947672